Other Books by Arlene Kay
from
ImaJinn Books

The Boston Uncommons Mystery Series

Swann Dive
Book One

Mantrap
Book Two

Gilt Trip

(Book Three: A Boston Uncommons Mystery)

by

Arlene Kay

IMAJINN

ImaJinn Books

IMAJINN

ImaJinn Books
PO BOX 300921
Memphis, TN 38130
Print ISBN: 978-1-61194-467-9

ImaJinn Books is an Imprint of BelleBooks, Inc.

ImaJinn Books was founded by Linda Kichline.

We at ImaJinn Books enjoy hearing from readers. Visit our websites
ImaJinnBooks.com
BelleBooks.com
BellBridgeBooks.com

10 9 8 7 6 5 4 3 2 1

Cover design: Debra Dixon
Interior design: Hank Smith
Photo/Art credits:
Woman © George Mayer | Dreamstime.com

:Ltgy:01:

Dedication

For Jo Ann Ferguson, mentor, model and friend. Thank you

Chapter One

ONE CLOUDY APRIL morning, I ambled along Boston's Newbury Street toward Boylston Station, deep in thought. Despite two months of scouring every boutique and website in the Back Bay, my quest for the perfect wedding gift had failed. That special something was as elusive as anything Cervantes ever dreamed up. Impossible! After all, my fiancé Deming Swann was heir to a vast fortune, a man who already had everything. Our impending nuptials loomed over me like an evil genie, taunting and sneering. It wasn't a matter of money—Deming knew the sad state of my finances. I pride myself on creativity. After all, I'm a writer, expert in flights of fancy, second to none in imagination. Couldn't I devise just one memorable gift that wouldn't break the bank?

I stumbled on a broken bit of pavement and suddenly found inspiration. Deming Swann has several passions in life. Fortunately, I happen to be one of them, however, his zeal for physical fitness is a close second. I try my best to measure up, but although my mind is a mighty fortress, my flesh lags far behind. Starvation is my weapon of choice when the pounds creep up. To Deming, a dedicated gym rat and possessor of the body beautiful, that is sheer heresy.

"Conditioning, Eja," he lectures. "Keep up. Writers need to sharpen their physical senses too." Blah, blah, blah.

The solution was etched on a discreet plaque beneath the sign for Back Bay Comics. Shaolin City, Sound Mind, Toned Body.

It was perfect. The wedding gift I'd labored over. Considering Deming's Eurasian heritage, the tie-in was even more perfect.

I visualized the whole thing. I'd surrender myself to the staff at this dojo, and a new Eja Kane would emerge. Forget the flab. I would stride down the aisle like a warrior princess ready to claim her liege lord. My backup plan also had a certain appeal. The martial arts made an inspired setting for a murder mystery—quite alluring to a published author and practitioner of the genre where every experience is fair game. It was kismet, or something very like it.

I summoned my courage, entered the dojo, and came face to face with an astoundingly handsome man. He was a tall, Asian, impossibly fit specimen dressed head to toe in black wushu garb. Excluding his air of smoldering sexuality, what struck me first was his seismic sense of calm and the bemused twinkle in his almond eyes.

"May I help you?" he asked in a velvety baritone. Men with deep voices exert a gravitational pull on most sentient females, even a betrothed woman such as myself.

I grabbed a brochure from the desktop and stammered, "I've never tried this before."

He chuckled and gazed down at me. "Ah, I see. You want the introductory class. My name is Justin Ming. Perhaps I can answer some of your questions."

"Are you a student or a teacher? A sifu?" I hate babbling, especially when I'm the babbler in question. "I'm Eja Kane, by the way."

He waved me toward a bench. "I assist Master Moore with instruction. Tell me about your goals."

Two disturbingly trim women bowed to Justin and marched past us. He nodded without taking his eyes off me. I had his full attention, and that ratcheted up the tension big time. I'd never master even the rudiments of martial arts in six years, let alone six months. Why kid myself?

"I'm getting married in six months, and I thought, that is I hoped, to surprise my fiancé by taking instruction." I glanced down at somewhat wobbly thighs that would easily fail the pinch test and arms that spelled computer bound.

"That's ambitious," Justin Ming said. "Every student progresses at his own pace at Shaolin City. The important thing is to actualize your true potential." He spread his hands in a graceful gesture. They were large, well-formed hands with carefully manicured nails. "The master emphasizes traditional kung fu values as well. Synergy, you know, between mind and body."

I realized immediately that this was a mistake, another harebrained scheme from a writer's fertile brain. Obviously, Master Moore had never heard of the digitalized, download approach to acquiring skill sets. I eyed the door, planning a quick escape.

Justin Ming must have read my mind. He flashed a puckish grin and locked eyes with me. "What is your profession, Eja Kane? Something creative, I bet."

"I'm a writer, a mystery writer."

His smile was infectious. "No kidding? I'm a crime buff myself.

2

Maybe I've read some of your books." He stopped midsentence and leapt to his feet as an imposing figure walked our way. Although small of stature, the hooded man projected authority and something more—serenity, a near saintly, Dalai Lama-ish quality that was in short supply these days.

"Master," Justin Ming said, "may I assist you?"

The man shook his head and glided toward me. "I won't disturb you, Justin. This young lady is new to our dojo. A recruit, I presume."

I grinned foolishly, unable for once to speak for myself.

"Ms. Kane, Master Avery Moore. She is a writer, Master, seeking enlightenment."

I dared not correct the magnificent Mr. Ming, but my quest for firm thighs and great abs seemed far afield from enlightenment. Thank heavens Deming wasn't there to gloat.

Avery Moore's handshake felt firm enough to shatter bone if he chose to do so. His shaved scalp blended seamlessly with an expanse of smooth café au lait skin and a full black mustache. Although the rest of his person was worth noticing, I was most captivated by his large green eyes. They radiated wisdom and something more—compassion. The multi-cultural combo of skin color and eyes was quite common in Louisiana. Wisdom and compassion less so.

"You're uncertain, aren't you, Ms. Kane? I hope Justin hasn't frightened you."

"No, no. It's just that I'm clumsy, always have been. Everyone here looks so graceful. I'm afraid I won't fit in."

He squeezed my hand and shrugged. "Come to our seminar tonight. Dress comfortably and get a sense of what we are all about. A writer such as you must be very curious about the unknown."

I nodded, afflicted by uncertainty, too cowardly to demur. "Thank you, I will."

As Justin Ming plied me with a battery of forms, Avery Moore slipped away. A petite woman with a stylish pixie cut ambushed him before he got far. I could tell by looking that she was a gusher, one of those determined females who ooze confidence like an open hydrant. To his credit, the master sidestepped her, patted her shoulder, and continued his journey to the back of the dojo.

"All set?" Justin asked. "Class starts at 7:00 p.m. The first few sessions are simple: stretching, conditioning, and lots of theory. Think you can handle that?"

With a confidence born of desperation, I nodded, stuffed the paperwork into my backpack, and made my escape. I would never survive Shaolin City without a partner. Time to call in reinforcements.

PURVEYORS OF TIRED mother-in-law jokes have never met Anika Swann. I'd known her since my preschool days, and in all that time, the gorgeous former model and Boston socialite had shown me limitless kindness and affection. She also knew how to keep a secret.

After checking her schedule, I sped straight from Shaolin City to the Swann manse, a swanky five-story colonial nestled in the heart of Back Bay. The Swanns called it home, but to members of the proletariat like me, it was a palace.

Po, the Swann's houseman, major domo, and fierce guardian, greeted me with a wintery smile that never reached his eyes and ushered me in. His devotion to the Swann family was legendary, and I felt certain that he would happily sacrifice his life for them. Po's impenetrable air of reserve repelled outsiders with the ruthless efficiency of the immune system vanquishing germs. Despite being a fixture in the Swann household for almost thirty years, I still felt like an interloper whenever I stepped over the threshold, especially when I encountered Po.

Anika Swann sat in the parlor calmly sipping oolong tea and reading. The sun's rays bathed her face in gold, creating a halo effect that rendered me speechless and envious as hell. Vermeer couldn't have found a more exquisite model if he'd scoured the earth.

She looked up and beamed a radiant smile my way. "Eja! I'm so glad you came over." Anika patted the cushion next to her. "Here. Sit down and have some tea."

"Gladly, but I have a favor to ask."

"Anything. You know that." She poured my tea and shook her head. "Is it an adventure? We haven't had one in a while."

Anika and I had joined forces in a few escapades that had left Deming fuming. Naturally he blamed me for endangering his mother, even though she'd insisted otherwise.

"Say no if you don't want to," I said. "Just don't tell Deming or even Mr. Swann."

"Bolin, darling. You have to get used to calling him that. After all, in six months you'll be part of our family. Not that you haven't been for ages." Her eyes misted over, and I knew that she was thinking of Cecilia, her murdered daughter and my best friend. We'd been inseparable from preschool up until her death. No one who'd known or loved CeCe would ever fully recover from losing her. Deming and his dad controlled their feelings, but I knew they felt the same way. Some wounds never fully heal.

"Okay, here it is. I finally found the perfect wedding present for Deming, but I need your help. Your support, actually." It sounded absurd saying it that way. After all, I'm a grown woman, a bit long in the tooth for a sidekick.

Anika's hazel eyes glowed. "Come on. Stop teasing. Don't keep me in suspense."

I explained my kung fu scheme and the misgivings that accompanied it. "I'm so clumsy. I'll probably make a fool of myself."

"Oh, I get it. The buddy system. We'll both enroll in the class." She clasped her hands together. "Sounds like fun. I know a little wushu—just a few moves—but a refresher would be good for me."

"What about Mr. Swann . . . Bolin? What will you tell him?"

Her laughter spoke of confidence and years of managing her smoking hot hubby. "The truth, of course. That you and I are going to exercise classes."

"Better add a girls' night out to the mix," I said. "Deming is the suspicious type. He knows I'm allergic to sweat."

Anika nodded and tapped her iPhone. Soon she was speaking to the man himself, Bolin Swann, billionaire industrialist, loving family man, and supreme hottie. Their relationship was both tender and passionate, a rare, almost non-existent combination in a mature marriage. If Deming and I followed suit, I would be one happy woman.

"Go home and change, Eja, and I'll buzz by your place around five thirty. Po will drop you off." Anika chanced a mini-frown. "Better let Dem know our plans, otherwise that boy will erupt. You know how he worries."

She was right, of course. Deming had a tedious habit of monitoring everyone's life and activities, especially mine. Naturally I ignored half of his blathering and did whatever I pleased. Still, better to avoid conflict where I could.

On the short trip to my condo, I leaned back in the Bentley cocooned in sleep-inducing, womb-like leather. Hard to believe that people actually rode around in a six-figure auto and considered it normal. As usual, Po maintained his stony silence, ignoring my attempts at conversation and humorous asides. For years I'd thought he was mute, until one evening when I'd witnessed a frenzied exchange in Mandarin between him and Bolin. CeCe called Po a sneak who spied on her and reported everything directly to her father. No doubt she was correct.

My gracious home in the Tudor, a bequest from my late friend, still feels somewhat alien to me. It is prime real estate, a historic part of Boston's Back Bay located right where Commonwealth Avenue kisses the nape of the Public Garden. In short, my condo encompasses 4,000 square feet of sheer luxury, complete with priceless antiques, paintings, and accessories. Chalk it up to CeCe's exquisite taste and limitless checkbook. I had nothing to do with it.

There's also the matter of Cato, a less desirable inheritance. He's an irascible spaniel, a rescue with sharp teeth and a fierce snarl for almost everyone. Cecilia Swann doted upon him, and Cato in turn adored my friend. With me, he maintains a spirit of détente, eyeing my ankles whenever I offend and confronting Deming with fangs bared.

I wrestled with the Medeco lock and stepped inside to the insistent shrilling of the phone. After fending off Cato with a treat, I lost myself in the mellow voice of my fiancé.

"Been busy today," he observed. "Dad said you and Mom are planning something."

So much for stealth. I opted for door number three—truth, or a reasonable facsimile of the same. "We're planning an excursion," I said. "Want to join us?"

"Wish I could, but I'm swamped with work. A very demanding client wants my personal attention." Deming's law practice was booming, a consequence of Boston's thriving business sector and his brilliance, not necessarily in that order.

"Hmm. Is this client male or female?" I was only half joking. Deming had been quite the Lothario before we got together. Even now, needy women constantly swarmed him. His manner hardly encouraged intimacy, but his film star looks, an exotic Asian/Swedish combo, prompted normally reserved females to forsake dignity and decades of breeding in the name of passion.

Chill, Eja. Your insecurity is showing.

Deming answered my question without pause. "Horton Exley. Horty. You've met him. Hasn't changed a bit since his days at Yale."

I racked my brain for memory crumbs. "I don't recall any Horton Exley. The one I knew was Ames. Younger brother or cousin probably. Smart, downtrodden, moderately good looking."

"Watch your step, Ms. Kane. You're spoken for."

"Don't I know it." A warm sensation surged through embargoed parts of my person as I envisioned his arms around me. My voice grew husky at the promise of things to come.

"Drop on over when you finish work."

Deming chuckled. "I might be late. Very late."

"No problem. I'll leave the light on. Use your key."

"Will you make it worth my while?"

I took a breath and whispered words of sweet surrender. "Count on it, big boy."

Chapter Two

I SEARCHED IN vain for a loose-fitting garment with some hint of style. My closet was awash with sweat pants and jogging outfits too unsightly to even consider. Since I loathed the mere concept of exercise, the pickings were slim. Unfortunately, I was not.

A sudden brainstorm made me plunge into the back of the spacious closet where CeCe had once stored her shoes by type and season. I took a more minimalist approach to shoes and every other wardrobe staple. Unlike the Swann tribe, Eja Kane was stylistically stunted. It took persistence, but I found it: a pristine black jogging suit with white piping and tons of attitude. I'd purchased it in a fit of conscience after glimpsing a particularly unflattering photo. Almost immediately, buyer's remorse had set in. The offending garment stared reproachfully at me until I'd banished it untouched to closet Siberia. Tonight it would finally get a star turn.

The phone rang at 5:45 p.m., announcing Anika's arrival in the lobby. Her attire, a loose-fitting emerald number, was as flawless as her complexion; her blond hair was pinned in a loose chignon that accentuated spectacular cheekbones. Both of us wore athletic shoes, although hers appeared to have been used before, probably during sessions with her personal trainer. Neither one of us wore jewelry.

"You look perfect, Eja." Anika lowered her voice. "But you might want to tie your hair back. Exercise is a messy business, you know."

Hair is my one point of vanity. While many women bemoaned their thinning locks, mine remained thick, dark, and wavy, a legacy of my staunch Russian forebearers.

Anika gave me a conspiratorial grin. "Tell me. Are we really there to exercise, or is this an undercover assignment?"

"No tricks," I said, "strictly legit. If I get some background material, that's a bonus. Trust me, this is a crusade."

"Fine, dear," Anika said. "I sent Po back home. We can walk down Newbury and get there in plenty of time if we hustle."

Hustle we did. It's shameful, but her sixty-year-old form floated comfortably ahead of my heaving body. We arrived at Shaolin City as the church clock boomed the hour and the dojo door closed.

"You made it," Justin Ming said with an easy smile. "And brought a most welcome guest." He bowed to Anika. "Greetings, Mrs. Swann."

"You know each other?" I asked, gasping for breath.

"I had a small part in the fitness event she sponsored at the Boys and Girls Clubs." Justin flashed a fetching pair of dimples. "Nothing particularly memorable."

Anika extended her hand in a charming gesture. "Nonsense, Mr. Ming. The children loved you. I was merely window dressing."

Justin waved us in toward a well-appointed room where supplicants were seated in a circle around Master Avery Moore. There was absolute silence as if they were praying or meditating. I gave Justin a puzzled look.

"They are expressing reverence for the master and freeing their minds to learn." He raised his eyebrows. "Worth trying on occasion, wouldn't you say?"

Avery Moore nodded a welcome and addressed the group. There was a mix of genders and ages, but the common factor appeared to be total absorption in his words. This crowd was intense and very fit. Even the women had plenty of muscle. I noticed the gusher, the shapely brunette I'd seen earlier hovering about the master. Tonight she wore a red bandanna that highlighted her olive complexion. She occupied pride of place next to Justin and directly across from Avery Moore. From her air of familiarity, I supposed she was a regular.

The master stood slowly and started speaking. "How many of us truly know ourselves? Kung fu is a discipline, something that will guide you to a path of health and happiness." He inhaled and gazed at us with omniscient emerald eyes. "Learn the ten Shaolin Laws, and they will set you free. They bind us as a community." With a flick of his hand, he summoned Justin Ming, who leapt to his side ready to obey. "Confidence. Awareness. Agility. These things lead to self-control and mastery. Study Sifu Ming for inspiration."

Justin Ming executed a series of quick, graceful maneuvers worthy of a dancer. For a big man, he certainly knew how to move. It wasn't spiritual inspiration I saw on the faces of other women in the group as they watched Ming's performance. They seemed transfixed, mesmerized, and thoroughly turned on, a carnal triumph of the flesh.

The quest for his favors heated up as the snarky brunette turned febrile eyes on her competitors. One willowy blonde almost drooled. Their behavior was a common ailment that I understood so well.

Deming also has a black belt in karate. A lithe, flexible man is capable of incredible acrobatics and can be dynamite in the sack.

Master Moore ended his soliloquy and urged us to grab a mat and start stretching. Justin stood in the center, serving as our coach, cheerleader, and examplar of clean living. Anika dove right in, showing exceptional skill and zeal. While I was no superstar, I managed to finish the routine without disgracing myself or sustaining injury. Meanwhile the master walked about, complimenting and encouraging each student with a friendly smile or pat on the back.

"This is not new to you, Mrs. Swann. Perhaps you will not be challenged." Avery Moore pointedly omitted me from his comment. The man obviously valued honesty and feared that any greater challenge would kill me.

"My skills are rusty, Master. Your guidance will be most helpful." Anika knew how to ladle up praise when it suited her. Humility was prized in this community.

"Private lessons might suit you better. That has been the preferred method through the ages, and progress is faster." For a saintly guy, Avery Moore had a smooth sales pitch. Private lessons were a costly venture for anyone other than a Swann.

"My daughter-in-law would join me," Anika said. "Is that possible?"

"Of course. Justin will accommodate your schedule." With a quick bow, the master glided away and out the door.

"Private lessons?" I asked. "They'll laugh me out of here."

Anika patted my cheek. "Don't sell yourself short. You're doing fine." She swiveled toward Justin Ming. "I guess class is over now. Mr. Ming is occupied with his admirers, so we'll speak with him tomorrow."

Occupied, indeed. The sexy sifu was holding court, doing his best to avoid bloodshed while accommodating both the eye-popping blonde and the predatory brunette.

"I know her," Anika whispered. "We've met at several charity events."

"Which one?"

"The blonde. That's Heather Elliot Exley, Horton's wife. Isn't she lovely?"

There was that name again. Horton Exley was Deming's frantic client. If her behavior towards Justin was any indication, Heather was the clingy type who needed constant reassurance. No wonder her hubby was antsy.

"Let's stop at Starbucks for some chai," I suggested. "We need to coordinate our story in case Deming gets suspicious."

INSOMNIA AND I are old friends. Small wonder that I embrace the Sandman's visits as a gift. After the evening's exertion, I fell into a fugue state from which nothing and no one except Deming Swann could rouse me.

Sometime after midnight he slipped under the covers, put his arms around me, and gently kissed my neck. I'd deliberately worn a slinky black number in hopes of just such an encounter. Some women sleep in the nude, but I have curves to spare and serious issues with self-esteem and body image. I address them by wearing a dark, filmy silk that hides a multitude of flaws. It's cowardly, I know, but an MFA from Brown is cold comfort to a struggling endomorph like me whose first husband dumped her for a sylph.

"Hush, baby," Deming said. "Go back to sleep." He slid the strap down my arm and stroked my skin. "So soft. So beautiful." He touched the lacy undergarment beneath the silk. "Hmm. What is this? Feels like satin." He slipped the thong off me, slowly, sensuously, and dangled it in the air. "Flimsy, isn't it, for such a pricey little thing?" Deming's voice grew low and husky. "Worth every penny."

Suddenly sleep was the last thing on my mind. Even darkness couldn't hide my full throttle flush. I leaned back against a wall of rock-hard muscles and sighed. "Don't stop. Please. It feels so good."

"This?" he asked, letting his lips wander. "Or maybe this." Deming has large graceful hands with the long, slim fingers of a surgeon. When those fingers explore my nether parts, I melt faster than cheap chocolate.

"I missed you today," Deming whispered. "I'll be glad when this wedding spectacle is over, and we can start a normal life together."

I studied his face in the pale glow of the night light. No surprise that he had worked his way up two coasts, devouring debutantes like salty snacks. His thick black mane curtained off the perfect profile of a film star. Deming had been the dark angel to his twin's blond beauty, but they shared their mama's beautiful eyes. I glanced away, unable to face the heat of those hazel orbs.

"Hey . . . not getting cold feet, are you?" He moved closer, his lips parting.

"Never. In fact, my feet and every part of me are toasty warm." I'd never spoken truer words. My body temperature soars whenever he comes within striking distance. I'm emotionally vulnerable, out of control, ecstatic.

I cuddled even closer to him and pressed my lips against his. "I may be a little bit rusty, though. Let's spend tonight brushing up on basics."

Chapter Three

THE SIFU DIDN'T waste any time. The next morning, soon after Deming departed, Justin Ming phoned to schedule our private lessons.

"What time best suits you and Mrs. Swann?" he asked.

We agreed that 3:00 p.m. would work and that at least two lessons a week would be required. Luckily, after completing my most recent manuscript, I had time to spare and some extra cash as well. Weekly sessions were a bit of a letdown for someone who hoped for instant success, but even incremental progress was better than nothing.

"Then we can assess your situation," Justin said without a trace of irony.

"Should I practice in between sessions?" I asked. "Remember, I'm on a tight schedule."

"Ah, yes, your wedding." He made a noise that from anyone else might have been a chortle. "Perhaps you can also attend some of the group sessions in the evening. Many students find that helpful."

"Sure. Sounds great." My mind wandered as luscious Mr. Ming launched into the sales spiel about uniforms and gear. After all, how much happy talk can one woman absorb in a phone call?

"I'll start this evening," I said. "Mrs. Swann might not be available, though." From what Deming said, his caseload would keep him occupied for most of the week. Bolin, however, liked his wife at his side and seldom missed dinner at home. As the guiding force at Swann, Sevier and Miles, he could do whatever he pleased.

Afterwards, I immediately contacted Anika. Three o'clock worked for her, and we agreed to meet at Shaolin City that next afternoon. As I planned my schedule, I daydreamed a bit, did some maintenance chores, and walked Cato around the Common at such a brisk pace that he protested vigorously.

My group session at the dojo would be a solo act, but I felt less anxious about that since the steamy night with my fiancé. It sounds reactionary, especially coming from a card-carrying, fire-breathing feminist. A woman's self-esteem should never be dependent on a man, even a spectacular specimen like Deming Swann. But having him at my side buoyed my confidence more than the burgeoning sales of my last three novels. Hard to believe that for two decades we were adversaries who derived great pleasure from avoiding and taunting each other.

Perhaps exercise really does release endorphins. After returning home, I spent three productive hours outlining the plot for my next mystery.

I resisted the temptation to browse Internet sales or to Google wedding sites. Even the telephone kept its vow of silence. When five o'clock rolled around, I leapt up, ready to storm the dojo in search of perfection.

I trotted through the Back Bay as if I owned it, smiling at strangers, jaywalking with abandon. As I approached Newbury Comics I noticed a couple in the doorway locked in a passionate embrace. The man was a stranger, but something about his partner's expert haircut jogged my memory. Of course. It was the saucy brunette who had slobbered all over Justin Ming. She had an odd name that I couldn't quite recall, something Greek I think. This time she confined her favors to the slightly paunchy middle-aged man at her side. Here was a woman who took Shaolin Law number one very seriously, especially the part about loving your fellow disciples. I added *fickle* and *nympho* to my mental image of her and shrugged it off.

Following orders is a skill set of mine, ever since Catholic school. I entered the Shaolin City pro shop and dutifully extracted a list of must have items. Justin Ming hadn't stinted on anything, and despite my good intentions, the resulting tab gave me sticker shock. I surrendered my credit card, signed a disclaimer, and was given an official locker key that conferred an immediate sense of belonging. Maybe I *could* achieve my fitness goals and pass for one of the Swanns' social set. Stranger things have happened.

Back in the changing room I donned roomy black pajamas and preened in front of the mirror. Was it my writer's imagination, or did I already look lean and mean? Speaking of mean . . . a heated conversation, conducted in furious whispers, caught my ear. I never deliberately eavesdrop, but writers learn so much by observing others that it is almost their duty. In this case, the female antagonists from the other night were at it again. Heather Exley was pinned to the back wall by the pointed talon of the unnamed brunette. She sprinkled expletives into the mix and growled the name Justin along with a puzzling reference to bullion. I leaned in, trying to make sense of a tricky situation. Unfortunately, just at the point where blows might have been struck, a gong sounded. As both women stopped the fracas and filed into the main meeting room, Mrs. Exley fired a passing shot at her adversary.

"This isn't over, bitch," she hissed. "Fuck with me, and you'll be sorry."

I scrunched into a corner, yearning for a cloaking device. Innocent bystanders can easily become victims, and I was a stranger in a particularly foreign land. My scheme seemed to work until something alerted the brunette. She turned and snarled a warning at me. "Mind your own business, whoever you are. It's healthier that way."

The encounter robbed me of enthusiasm for our group session. I filed in like an obedient serf after keeping a weather eye out for trouble. Master Moore explained that we were exploring the second Shaolin Law that required students to be diligent in pursuing their art. He mentioned something alarming about physical and mental fitness too. I tried to observe the two combatants, but they were positioned on opposite sides of the room beyond my line of sight. Besides, I was there to improve my conditioning, not to stir up controversy. I stretched valiantly and made a tentative, somewhat feeble effort to learn a basic kung fu pattern. Justin Ming appeared and strolled down the line, observing each participant. He paused when he reached me.

"How are you, Ms. Kane?" He stepped behind me and moved my hands into the correct position. "There. That's much better. Side stretch, there you go. Now try a thrust." The bland expression on his handsome face called the double entendre into doubt. Was I suspicious, too inclined to tar everyone else with my own lascivious brush?

"Much better. Keep practicing." Justin whisked away and returned to the center of the room.

Heather Exley curled her lip and refocused on the sifu. I envied her limber body and the way she maneuvered it so effortlessly. Even in my youth, I was ungainly, despite lessons in tap and ballet. During gymnastics class, I earned the distinction of being the only child unable to perform a cartwheel or climb a rope. Talk about humiliation.

A sudden thought brightened my gloom. According to Deming, Heather Elliot Exley was one of least intelligent females on the face of the earth. Perhaps the Creator had compensated for mental deficit by awarding her great beauty and a kick-ass body. I'm uncertain which of us got the better bargain.

Justin Ming clapped his hands and gestured for silence. "Now we try the squat and kick." He modeled the exercise for us, moving in a rapid, sensuous blur that was worth watching but impossible to follow.

Apparently most of the class shared my view.

"I will ask our student, Miss Phaedra Jones, to also demonstrate. Learning is facilitated by viewing another student."

I experienced one of those "aha" moments as the brunette brawler from the locker room stepped center stage. Phaedra Jones. So that was her name. I had to admit it was pretty cool, a Greek morality play straight from the pen of Euripides. His Phaedra also failed to control her emotions and had paid the ultimate price. I hoped that her modern namesake would fare better.

All that ruminating cost me. I totally missed Phaedra's little show and Justin's narrative. When we were told to replicate her movements, the rest of the class sprang into action. My version was woefully inadequate, but I was shielded from shame by a sizable pillar. My relief was short-lived when I glanced behind me and spied Master Avery Moore, beaming gently, missing nothing. I had skated by the first Shaolin Law, but with my lackluster performance and spotty record, commandment number two was a problem. I had a bad attitude.

Class ended at 8 p.m., and I prepared to flee. My escape plan was perfect. Only the master's smiling visage stood in my way.

"You are troubled, Ms. Kane. Frustrated?" His voice was gentle, but the words had bite.

"This is difficult for me, Master. I must try harder. Tomorrow I start private sessions."

"Fine. Guidance is something we all require. But it must be reinforced through discipline and practice." He patted my shoulder and glided toward Justin Ming, the sizzling sifu, who was surrounded by his honor guard of doting females. Heather Exley led the pack, but the one called Phaedra was nowhere to be found. Had she slipped out to tryst with her other sweetie, or was she nestled in Justin's office awaiting a very private lesson?

I puzzled over that while walking up Newbury Street. Thus far, my quest for improvement had hit some major snags. Most of them were attributable to my own sloth and inertia. On the other hand, material for my next novel was plentiful. Lust, love, and jealousy combined with exertion and sweat—a virtual Pandora's Box lay open at Shaolin City.

Several blocks from home, he cornered me. As I passed an alcove, a pair of strong arms encircled my waist and pulled me close. I didn't scream or even panic. Those arms were very familiar as was the faint scent of Creed's Royal-Oud.

"Okay, Mystery Minx, what's the story?" Deming used a stern

courtroom voice, an outgrowth of his youthful obsession with Perry Mason.

"Alert the media. I'm taking a walk." I wiggled free and trotted up the street with Deming at my heels.

"Not so fast, missy. You're up to something."

Here's a tip for confounding a lawyer. Go on the offensive and admit nothing.

As we waited for the stoplight to change, I whirled around, hands on hips, and faced him. "I thought you were working tonight. You owe me an explanation."

Deming showed the advantages of multi-culteralism by sputtering outraged comments in three languages. "Don't get mad. I finished early and came over to find you." He raised his finely chiseled chin and glared. "You weren't home so I decided to take a walk too. That's it."

I shivered as a brisk wind ravaged my hair. "I'm hungry, but I need to freshen up and walk Cato."

"Ugh! That little brute gets more attention than I do." Deming is adorable when he pouts.

We entered the lobby of my building under the watchful eye of the concierge. The Tudor ranked among Boston's most august structures. It had everything I lusted for and aspired to in a sanctuary: privacy and pristine surroundings. Who could argue with beautiful dentil moldings, high ceilings, and location, location, location? The corridors were whisper-quiet, ultra-thick walls redolent with fifty years of glitz and glory. Each floor contained only two spacious flats, or residences as they were called.

Much to Deming's delight, the Medeco lock gave me fits. "Here. Let me handle that," he said with an unmistakable note of triumph in his voice. "You're hiding something. Come on. Out with it."

Fortunately, the door swung open, and Cato charged, giving me some thinking time. He made a beeline for one of Deming's pant legs and held fast to the cuff.

"Stop it, you little bastard! That suit is brand new." Deming prided himself on sartorial splendor and was especially fond of anything made by Kiton. The suit was pricy, and teeth marks were not an approved accessory.

I lured Cato away with a treat and faced the accusing stare of my fiancé. It was hard to ignore those hazel eyes, particularly when they blazed with passion.

"You were saying . . ." I folded my arms.

Deming assumed his bland courtroom face and eyed me. "You hate exercise."

"You're always nagging me to improve. Some thanks I get for listening."

He put his arms around me and squeezed. "You never listen to me, Ms. Kane. I still think you're up to something."

"How about a drink?" I asked. "You're terribly cranky."

Deming sighed and pointed toward the scotch. Personally, I loathe the nasty stuff, but he considers Johnnie Walker Blue mead from the gods.

"We can order out if you want to relax," I said. "Let me loosen your tie." I spent some time playing with the silken fabric, slowly unfastening the buttons on his shirt. By the time I brushed my lips over his collarbone, he was half asleep, and I was awash with sensation.

"I'll go freshen up," I whispered, covering him with the cashmere throw. "Won't take long."

I soothed my aching muscles in the steam shower and loaded up on French honey gel. My feeble efforts at the dojo had antagonized body parts I didn't even know I had. Master Moore's homily echoed in my brain: discipline and practice. Tomorrow was another session, this time a private one under the gimlet eye of Justin Ming. His wary look this evening told me that he hadn't bought my act one bit. Perhaps with Anika's help, I could pass the second Shaolin Law and keep in step. Diligence and practice—my new watchwords.

Chapter Four

DEMING WAS WIDE awake, clutching his iPhone when I entered the living room. After issuing a series of terse commands, he ended the conversation and looked me up and down.

"Hmm. Nice cleanup job, Ms. Kane. Why waste that beauty by staying indoors?" He jumped up and held out his arm. "Come on. We can make No. 9 Park if you're quick about it. It's only two blocks away."

"But we don't have reservations," I protested.

Deming gave me a pitying look reserved for the uninitiated. I'd forgotten. Swanns never need reservations. "Chop, chop. Can you walk in those heels, or shall I carry you?" The gleam in his eyes said he would do just that.

I gave Cato a quick hug and sped out the door. "Bet I beat you there," I said. "This is a challenge."

Deming laughed all the way to the elegant townhouse that was No. 9 Park. He was no stranger to the hostess, who beamed like a searchlight and immediately seated us. I should be used to it by now, but it doesn't seem fair. The queue of diners waiting patiently in the bar probably agreed with me.

I chose a tuna appetizer and asparagus, but Deming went whole hog. Kind of. He avoided pork but chowed down on halibut and a potato so large it needed its own dinner plate. When he finished chewing and swallowing, I made my move.

"Why so upset? You usually blow off whiny clients."

Deming sighed. "It's not that simple in this case. Sometimes you just can't save them."

If a client went down for the count, Deming took it very personally. Since he specialized in uber-rich, overly-indulged juveniles, it wasn't surprising. He couldn't tell me much without violating his attorney/client relationship. Just as well. I never disguised my contempt for spoiled brats insulated from the facts of life.

Deming suddenly snapped his fingers. "Hey! Don't you have a friend who's a big deal in the FTC?"

"The Federal Trade Commission?" I surfed a wave of temporary amnesia and drew a blank. Very few graduates of Brown University choose a government career. Fewer still cross over to the dark side and join the Feds.

"You know. The redhead. Always popping up when you least expect her."

"Fleur Pixley? You've got to be kidding. I haven't talked to her since CeCe's funeral. Besides, you know her too. She shadowed you for three years." I patted his cheek. "You scraped her off your shoes like chewing gum, as I recall. Quite brutal."

"Come on. I need your help. Give her a call and set something up."

"What? She'll ask, you know. Fleur's a bright woman. Got her CPA and graduated from Georgetown Law."

Deming grunted with the disdain a Harvard man felt for lesser institutions. "My client has a problem with the IRS, but it involves the FTC as well. A friend at court would help."

I felt my heartbeat quicken. "A criminal? You're talking about Horton Exley, I bet. Tell me more."

He gulped a slug of scotch. "He's no criminal, unless stupidity is a felony. Look, forget I said anything."

I know Deming's game. He's accustomed to women falling over themselves to do his bidding. I refuse to play. Indifference is an effective weapon against him when wielded judiciously.

"Okay. Sorry."

He leaned forward and clasped my wrist. "You're serious, aren't you?"

"Absolutely. I can give you her phone number though. She's right over at the JFK Building. Something to do with consumer protection." This time I pinched his cheek. "That's all I know, unless you read me in on more details, of course."

Swanns are notoriously poor sports. Losing at anything makes them peevish.

"Oh, for Christ's sake, that will have to do. I can't divulge confidential information, and you know it. Give me her number when we get home." Deming retrieved his platinum card from the tray, added the gratuity, and watched as the waiter noiselessly whisked it away.

He was seething, that was obvious. I ignored his behavior and waited as he gathered my things and helped me out the door. Tenderness is a secret side of Deming Swann that few people see. His outward demeanor is crusty, but he is devoted to those he loves. Whenever I can,

I prod him to loosen up and relax. He never listens.

My mind replayed long ago college scenes when Fleur Pixley made a grab for Deming. She wasn't alone in that of course, but CeCe and I found the whole situation hilarious. Just thinking of it made me smile. "Better wear your chastity belt, big boy. Fleur probably still has designs on your virtue. Always did."

Deming huffed at the very thought of it. "I assure you this is a professional matter. No danger of anything happening." He squeezed my hand. "You know I'm not interested in other women, Eja. Only you."

Nice words, but I judge people on actions. Deming had a well-deserved *reputation* in Boston social circles as a rake. He'd earned it by breaking hearts and dodging at least one paternity suit and several angry husbands. That happened long ago, but it was worth considering. Something about a leopard and his spots.

"Don't blame me if you hear gossip," Deming said with a faint sneer. "I'll offer to take my old classmate out to dinner. Soften her up."

"Not a problem," I said with a sweet smile. "Your mom and I have stuff to do tomorrow."

"Oh?" I could almost see his antennae rising. "You two are magnets for trouble. Remember, I won't be there to save you if you get involved in some harebrained scheme."

"I thought wedding plans made you crazy," I said. "If you insist on being involved, we can postpone our trip until you're available."

The alarm on his face was comical. "No, no. You handle it. I'll swing by after dinner."

I looked up at him and sighed: smooth golden skin, sculpted features framed by clouds of raven hair, and seventy-four inches of muscle. Star quality for sure.

"Oh, I forgot. I met Heather Exley the other day when I was with Anika. She's breathtaking. Heather, I mean, although your mother is too."

"Eh. Heather's been brain-dead for years. Their sons aren't much brighter, so I hear." He brought my hand to his lips and kissed it. "Not like you, my love. Our sons will have it all—looks and intellect."

That kind of talk made me flush, with either pleasure or alarm, I wasn't sure which. I'd never envisioned myself as anyone's mother, but Deming had definite ideas to the contrary.

"Are you spending the night?" I asked. "Cato will miss you."

"Don't get me started. I'll wait until you walk the little bastard and then leave. Tomorrow's an early day for me."

I DID MY BEST to practice the next morning by studying the YouTube video featuring Sifu Ming. Progress was slow, almost non-existent, but I kept at it, awarding myself points for pluck and sheer stubbornness. When two thirty rolled around, I met Anika at Starbucks with a clear conscience and some semblance of hope. As usual, she looked like a dream—perfectly coordinated in head to toe peach, including her gym bag.

"Tell me about last evening," Anika said. "Did I miss anything?"

I dished about the catfight and the amorous antics of Phaedra Jones.

"Phaedra. Hmm. It's so perfect." Anika leaned her head back and closed her eyes. "Of course, women are no different than men when it comes to defending their love interests. No telling how bullion came into the picture though. I can already see your new book title, Eja. *Shaolin Screams*. How does that sound?"

"Great, except I'm there to learn, not write. No distractions."

"Good point. I'll take notes in case anything interesting arises." Anika waved a small Hermes notepad my way. "One never knows."

We hustled into the dojo and quickly changed into wushu gear. Last night's bad vibes had vanished, and the locker room was a place of serenity. The Shaolin virtues of peace, harmony, and good cheer ruled the day.

"Maybe we should stretch," Anika said after we reached the practice room. "We must be early."

I kept any misgivings to myself. Justin Ming seemed like the punctual type who would abhor any breach of manners. Suppose he were indisposed—permanently silenced—by one of his female admirers or their male lovers? I shivered just thinking of it.

"Forgive me, ladies," a deep voice said. "I lost track of time." Justin Ming beamed his soft, sensuous smile, but his manner was slightly off key. A lock of shiny black hair hung in his eyes, and sweat dotted his brow.

"We shall start with a basic Shaolin pattern, a review of last night's session. I will demonstrate for both of you."

Once again, his movements were an elegant blur of man and muscle. He slowed down and repeated step by step, more for Anika's benefit than mine. Unbeknownst to my sifu, I had mastered that pattern with the aid of YouTube. For once, Justin Ming lost his inscrutable look. The man positively gaped as I executed the moves in question with a grace that astonished even me.

"Very nice, Ms. Kane. Much improved. The master will be pleased."

Anika's first effort surpassed my practiced moves, but I expected that. We both flourished with the one-on-one approach, and the hour sped by. Justin Ming was untroubled, so composed that his earlier behavior seemed like a figment of my imagination.

"At our next session, we will explore basic self defense moves," Justin said. "Meanwhile, practice your stretches and kicks. They are vital."

He patted our shoulders and vanished through an inner door. Anika and I gave each other a high five before we showered and retrieved our belongings from the locker room.

"You're really good at this stuff," I said. "Why didn't you warn me?"

"Oh, Eja, it's not magic. Besides, I have a quarter century head start on you. I've been practicing with Bolin for a long time." She unpinned her chignon and fluffed her golden locks. "Come on. We're not far from the Fairmont. My treat."

I'm pathetically easy to bribe, particularly when it involves a snack at a watering hole of the beautiful people. After all that exercise I almost qualified.

"It's early for dinner but late for lunch," I said. "Almost five."

Anika shrugged. "We don't have to eat much. Besides, I haven't been there since they renovated the place. The Long Bar is supposed to be very cool."

The Copley Plaza Hotel is one of Boston's grande dames. Like most ladies of a certain age, it had needed a tasteful facelift, and the Fairmont people had provided that. Nothing splashy, just an updated, freshened look. Anika and I slipped into soft seats of red leather, propped our elbows up on the bistro tables, and scanned the menu.

"I'm ordering a sidecar," she said. "So atmospheric."

My palate is untested, despite Deming's constant efforts to improve it. I seldom drink, and when I do, the results are unpredictable.

"Make it two," I told the waiter. After all, Boston has plenty of cabs, and this was a celebration of sorts.

We added a plate of raw oysters, sipping and slurping the feast until our hunger and thirst were slaked.

"Dem is getting nervous, I think." Anika took a delicate sip of her sidecar.

My heart sank. "Changing his mind?" I gulped.

"About you? Of course not. About some client I think." She rolled her eyes. "You've had his heart since preschool, Eja. Cecilia and I always laughed about it."

As usual, her eyes teared up when she mentioned her slain daughter. CeCe was very much alive to those of us who loved her, and Anika refused to "get over it" or "move on" as some well-intended friends had urged.

Anika checked her watch and signaled for the check. "Oops. It's almost six. Bolin will be getting home soon." A strange look flashed over her as she reached into her satchel.

"What's wrong?" I asked.

"My wallet! I must have left it at the dojo. It probably fell into my locker."

Fortunately, I had both cash and credit cards. "Not a problem. We'll run back and get it after I pay."

I flung Generals Jackson and Grant on the table and hustled Anika out the door. "Come on. No need to tempt anyone prowling around the locker room."

Anika seldom lost her composure, but this was one of those times "I'm so embarrassed, Eja. Some hostess I am."

"Forget it."

By maintaining a pace that would have pleased and astounded my fiancé, we reached Shaolin City just after six o'clock. Class was in session, so we tiptoed down the hallway into the ladies' locker area. The room was deserted but dimly lit.

"Where's the light switch?" I groused. "Someone might trip." Since I was the likely victim, my grievance was personal. Fortunately, Anika had a small but powerful flashlight on her key ring that guided us to her locker.

"Here it is," she cried. "Thank heaven! It's such a hassle replacing everything."

"No kidding." I leaned back against the locker and suddenly felt dampness on my sleeve. "Ugh! Someone must have spilled something. I thought they banned food in this area. At least they should pay their electricity bills."

Anika shone the light on my coat and grimaced. "Might as well get a rag and wipe off the floor. No need for someone else to suffer." She aimed the flashlight toward the wall. "They probably have something in the utility closet."

My sunny mood evaporated fast. Sticky substances didn't bode well for a new suede jacket. I'm normally a miser about clothing, but this had been my spring splurge. I stalked over to the closet and rattled the knob. "I think it's locked or maybe just stuck."

Anika sped over and gave the handle a mighty tug. Our teamwork paid off as the utility closet yielded to girl power, disgorging a mop, pail, and something unexpected.

Anika's screams harmonized with mine as the crumpled corpse of Phaedra Jones sprawled at our feet.

Chapter Five

IN MY PANIC I misspoke. Phaedra Jones wasn't really a corpse. Not yet.

"She's still alive," Anika said, taking Phaedra's pulse. "Barely. Stay with her while I run for help."

I couldn't protest even though my heart convulsed at the thought of babysitting a body. I slid my bag under Phaedra's head and grasped her hand. She wasn't bleeding. At least I couldn't see any evidence of blood. Her eyelids fluttered, fanning false lashes like convulsing caterpillers. When she gripped my hand, her icy fingers showed surprising strength.

Suddenly she opened her eyes and stared straight at me.

"Help is coming," I said. "Don't worry. You'll be fine."

No character in my novels would utter such senseless, banal dialogue, but this was no time for editing. Phaedra Jones glared at me as she edged toward the darkness.

"Dim Mak," she whispered. "Promise."

"What? Who did this to you?" It was important, a dying declaration that made no sense. I leaned closer putting my ear against her lips as she said it once again. *"Dim Mak."*

Then with a final shudder, Phaedra died.

I NEVER FAINT. Hardly ever. Alcohol consumption, not shock, made me black out that night, and I'll swear to it. I revived and sat up amid a sea of anxious faces. Anika's arms encircled me, chafing my wrists, speaking in a calm, finishing-school voice.

"It's okay, Eja. Everything's under control, and Bolin is on his way."

"Deming?"

"Po will pick him up."

I shivered as the dampness claimed me. "My jacket?"

"Evidence, Ms. Kane. How are you, by the way?" That familiar voice belonged to Lieutenant Euphemia Bates, a solid forty-something fixture on the Boston homicide squad, who knew us all too well. She hadn't changed much: still impeccably dressed, tall, slender as a sapling, and improbably poised. Her hairstyle was different, combed straight back with a hint of grey. It suited her, framed her smooth bronze skin and high cheekbones with an artist's touch.

I met and held her steely gaze. Mia Bates was an intimidating presence at any crime scene, especially when civilians interfered. She really hated that.

"It's been a while, ladies. Frankly, I never thought we'd meet again. At least not professionally." As she acknowledged Anika, Mia's eyes softened. While investigating CeCe's murder, she'd gotten to know and even like us. I'd always admired her blend of cop toughness tinged with compassion for the bereaved.

"Feel up to some questions?" Mia asked. Her tone made clear that it was purely a rhetorical question. Like any crack investigator, she tackled witnesses as soon as possible after the crime occurred.

"Please use my office, Lieutenant." Avery Moore's soft voice was steady, but his green eyes evinced pain and something else that I couldn't identify. He led the way past the body of his student, never looking, staring straight ahead as we entered the hallway.

The master's workspace was austere, a cubbyhole barely large enough to accommodate three adults. His desk was a simple oak table, cleared of clutter, adorned only by a vase with a single orchid stem. No pictures, personal items, or papers.

"I'll have tea sent in," he said. "A restorative." Avery Moore vanished into the ether before we responded.

Euphemia Bates crossed her arms as she watched him disappear. To homicide detectives mired in human depravity, spiritual beings such as the master must seem like a foreign species.

Anika closed her eyes, taking several deep yogic breaths. I tried to emulate her, but somehow my lids flew open, afraid of missing something.

"Let's get to it," Mia said, pointing to me. "What's your connection to the deceased?" She consulted a printout. "Phaedra Jones. That's the name I was given."

"None at all," I said. "That is, I didn't *know* her. In fact, until last night I didn't even know her name. But we were there. I held her hand and watched her die." I closed my eyes and took a big gulp of air. "That does something to a person. I can't forget the look on her face. She knew she was dying, Lieutenant."

I ignored Mia's narrowed eyes and cynical grunt. Staying silent was a tough proposition for me. I yearned to blurt out everything I had observed, concluded, or speculated about Ms. Jones, but I remained strong.

"Did she say anything, Eja? Anything at all."

I bit my lip, not trusting myself to speak. "She mumbled something, but I couldn't understand it."

"Try." Mia issued a command, not a suggestion.

"I don't know. Dim something. Probably the fading light as she lay dying."

"That's a writer talking, Eja. Fanciful talk. Think about it awhile." Mia turned to Anika, using an official impersonal voice. "What about you, Mrs. Swann?"

Anika stayed calm. For a pampered socialite she was far more self-possessed than a writer of murder mysteries like me.

"I'm afraid I know even less than Eja. Two nights ago was my first time at the dojo."

"I've got to ask. What were the two of you doing here anyway? You're the last person who needs exercise, Mrs. Swann." Mia pointedly excluded me from that statement.

"I'm here to support Eja," Anika said, "and to brush up on my wushu moves as well. I left my wallet in the locker. That's why we came back."

"How about you, Ms. Kane? More research for your novels?" Mia shed her lieutenant's mask and used a homey air. "I read your last book, by the way. *Swann Dive*. True crime, isn't that what it's supposed to be?"

I nodded, too intimidated to ask if she'd enjoyed it. "I'm trying to learn martial arts before my wedding. Sort of a gift for Deming."

"Hmm." Mia's comment was one inch short of a sneer. "You usually have a unique take on things. What do you know about the victim?"

I learned long ago to dispense with social niceties, especially that nonsense about speaking no ill of the dead.

"Phaedra was unpleasant. Not the type of woman you'd want for a friend."

"Man crazy," Anika offered. "The kind who is always on the prowl."

Mia leaned back in the chair and crossed her long legs. "Any man in particular?"

"Several," I said. It seemed like the appropriate time to mention the doorway lover, but I started instead with the esteemed Sifu Ming. Mia took notes and raised her head.

"Justin Ming, the assistant here? Why him?"

Anika and I faced each other and grinned.

"Wait 'til you meet him," Anika said. "You'll understand."

Before I launched into an account of the catfight, or described the other man, someone rapped at the door and poked his head inside.

"We have a development, Lieutenant. A suspect." I recalled that the freckle-faced redhead was Officer Jennings, Mia's personal driver. He'd bulked up a bit but couldn't shed that golly-gee-whiz, Opie look straight from *Mayberry RFD*.

Euphemia Bates excused herself and strode out the door. Anika and I followed right behind her.

That's when everything went haywire. I recognized the man in the grasp of two burly officers as Phaedra's phantom lover. Simultaneously, Bolin and Deming Swann converged on the scene, followed by Justin Ming.

The prisoner stopped struggling, Anika melded into Bolin's arms, and Deming gasped my name.

"What the *hell* are you doing here, Eja? You too, Mom!"

The prisoner straightened his shoulders and glared at the cops with naked contempt. "I have nothing further to add. My attorney will speak for me."

As I swiveled toward Deming, I heard him say. "That's enough. Lieutenant, this is my client Horton Forbes Exley. May I confer with him alone?"

"We'll do that downtown, Counselor." Euphemia Bates listened as an officer recited Miranda rights to Exley, then moved to take him away. Deming followed his disgruntled client to the police car, and with Mia's permission, stepped in beside him.

"There's no need for handcuffs, is there? My client isn't under arrest, I presume, despite the Miranda routine." Deming's tone was exquisitely polite but pointed.

Mia's nostrils flared, but her response was measured. "We tend to read rights to any suspicious person we find at the scene of a murder. Saves confusion later." She nodded to the officer. "You needn't cuff him, Officer. Mr. Swann will stay with his client."

"May I take my wife and Ms. Kane home, Lieutenant? They may be in shock." Bolin proved his membership in the legal tribe by glibly lying. I averted my eyes while Anika sagged against her husband's shoulder.

I doubt that we fooled Mia. However, she waved us out after firing a parting shot. "I'll need their statements tomorrow, Mr. Swann. As early as possible."

Bolin shook her hand and slipped her his card. "We'll be at your disposal any time. Thank you for your consideration."

He led us out the back way where Po had parked the Bentley. The coroner must have moved the body while we were being questioned, because both the van and the remains of Phaedra Jones had vanished. Anika still clutched her gym bag in a death grip, but my purse was among the missing.

"My things," I cried. "I need the house keys and my wallet. Cato must be starving." A hungry Cato is a fearsome prospect indeed. I envisioned the results, and they weren't pretty.

"Don't worry, Eja. Po will handle it." Bolin's gentle voice soothed my spirits, making me believe for an instant that everything was okay.

"Besides," Anika said, "you're shivering. Come on over to the house and get some cocoa. Dem will join us when he's through."

Unfortunately, I'd had some experience with murder. Too much. It didn't dull the shock, even though in this instance I neither knew nor particularly liked the victim. Seeing the life force ripped from a formerly vibrant being was a sobering experience. I accepted the Swanns' invitation, grateful to stave off loneliness for yet another night.

WE SIPPED COGNAC by the fireside, listened to Mozart, and waited for Deming until almost midnight. Anika dozed against her husband's shoulder while I propped myself up in a wingchair and brooded. Cato displayed unusual empathy by curling up in my lap.

Finally, Bolin gently tapped my shoulder and roused me. "Dem called, Eja. He's still at the station with Horton. I told him you'd stay here tonight."

"Oh, okay. I'll walk Cato first." Every muscle in my body screamed for mercy as I slowly uncoiled and stretched.

Bolin helped me up and grinned. "Don't worry. Po will handle Cato. Remember, we're familiar with his ways."

Guesting at the Swann manse is equivalent to a month's stay at the best five star resort—times ten. I've often wondered if even heaven could match the eiderdown quilt, Porthault sheets, and Loro Piana cashmere that graced each bedroom. An exquisite nightdress and matching robe were neatly folded on the bench. The adjoining bath was crammed with every imaginable potion, cream, and scent.

I washed my face, brushed my teeth, and crawled under the covers in a fog so deep that only the morning sun and the sublime fragrance of espresso roused me.

Anika had recovered from our drama much earlier and was eager to plot our strategy. She knocked on the door and glided in, clad head to toe in buttercup yellow.

"Sorry to wake you," she said, "but Lieutenant Bates called earlier. She'll be here in forty-five minutes."

"Here? Isn't that a bit unusual?"

Anika blushed. "You know how protective Bolin is of his family. He asked her to come. As a favor."

Euphemia Bates was no fool. In Boston, as in every other place on earth, money talked, and Swann-size money shouted. Besides, the crafty lieutenant probably wanted to keep me as far away from the action as possible. I'd learned to never underestimate her.

"What about Deming?"

"He spoke with Bolin around nine o'clock. Apparently, their session was grueling, but at least Horton wasn't arrested. Yet."

I took a mighty swig of espresso. "Deming doesn't handle criminal cases."

Anika nodded. "Dem said he'll refer the case to a specialist at the firm. He's still involved in some financial scrape of Horton's, though. I knew that boy's parents. They were older of course, but very upright, responsible people. Uptight, too, I guess you could say. Funny, I always thought Horty took after them."

I recalled Deming's sudden interest in Fleur Pixley and the FTC. "Listen, Anika. Is Bolin still home? I've got a tricky situation to ask him about, and I need to do it before Lieutenant Bates arrives."

She was curious, but good breeding prevailed. "Sure. Get dressed, and we'll discuss it downstairs. Po's making breakfast, or I should say, brunch."

I checked my watch. Egad! It was almost ten o'clock. I padded to the bathroom and jumped into the shower, trying mightily to revive my flagging wits. I hadn't mentioned the Phaedra/Horty lip-lock that I'd witnessed. Everything had happened too fast for that. Now I faced an ethical dilemma—volunteer the information to Mia or wait for her to raise the issue. Most lawyers would answer that immediately: never lie, but don't volunteer when dealing with the cops. Unfortunately, I'm the world's most inept liar. Years of nuns thundering threats about hell clogged my subconscious. I'd given up on sins of the flesh long ago, but lectures about sins of omission and eternal damnation stuck. If I showed any vulnerability, Euphemia Bates would nail me to the wall and skewer me in a New York minute.

After fluffing my hair and applying a touch of makeup, I slipped into yet another of the seemingly endless outfits that Anika kept at the ready. This time, it was a cashmere jogging suit in a flattering shade of aubergine. My clothes from last evening were freshly laundered and neatly folded in a Vuitton tote. By some miracle, my purse was also with them. I never question Swann magic, especially when Po is involved. I just shudder and enjoy it.

I hustled down the stairs, lured by the scent of crabmeat quiche wafting outside the breakfast room. Bolin, Anika, and Deming were already seated in the bright, beautiful room, sipping espresso and waiting patiently for me.

"About time, Sleeping Beauty." Deming had changed his suit and shaved, but his weary eyes told me that he hadn't slept. His attitude could have used a tune up too.

"Don't tease her, Dem. Eja had a horrifying experience. So did your mom for that matter." Bolin squeezed Anika's hand.

"Ha! Don't be naïve. Both of them reveled in it. They think they're some sort of detectives, like the ones Eja dreams up in her books." Deming's frown was worthy of Zeus incarnate. "What in the hell were you doing at that dojo? Don't lie. Either of you."

"Hold it, son. Let's have a civilized breakfast before Lieutenant Bates gets here." Bolin's tone was genial, but it contained a warning. Bolin Swann was very much the patriarch of the Swann clan, and Deming knew it.

Po divided up the quiche, serving each of us a slice of carb heaven. I followed Anika's example by ignoring toast and spooning fruit into my dish. Deming and Bolin heaped smoked salmon and sausages on their plates.

"I have a bit of a conundrum to resolve, and I'm not sure how to handle it."

Deming rolled his eyes, dismissing my attempt at girlish charm. "Does this concern the murder or my client?"

"Both, maybe. Besides, I thought someone else was representing him now. This is only a hypothetical." I blew him a kiss.

"Cut the shit, Eja. This is serious." Food hadn't improved Deming's temper one bit.

"Children, please." Anika wagged her finger at us. "You both act the way you did in preschool. Always nipping at each other's heels."

"What's your question, Eja?" Bolin waved me on. "We don't have much time."

I explained the lip-lock between Phaedra and Horton Exley and his wife's fracas with the victim. "You see how delicate the whole thing is. Either way, the Exley family is up to its patrician neck in murder."

"Don't be a drama queen," Deming said. "Horty might have been comforting her. As far as Heather goes, take it from me, she hasn't a jealous bone in her body. Not where her husband's concerned. She's indifferent to anything except her own comfort."

"I agree," Anika said. "From what I've observed, money and position motivate her. She was originally an Elliot, you know. From the poor side of the family, of course, but still."

"Maybe both of you are right," I said, "but she looked like she wanted to thump Justin Ming like a ripe melon, and she wasn't the only one."

Deming curled his lip. Gorgeous from birth, he dismissed other men's charms with a shrug. "Nice talk, Eja. What's so great about Ming? He looked normal to me."

Anika and I locked eyes and smiled.

Po slithered over to Bolin and whispered something in his ear. "Show her in," Bolin said. "And Eja, here's my advice as an attorney. Answer the lieutenant's questions truthfully."

Deming stabbed an accusatory finger my way. "And for Christ's sake, don't volunteer anything."

Chapter Six

EUPHEMIA BATES was a study in scarlet. Red, actually, but the literary allusion still applied. Her blood-red suit had a modest side slit exposing dominatrix boots that promised pain, pleasure, or both to the recipient. A guarded expression left her eyes unreadable. She greeted us with the serene smile she often used to disarm adversaries. I'd bet that many a fool had been lured to his doom by that siren song.

We adjourned to Anika's parlor for the Inquisition. Truthfully, that's a misnomer—Torquemada never had it so good. Leather wingchairs bracketed the fireplace, while plush down sofas made the room feminine but inviting. Po had positioned a trolley laden with espresso, tea, and Perrier at the entryway.

After observing the proprieties, Mia Bates got right down to business. Officer Opie stayed glued to her side, furiously typing notes into an iPad.

"Ms. Kane, you said that the victim seemed unpleasant. What made you think that?"

"It was just an impression. I never actually spoke with her." I gulped. "Until the end, that is."

Mia tapped her foot. "Come, come now. Writers are keen observers. What gave you that impression?"

"She scowled a lot. Especially when someone got near Justin Ming."

Anika nodded her concurrence.

"Did anyone in particular annoy her? You don't have to know names."

I hesitated, just long enough to alert Euphemia Bates, who immediately pounced. "We're talking murder here, Eja. So far Ms. Phaedra Jones is rather a mystery woman. I need information to piece together the facts."

"There was a blond woman who hung around Justin, but I never met her. A tall, attractive woman."

Mia donned reading glasses and scanned a printout. "Does the name Heather Exley ring any bells?"

Bolin and Deming wore the blank, expressionless masks they award in Law School 101. While I sat frozen, trying not to squirm, Anika plunged in to save me.

"I know Mrs. Exley, Lieutenant. Not well. Through charity things and the like. She was one of the students, although I can't speak to problems she might have had with anyone." Anika radiated charm and sweetness buttressed by a spine of steel.

"She seemed interested in this Justin Ming?" Mia asked.

"Most women were," Anika said. "He has quite a following."

Mia nodded and consulted her notebook. "Last evening you mentioned some romantic encounter, Ms. Kane. The victim and another man who was *not* Justin Ming." She took a delicate sip of Perrier and smiled. "We were interrupted before you finished. I want you to describe this man now."

I gave her the basics: white, forty-ish, brown hair, and a beige trenchcoat. It looked like a Burberry, but I didn't mention that. Horton Exley wore a Burberry.

"How about his face?" Mia asked. "Did you see it or hear anything?"

This time, truth was my friend. I never actually saw Horty's face, and his tongue was so far down Phaedra's throat that he couldn't say a word.

"How about his build? Surely you saw his back."

"Nothing memorable," I said. "Kind of lumpy. Not fat, exactly. Certainly no hottie."

Deming narrowed his eyes at that but kept silent. Believe it or not, he gets jealous if I look at another man, as if any other being could measure up to him.

Mia tapped that toe again. She suspected I was lying, or at the very least hiding something. I pictured her boot giving my behind a hard, swift kick. Once again, she asked both Anika and me to retrace our steps from the time we left class to our return.

"How did Ms. Jones die, Lieutenant? I didn't see any blood on her face." Anika casually lobbed the question, as if she were asking the temperature.

Euphemia Bates moistened her lips and hesitated. "The medical examiner gave us a preliminary finding. Pending toxicology tests, of course. It appears that Phaedra Jones died from a broken neck."

My mouth opened, and I blurted out a comment before I could

stop myself. "Like a martial arts blow. You know, a death chop. Bruce Lee did it all the time. So did Ranger Walker."

Bolin leaned forward, calm but engaged. "Not really a chop, Eja. A simple side kick to the back of the throat would accomplish that. Of course, there are other more elaborate moves as well."

Mia's fleeting smile was forced. "We're checking out all possibilities."

"What about that sticky stuff on Eja's jacket? Wasn't that blood?" Although Anika radiated innocence, Euphemia Bates didn't rise to the bait.

"The lab is testing that, Mrs. Swann. Lots of DNA there. Fortunately, the suede jacket was logged in as evidence." Mia's tone told me she wasn't worried at all. She turned toward Deming as she prepared to leave. "We found out one thing about her. It seems that Ms. Jones had a curious profession."

"Really." I expected the words madam, hooker, or escort to pop up, but I was wrong.

"She was what they call a *fixer,* someone who brings interested parties together to consummate deals. Ever heard of her, Mr. Swann?"

Bolin shook his head. "What about you, son?"

"I hear lots of names, Lieutenant. Hers does sound familiar. When I get back to the office I'll check my files."

"You do that." She handed him her card. "Call or text me when you do. By the way, I understand Mr. Exley has a new attorney. Ms. Schwartz, I believe."

The name Pamela Schwartz made me recoil. She was a former lover of Deming's, the kind of woman who aroused every ounce of insecurity within me. Poison Pam, pernicious Pam, predatory Pam—I had a dozen descriptors for her, none of them good. I studied the small Boucher painting above me while counting way past ten. As with all the items in the house, it was rare, beautiful, and genuine, very much like Anika Swann herself.

Deming said, "As you know, I don't practice criminal law. Ms. Schwartz will handle any legal issues. I am Mr. Exley's personal attorney, though. Consider us a team."

Mia Bates got the last word in. "I will, Mr. Swann. You can count on that."

"COME ALONG, EJA," Deming said, after we'd fortified ourselves with more espresso. "I'll drive you home." It was more order than offer, and that annoyed me.

"You go on," I said. "I've got errands to run."

Deming folded his arms and shot his Lord High Executioner glare my way. I've never been a Gilbert and Sullivan fan, so I ignored him. It's a useful skill when he has tantrums. Even as a child, he expected every sentient female to do his bidding. Smart lawyer that he is, he tried another tact.

"Eja, please. We have to talk. Besides, what about Cato?"

Lawyers are a cagey crowd. They find your weak spots and turn the screws.

"Very well," I said tartly. "Let's go." I winked at Anika and gave Bolin a hug. Soon Cato and I were wedged into Deming's beloved Porsche Panamera, dodging homicidal Bay State drivers.

"Tell me everything," Deming said. He stroked the leather steering wheel as if it were a lover.

I can be obstinate when it suits me. "Nope. Not unless we trade. Call me your consultant or whatever else you need to do, but I want the whole magilla."

"For Pete's sake! You sound like a lowbrow Damon Runyon. Is that what they teach at Brown University these days?"

"Absolutely." I moved alongside him and pinched his cheek. "Come on, big boy. Spill."

He growled something unprintable, but by the time we reached my condo he'd settled down. Deming loosened his tie and flopped lengthwise on the sofa, activating all sorts of libidinous thoughts in my mind. I forced myself to stay strong and focus on the mission. If we headed for the bedroom, coherent thought was out the window.

"What's going on with Horton Exley?" I asked. "It must involve fraud of some kind, and sex of course. That goes without saying."

Deming threw his hands up in the air and sighed. "Tell me how much you already know. Then I can calculate the risk. As it happens, Horton authorized me in writing to share information with you. For some reason, he thinks you're a crack investigator."

I try to be a good sport whenever possible, so I played along. "Really? He must have read my books. Anyhow, that was definitely your client pinning Phaedra Jones, a.k.a. the victim, to the wall of Newbury Comics. His energy shattered all my prejudices about frigid WASPs. Horty was really into it, and he obviously didn't care who saw him. Phaedra seemed to be enjoying herself too."

Deming sat upright, more lawyer than lover. "That was the night before her murder. Correct?"

I nodded. "Double feature for the Exley clan that night. Heather had a catfight with the same Phaedra Jones in the locker room. Threats were made."

"You actually witnessed this?"

"Yes, Counselor. Not all of it, though. I caught round two. Phaedra was livid, stabbing those talons at poor Heather. Could have blinded her."

"What did they say?"

"Lots of trash talk. You know the drill—bitch this and that. Oh, and something about bullion. That didn't make much sense."

Deming exhaled but continued the interrogation. "Was Horton mentioned at all?"

I closed my eyes and concentrated. "Nope. The only name I heard was Justin's. Totally understandable, of course. There's no comparison between Horton Exley and Justin Ming, unless you factor in the bank balance."

My fiancé said a very naughty word while raking his fingers through his thick black hair. "Between you and my mom, all I hear is Justin Ming. Are you suggesting that Heather Exley and Phaedra both were interested in him? Carnally?"

Suddenly, I realized that I was giving all the information and getting nothing in return. "There's more, but not until you fill me in. Trust. Remember? I'm part of your team."

Deming narrowed his eyes in the classic intimidation pose one sees on Court TV.

"Okay. Horton is a decent guy, but he's no shining star, and he's been insulated from reality all his life."

"Wait a minute," I said. "Doesn't he have a JD from Yale?"

Deming rolled his eyes. "Meaningless. Horty was a legacy. You know how that works. Exleys are old Yale alums—Skull and Bones, the works. Horty and his cousin were both Bonesmen, and the Forbes side of the family financed half the rooms in the law school. Those kind of people don't flunk out, Eja."

For once I kept my opinions to myself. I was an anomaly, a scholarship student who won every academic prize through intellect and hard work. Pampered slugs got no sympathy from me.

Deming's eyes sparkled as he held out his arms to me. "I know what you're thinking, smart girl, but not everyone has your IQ. For years,

Horty managed to do a decent job of managing the family finances. It wasn't that easy, either. Ames is always at his throat, and Heather spends money at the speed of sound."

I cuddled happily in his arms as the narrative continued. "Tell me more."

"Most of Horton's finances are tied up and out of his control. Dad saw to that."

"Bolin?" I asked.

"Of course. He and Horty's father were close friends. Business partners for a while." Deming clenched his jaw. "The Exley Foundation was the one exception. Horton chairs and controls that independently. It's one of Boston's biggest philanthropic organizations."

Lightning struck with a thud, and I made the connection. The IRS took a major interest in high-end foundations and the boards that supervised them, especially when someone played fast and loose with the cash. If Horty was involved in a scam, that might interest the FTC as well. That ensured a slow, steady decline, a messy death, and lots of taxable income for the one in charge. Now I understood Deming's sudden yen for Fleur Pixley.

"You're trying to butter up Fleur Pixley, you swine! Very devious."

His look of injured innocence didn't fool me for a minute.

"I get it—he absconded with the foundation's cash." I envisioned Horton Exley on the lam, adopting the grunge look, while the newly impoverished Heather rang up customers at the CVS.

"Are you listening to me, Eja? He did no such thing. Horty is dense, not dishonest." Deming stammered a bit. "He's my client, and he needs my help."

"Where does the FTC come in?" Two can play the intimidation card. I channeled some of the tough female prosecutors from legal thrillers.

"This is strictly confidential. Horton made some poor investments. He had the best intentions, thought he could triple the foundation's principal, hedge inflation." His voice trailed off, igniting my suspicions. "Naturally, he made a mess of it."

"Let me see if I've got this. Horton Exley, who probably never balanced his own checkbook or had a budget in his entire life, tried to play big stakes finance. What was it? A Ponzi scheme . . . or some can't-fail stock tip?"

"Nothing like that." Deming jumped up so suddenly I almost hit the floor. "It actually wasn't a bad plan, but Horty was overly enthusiastic. Vulnerable."

Good mystery writers have suspicious minds. When I hear *vulnerable* coupled with a forty-something male, only one phrase springs to mind: cherchez la femme. From what I witnessed two nights ago, the femme in question could be only one person: Phaedra Jones, the fixer who helped consumate deals and so much more.

"So Phaedra screwed him literally and figuratively," I said.

Deming wrinkled his perfect nose. "Rather a crass description, Eja."

"How would you describe it?"

"She interested Horty in a business opportunity and connected him with someone she knew. Unfortunately, it was a scam."

My curiosity was at flood stage. I might wheedle or cajole, but I refused on principle to beg. "Okay. What was the con?"

"It wasn't some pie in the sky thing. Horty's not a total idiot, you know. Gold. Precious metals. You've heard all those ads on television. Celebrities hawking gold, average Americans panicking. And the price kept rising."

I bit my lip both as a distraction and a way to calm myself. No wonder Mrs. Horty freaked about bullion. "What was the problem?"

Deming sighed. "Just think. There are different ways you can invest. Gold stocks, coins, or bars. Some daredevils even take a flier on gold mines. The field is wide open right now and it's damn complicated. I've studied it, and even then, I'd never invest without one of our financial guys advising me. Dad is even more rigid."

I'd seen the ads, of course, and my suspicious mind kept gnawing at one big question: how would the average Joe or Josephine know that the glittering stuff was really gold? Prospectors have been deluded about that since the Gold Rush days.

Deming continued his narrative as if he were instructing a particularly dull pupil. "You mentioned bullion—that's just a term for bulk metal, usually coins or bars. Nobody advises you to buy coins unless they're issued by the US mint. Otherwise you pay an outrageous premium."

His emotion was laughable. Swanns have absolutely no sense of humor concerning money matters. That probably explained how they made and kept their enormous fortune.

"What did Horton choose?" I asked.

"Initially, he went for gold stocks and futures, you know, mines and the like. Risky, but relatively safe. But then, as with so many other romantics, he became a gold-bug."

"Huh?" The term was unfamiliar except for its usage in the famous Edgar Allan Poe story. Come to think of it, there may be similarities after all.

Deming drummed his fingers on the table and sighed. Patience has never been his strong suit. "Keep up, Eja. I haven't got all day."

"I assume you mean Horty was obsessed by gold."

"Correct. Acquiring it, talking about it, and what's worse, touching it. He insisted on buying bullion—coins and bars. The man thought he was Midas, for Christ's sake, or Croesus, running his fingers through the stuff."

I sorted out the myths separating King Midas from Croesus and refocused on Deming. "Wait a minute. Isn't there a storage issue? I read something about complications and the dangers of theft."

Deming narrowed his eyes into glorious hazel slits. "Not for him. Horty rented an entire vault, if you can believe it. Had the stuff trucked in all the way from Manhattan."

I had to hear the whole story, even though I could predict the ending. Somewhere, Deming had to connect the Exley Foundation, its entire portfolio, and the Feds.

"How much did he invest?"

The glum expression on Deming's handsome face said it all. "About five million dollars. Not the entire endowment, but a significant chunk of it. Enough to trigger an audit and attract the attention of the FTC."

I took a deep breath and plunged right in. "He could reimburse the foundation. But it's more about his reputation, I bet. Did someone rob him?"

"Nope," Deming said. "You see, the Board of Directors got involved. Insisted on an independent appraisal for insurance purposes. Horty found out that his precious coins and bars were phony—fool's gold. He'd been taken, snookered, hung out to dry."

"Let me guess the rest," I said. "The person responsible for the fraud was none other than Phaedra Jones."

He nodded. "Now you've got it."

Chapter Seven

HORTON EXLEY WOULD be skewered when Euphemia Bates found out. King Midas, indeed! Even Pam Schwartz couldn't deny the money motive and the connection to Phaedra Jones. Still, why would Horton murder Phaedra? He obviously still lusted after her. I'd seen ample proof of that with my own eyes.

"He didn't seem to hate her," I reminded Deming. "Quite the opposite."

Deming poured Pellegrino into a crystal tumbler and sipped. "Men are like that, my love. Carnal instincts trump good sense every time, especially when a beautiful woman is involved. You above all people know that."

I closed my eyes and tried to be objective. Had Phaedra Jones been beautiful? Not really. Seductive and exotic certainly, but beautiful? Only if you consider sharp features and a smoking hot bod with more twists than a pretzel alluring. Most males would give an emphatic thumbs up to that one.

"Your eyes are closed," Deming said. "Ready for a little nap?"

I ignored the double entendre. When Deming and I napped together we seldom slept.

"Sorry. I have a meeting with my publisher and some details to work out with your mother." I patted his cheek. "Nothing that would interest you. Besides, doesn't Pamela need your help?"

His smug smile irritated me. "Pam still gets to you, doesn't she? Relax. We only hooked up for sex. It was never about love."

"Excuse me if that doesn't comfort me."

Pamela Schwartz was blond, beautiful, and tall. She was also meaner than a rattlesnake and twice as lethal. I both feared and envied her.

"I forgot to tell you," Deming said. "Tonight I'm taking Fleur Pixley to dinner at Bistro du Midi. She was dying to try it."

"Make sure that's all she samples," I said, stepping on tiptoe to kiss him. "You've become quite the man about town lately."

Deming wrinkled his nose. "You never explained that whole dojo thing. What were you and Mom doing there? Ogling Justin Ming?"

"Exercising. That seems fairly obvious." With Deming, less information is a better strategy. He has an annoying habit of expecting the worst and probing until he finds it.

"Well, don't go back there," he growled. "That goes double for my mom. A murderer is running around loose."

I arched a brow and laughed. "Pretty bossy these days, aren't you? Don't issue commands until we're married. Even then I can't guarantee anything."

Deming huffed enough to power a wind farm. "You never listen. I should know better by now and save my breath." He took my hand and kissed it. "At least be careful. Promise?"

One glance at those hazel eyes melted my defenses. "Of course. I'm only interested in exercise."

He released my hand slowly, bent down, and gently kissed my lips. "One more thing."

"I'm listening."

"No Ming mania, if you please. You're already spoken for. I'd be forced to dust off my wushu gear and fight him to avenge your honor."

I gave that scenario some thought. Any female would fancy having two hunks vie for her favors. On the other hand, Deming was man enough for any woman, and high drama made me edgy. Monogamy suited me very nicely.

"Justin is polite and friendly. Purely professional, nothing more. Besides, your client's wife would claw out my eyes if I even flirted with him." I reprised the locker room brawl between Heather and the late Phaedra Jones. "What *was* Horty doing there that night? Pretty risky juggling his wife and his mistress at one time."

Deming shrugged. "Ask him yourself. He invited us to his place for cocktails tomorrow night. Heather is quite a hostess, or so I hear."

"Will your parents be there?" Anika was a valuable ally in the information wars. She knew everyone on the social circuit and could charm information from a clam.

"Probably. Be ready about seven o'clock." Deming checked his watch and headed for the door.

"Will you stop by after your date, Mr. Swann?"

He wrinkled his brow. "Doubtful. I have tons of paperwork to do."

"Oh. Is that what they call it now?"

He dodged Cato, spun 'round, and winked. "Wish me luck."

PER ORDER OF the Boston police and Euphemia Bates, Shaolin City was closed until further notice. Every student received an email with the bad news, but I got a phone call as well. If Justin Ming's voice astonished me, his suggestion floored me.

"You know about the closure," he said. "We'll probably be out of commission for a few days, maybe a week. Lieutenant Bates wouldn't say."

"That's a shame." Caution was both watchword and friend. My response was neutral, noncommittal.

His voice sounded strange—subdued but focused. Weird. "I know you're under a time crunch," he said, "so I thought you might want a private lesson. Tonight."

I'm usually quick on the uptake, but that had me stumped. "Where? I thought the dojo was closed."

"There are other things we can do," Justin said. "Perhaps at your apartment?"

"Oh. Yeah, I guess so. Our living room has lots of space, and I'm not busy tonight. Should I call Mrs. Swann too?"

He paused, as if I'd broken protocol. "That's your decision."

"What time will you be here?" I checked the Swedish Mora clock in the corner. It was nearly two o'clock, and I had things to do.

"Does six o'clock suit you?" His velvety baritone seeped through the phone lines.

"Sure. I've been reading the material you distributed, and I do have a few questions."

No doubt Master Moore was eager to fill the empty coffers. Justin Ming, like many personal trainers, was trying to build his clientele and keep them satisfied. I phoned Anika immediately and explained the situation.

"Private sessions? Hmm. Very entrepreneurial. Unfortunately, Bolin made dinner plans, so I can't join you." Anika hesitated. "I'm sure you'll be fine, but maybe you shouldn't tell Dem about this. You know that boy has a short fuse when it comes to you."

"Really?" The idea thrilled me. "Call me when you get home, and I'll give you a full report."

I spent the next three hours running errands and reviewing galleys with my editor. No three-martini lunches for that girl. She was a workhorse who expected and got the same stamina from her authors. At five o'clock, I slipped into wushu gear and trotted Cato around the Common for his thirty-minute constitutional. As usual, his surly nature asserted itself, and he rebuffed all attempts to civilize him. Wise pedestrians gave our duo a very wide berth.

When Justin Ming arrived promptly at six o'clock, Cato charged the door, prepared to do battle. Then an amazing thing happened. The sifu entered, bent down, and spoke softly to Cato in a language I couldn't understand. It might have been Mandarin or magic based on the impact his words had on my dog. Instead of baring his teeth, the irascible spaniel licked Justin's hand and rolled over for a tummy scratch. Was this the technique Ming used to soothe the females who vied for his attention?

"You look like a serious student," he teased. "All decked out in your uniform. Even got your white sash." Justin's black belt, the highest rank in wushu, was draped around his trim waist in a toothsome display of male beauty. He surveyed the spacious living room and nodded. "A lovely space, Eja. Tranquil."

I'd pushed back furniture to clear the area, although I wasn't sure what Justin had in mind. CeCe, whose parties were legendary, had loved to entertain in that room. She had hosted fifty or more guests for cocktails with room to spare.

Justin motioned me into the center of the room. "We will start by stretching," he said. "Then we can try some basic kung fu patterns." He moved with a grace that any panther would envy, stretching, lunging, and twirling like a top. "Your turn," he said. "Stretch."

My attempts to imitate him were a dismal failure reminiscent of my worst childhood memories. Under Sifu Ming's watchful eye, I sank like the *Titanic*. The mirth-inducing strikes and lunges were pathetic efforts that even Cato would scoff at.

"Eja. Ms. Kane." He moved behind me and gently straightened my shoulders. "So much tension there. No wonder you are struggling." He took my hand and led me to the sofa. "Do you meditate?" he asked.

"Not really. My thoughts start swirling around, and it spoils the mood." I gulped a lungful of air. "I'd like to learn, though. Sometimes I have trouble sleeping."

Justin nodded. "That will be our task this evening. Decreased stress through mindful thought. Many of my clients find relief that way."

Mindful thought? Shaolin doctrine was centuries old, but this sounded like new age nonsense. Either way, I was up for anything that promoted sleep. It certainly beat hoarding Ambien like a miser's gold.

"Do I need to sit on the floor?" I asked.

"Not right away. We can manage right here. Bend your neck forward." He found the pressure points and massaged my back and shoulders until I purred.

"I didn't realize this was part of the process," I said.

"We adapt to the needs of the individual. Remember, the second Shaolin Law requires physical and mental health." His hands kneaded my muscles with a strength that banished every ache.

"Do you often make house calls?" I asked.

"Sometimes. For special clients."

Justin's hands moved slowly down my back and slid toward my breasts. Danger signals, vivid, flashing lights, interrupted my meditation. I wiggled out of his grasp and sat upright.

"Is something wrong, Ms. Kane?" His expression was bland and untroubled, the picture of innocence.

"I . . . I don't feel comfortable with this. Let's go back to stretching."

"As you wish." Justin Ming leapt to his feet with the agility of a feline. For the next twenty minutes he guided me through patterns so basic that even I excelled. When we stopped, I confronted the sexy sifu.

"Phaedra Jones was one of your private students," I said. "Heather Exley too."

"Why do you ask?" Justin Ming was the most self-contained man I'd ever met. "As you know, Shaolin Laws are never forced on followers. They are guides for spiritual and emotional cultivation."

I no longer felt fearful, awkward, or shy around Justin Ming. A surge of anger emboldened me beyond reason. "I assume there is an extra fee for special services," I said. "Emotional cultivation can't be cheap."

He permitted himself a small, measured smile. "My disciples are often generous. They donate as their circumstances allow."

"Master Moore approves of this?" I asked, unable to keep the scorn from my voice. Justin Ming was one sexy step up from an escort service. It galled me that someone I had admired, and yes, lusted after a bit, had me so completely fooled. I'm just a writer after all. Even one of our presidents lusted in his heart.

Justin's voice was soft but unapologetic. "The master is unworldly. He has no part in this."

"Phaedra Jones did. I could tell by the way she looked at you."

A faint blush stole over his cheeks as Justin Ming bowed his head. "Our laws oblige us to be chivalrous and spread love."

"Really?" I grabbed a folder and flipped through the Ten Shaolin

Laws. "You forgot the eighth commandment, Sifu. 'Forbidden to abuse power official or physical.' The rulebook says you can be banished for any violations." I slapped the folder down on the coffee table. "Someone might take exception to spreading that much love."

He locked eyes with me, sending a shiver straight down my spine. I'm a risk-taker, who doesn't always think before acting. Sometimes, audacity makes me stupid. Justin Ming, a powerful man who could snap my neck with one lethal blow stood only two feet away. Cato was my only hope, and he was firmly in the enemy camp. I flashed back to the crumpled corpse of Phaedra Jones. Would I suffer the same grisly fate?

Justin must have read my mind. "Don't be afraid. I am not a violent man. I have many failings, but never would I injure anyone."

"Small comfort to Phaedra Jones," I said. "Someone with your skills finished her off. It happens all the time in the movies."

He chuckled, a sound of mirth that seemed inappropriate and downright insulting. Villains in my books were awesome evildoers, not smiling hunks with dimpled cheeks.

"Ah. You are thinking of *Dim Mak*, the touch of death. It is true that I know the technique, but never would I use it, especially against a woman. It violates every principle of the Shaolin code." He stretched, treating me to a fine display of muscle magic. "Filmmakers have no such restrictions. They kill with impunity."

Dim Mak! The last testament of Phaedra Jones was suddenly clear. As a martial arts groupie, she knew all the kung fu hot buttons, including the one that killed her. *Dim Mak*. She had the chance to name her killer but chose not to. Surely that absolved Justin Ming.

The tension in the room dissipated, and my fight or flight instincts went from boil to simmer. Time to quiz the sifu about murder. After all, Horton Exley prized my detective skills. He was counting on me.

"I'll brew some tea," I told Justin. "We have to talk."

And so we talked over cups of herbal tea. He answered my questions without hesitation, even the personal, impertinent ones.

"Was Phaedra Jones blackmailing you?" I asked.

Justin laughed. "I have no money, Ms. Kane."

Our eyes met, acknowledging what each of us knew. The currency of blackmail was frequently power and control over others.

"Okay. What did she want?" I steeled myself for something sleazy, but the sifu surprised me.

"Phaedra thought she was in love with me. She wanted an intimacy I couldn't give." Justin cleared his throat. "Our time together was pleasant but unremarkable. At least for me."

"She knew there were others, I suppose?"

He nodded. Justin Ming used words sparingly and to great effect. He volunteered nothing.

"Were you involved in the bullion scheme? I heard all about it."

"Bullion? I don't understand. Our relationship was sensual, Ms. Kane, not business. Frankly, I had few discussions of substance with Phaedra or any of the others during our time together." He smiled again. "They preferred it that way."

His manner morphed from superior to arrogant, and it annoyed me. Good looks and incredible abs were no substitute for humility. There had to be a Shaolin law about that.

"How did you identify your 'special' clients? Some secret code?"

Justin shook his head. "Martial arts trains one to be observant, and I am skilled in nuance. I identified their needs during class," he shrugged, "and pursued it later."

Had I given off some needy vibe? I had to ask.

"What about me? I'm engaged, happily so, I might add. And my mother-in-law is totally in love with her husband."

He took a slight step back and bowed. "My mistake. Forgive me."

I yearned to smack that smirk off the sexy sifu's face, but good sense prevailed. He posed as the poster boy for customer service, but Avery Moore might see things differently. Justin had violated the Moral Way, the basic underpinning of Shaolin law.

"The master might have banished you," I said. "Then what would you do?"

His expression was one inch short of smug. "I am not without resources, Ms. Kane. Several of my clients have made generous offers."

"Really? You mean you'd go to the highest bidder?"

He bowed his head. "Exactly."

Chapter Eight

WHEN ANIKA PHONED later that evening, I fought a losing battle to remain calm and coherent. Despite taking yogic breaths and visualizing puppies, Justin Ming's treachery left me outraged.

She let me rant for a while, then spoke in soothing tones. "Hold on, Eja. I'm on my way."

That jolted me back to reality. At that hour, Bolin would insist on accompanying his wife. Before long, Deming would join the mix, and the entire incident would escalate into a Swann-sized mess. My big scoop wouldn't matter if Deming brawled with Justin Ming.

"Wait! I overreacted, Anika. Everything's fine."

She sighed. "Are you sure? Po can drive me over. It's no big deal."

I filled a brandy snifter and drained the glass. "There. I'm much better. Besides, we'll see each other tomorrow night. You'll be at Horty's party, I hope."

"Are you kidding? I wouldn't miss it for the world." Anika giggled. "Bolin tried to bow out, but I insisted. Horton's mother was a fine woman who was very kind to me. Just think. With a little luck, we might uncover a murderer."

Her euphoria froze me in my tracks. Horton Exley had the big three in the crime pantheon—motive, means, and opportunity. His mama wouldn't care for that.

"Does he know what we're up to?" I asked.

"Who, dear?"

"Bolin. Deming knows some of it, but not what happened tonight. You know him. He'd go berserk. He's already suspicious of Justin Ming."

Another laugh from Anika. "So sweet. That boy adores you, Eja. He takes after his father that way. Bolin protects those he loves at all costs."

"How well do you know Heather? I've never really spoken to her." I discounted the nasty looks that Mrs. Horton shot my way and her imperious snubs.

49

Anika paused. "Not well. Just social chitchat at different functions. I seem to recall that she is wild about fashion. That might be an opening."

"For you, maybe, not me. I met Horton's brother years ago at some literary mixer that Brown hosted. Ames seemed nice enough, and he was really into creative writing. Plays, I think. Maybe I can build on that."

"Just be careful, Eja, and remember, I've got your back."

Once again I thanked the Heavens for Anika Swann, my sleuthing partner and so much more. "Don't worry. I'll plot tomorrow's strategy and fill you in."

I heard Bolin call Anika up to bed. After we said our goodnights, I checked my watch. Eleven o'clock. Deming had had enough time to discuss and restructure the entire tax code with Fleur Pixley. Good thing I'm not the jealous type.

Armed with my Surefire Defender flashlight, I hustled Cato outdoors for his evening constitutional. Commonwealth Avenue was deserted beneath a magical sky carpeted with stars. The beauty of the night trivialized my fears, especially those of Justin Ming. He might be a high-end rent boy, but that didn't make him a murderer. Besides, in a contest between Phaedra's word and a respected sifu's, Master Moore would surely believe Justin.

Unless she had proof. If Phaedra Jones was wily enough to fleece men of their money, she might easily have kept a souvenir or two. That would up the stakes for both Justin and Horty, not to mention those private clients she rounded up. I crawled into bed and fell asleep counting motives.

FLEUR PIXLEY CALLED the next morning before I'd finished my espresso. It was still early, although to a bureaucrat, 9:00 a.m. might seem like the shank of the day. We spent a few minutes in meaningless chatter before she came to the point.

"I had dinner with Deming last night. He's so charming and better looking than ever."

"Indeed." I didn't trust myself to say much—spiteful comments were unworthy of me. I could picture Fleur fluffing her pixie cut as she sat entombed in her federal cubicle. The poor dear probably appreciated a good meal at a fine establishment.

"Have you set the date yet?" she purred. "I couldn't get any specifics from Deming."

"Soon. Very soon. Deming loathes fuss. He'd just as soon elope to-night, but his mother has other ideas." I kept my voice friendly, as if my former classmate's agenda were a total mystery.

"Oh. You lucky thing. He's a divine dancer, but I don't have to tell you that."

Actually, Deming and I seldom went dancing. Make that never. I love music but I'm not the most graceful gal on two feet. I laughed and muttered something in response.

"You know, we were very close to your place last night," Fleur said. "You've probably been to Rise plenty of times. It's right on Stuart Street. Such a cool club. I should have known that Deming Swann would be a member."

Now I knew why Deming hadn't called last night. That rat was up to his ears in something, and it wasn't paperwork.

"I'm glad you enjoyed yourself," I said. "Let's do lunch sometime soon."

"When?" Fleur had certainly cultivated her killer instinct. Maybe enforcement work demanded that.

"How about next week? I'll text my mother-in-law and call you back."

"Mother-in-law? Jumping the gun a bit, aren't you, Eja?"

Now was my turn to twist the verbal knife. "You know how it is. We are so close that Anika already seems like family. Bolin too."

"Wow! Bolin Swann is on the Forbes list. One of the richest billion-aires in the world, or something like that." Clearly, Fleur was staggered by my proximity to greatness.

"I know. He was really embarrassed when they issued that thing. Swanns like to keep personal matters low key. You understand."

Fleur soon made her excuses and ended our chat, leaving me very curious about Deming's tete-a-tete and the impact on Horton's money problems.

THAT EVENING I agonized over wardrobe options before settling on my old standby—a black scoop-neck Armani with matching lace jacket. It made me feel elegant and slightly decadent, especially when a strand of Grandma's pearls dangled near my cleavage. Fortunately, my minimalist approach to hair and makeup could be done on autopilot. I had no time and little patience for fussing.

Deming, or Twinkle Toes as I now called him, had texted our

departure time. At six thirty p.m. I was ready and waiting to embrace the Exley throng, if not my fiancé. With him, I was a bit miffed.

"You're lovely, Eja," Deming said, putting his arms around me. He looked pretty nifty himself in a charcoal grey Brioni suit. In truth, he looked spectacular. Deming had the dark, sizzling Byronic thing down pat. Constant praise from women was something he'd grown to expect, so I meted it out sparingly. Besides, I was confident that Fleur had shored up his ego last night during their dance session.

"Is something wrong?" he asked. "Sorry I didn't call you last night. Things got really hectic." He was fidgeting, and if he followed the script, he'd soon be cracking his knuckles. Despite an elegant facade, even Deming occasionally felt guilt. Mangling knuckles was his concession to nerves.

"No problem," I lied. "I was pretty busy myself." True enough, if you considered fending off a sex-crazed sifu and potential murderer all in a night's work.

We evaded Cato, caught the elevator, and were soon motoring to the Exley spread.

"By the way," I said. "Guess who phoned me this morning? Fleur Pixley. She wants to get together for lunch next week."

Deming's frown was a thing of beauty. "Bad idea, Eja," he growled. "This foundation matter is a delicate thing. Fleur agreed to look into it, but I think we should limit any other contact."

I shrugged. "Fine. I'll think up some excuse. After all, your dinner was strictly business, but our lunch would be personal."

Deming stomped on the gas pedal and sailed into traffic heading west on Storrow Drive toward Brookline. A pack of homicidal drivers jockeyed for position as they made their homeward pilgrimage. That focused Deming on road congestion, leaving me the opportunity to share a bowdlerized account of my session with Justin Ming.

"He came to your apartment?" Deming bit his lip as his complexion paled. "What were you thinking, Eja? The man might be a murderer."

"Your trainer comes to your place all the time," I said. "So does your masseur, as I recall. What's the harm?"

"Harm? For one thing, I am fully capable of defending myself." He narrowed his eyes and glared at me. "How would you fend someone off—with a cutting remark?"

"Good one," I said. "Let me write that down. Just stop fuming and listen for just a minute. You'll find this very interesting." I delivered a summary of events that was a model of brevity. When I finished,

Deming gripped the steering wheel as if he were facing a death squad.

"Why didn't you mention *Dim Mak* before? We need to notify Lieutenant Bates at once."

"Don't blame me. I'd never heard the term before. And Justin volunteered it. That's something a guilty man would never do." I folded my arms and rested my case.

"Let me get this straight," Deming fumed. "Maybe I didn't hear it right. Justin Ming is a prostitute? Is that what you're saying?"

I shook my head. "That's rather harsh. More like an escort or paid companion. No one thinks twice about it when some nubile girl does that. What's the difference? Let's just say, Justin learned to capitalize on his assets. With Phaedra Jones pointing the way, he identified receptive women who became his private clients, including our hostess, Heather Exley, wife of your client."

"How in the hell did you pry that information out of him?"

I shrugged and tossed my hair. "No problem. We drank tea and I just asked."

Deming massaged his temples as if he were fending off a migraine. "Unbelievable. Let me summarize. Horton was doing the murder victim, while his wife was schlepping the sifu. What else?"

"Don't forget that Justin and Phaedra were also an item. That man has plenty of stamina. Apparently she was in love with him and wanted an exclusivity clause."

"Christ!" Deming was seldom profane. His anxiety level must be stratospheric. "Don't mention this tonight. I'll broach it to Horton later on."

"Fine," I said. "I want to relax and have a good time. You know, mingle, have a few drinks. Maybe we can go dancing afterwards. Know any place good?"

His perfect profile turned to stone, but Deming gave nothing away. "Sure. Sounds like fun. It might not work tonight, though. I need some time alone with Horton about foundation business."

He turned up the music as a soul medley played on the Porsche's super-duper Burmester surround sound system. As luck would have it, Nina Simone added her two cents by belting out, "The Other Woman." I hummed along, word for word until Deming cracked.

"Listen, Eja, I don't know what Fleur told you, but everything was very innocent last night. We had dinner and dropped by a club to listen to music. Period."

"Okay. You know that I trust you." I hid my hands under my purse so that he didn't see my crossed fingers. "What's the story with the FTC and the Exley Foundation?"

He sighed. "They got a tip—anonymous source—that Horton was involved in a scam, using the foundation's treasury as his personal piggy bank. That alone is enough to trigger an inquiry, unless I can convince her that Horty is a fool, not a felon."

I gave his shoulder a friendly pat. "You can be very persuasive. Your client is one lucky guy."

The hint of sarcasm wasn't lost on Deming. His guilty flush proved that.

"Does Horton blame Phaedra for his problems?" I asked.

"Nope, that's just it. He thinks Phaedra was an innocent dupe."

From what I'd seen of Phaedra, she'd left innocence behind in her cradle. The woman had a lot going for her, if you like a sultry blend of sex and avarice, stirred not shaken.

"Mrs. Exley might see things differently. She's got plenty of muscle from her workouts and seemed more than willing to use them." I recalled her parting threat to Phaedra in the locker room. The venom literally spewed from Heather's lips.

"Just chill, Eja. Let Lieutenant Bates do her job, and you do yours. For tonight, just act like the brilliant novelist and loving fiancée that you are. Put that detective shit on hold." He pinched my cheek. "I know you can do it."

I had no time to react. My mind was boggled by the first glimpse of the Exley manse, an English manor house whose gabled roof and lush grounds resembled a movie set more opulent than Downton Abbey.

"Good Lord!" I gaped. "That house is huge. It must be fifteen thousand square feet."

"Twenty at least," Deming said coolly. "It's insured for a pile of money. Historic register and all that. Merry Meadow has lots of space, plus a gym, theatre, and fantastic wine cellar. The name's misleading, though. Not much joy in those rooms." He squeezed my hand. "What's the matter, my love? Overwhelmed by a stately home? It was built to house large families with plenty of kiddos running around."

I'd never considered Deming very child-centric. His preoccupation with progeny was recent and somewhat puzzling. Was he vying for father of the year? The thought sent chills up my spine. I fully expected him to paw the ground like a stallion in rut.

"Come along, Eja," he said. "I need to speak with our host before the others arrive. You can entertain Mrs. Exley."

Even after years with the Swanns, conspicuous consumption makes me uneasy. Blame it on my socialist parents who would have been scandalized by Horton and his crowd. They had loved CeCe and applauded Bolin's generosity to the poor even as they showered me with Marxist bromides and warnings against capitalism. In our household, Bertrand Russell, not Horatio Alger, was a role model.

"How many people live here?" I asked, as we walked up the cobblestone driveway.

Deming shrugged. "Horty's family, of course, and Ames too, I believe. He never married, although he's in his mid-thirties now."

"Really?" I said. "He was a ladies' man in college. Coeds considered him quite a catch."

That earned me an eye roll from my sweetie. "I seem to recall that a cousin lives here too. Priscilla, Orphelia—no, Portia. I knew it was something Shakespearean. Portia Amory Shaw, a first cousin or something. Disowned by the Amorys when she married beneath her. Divorced the husband and hasn't a cent to her name."

"Hmm. Everything is quite Victorian, wouldn't you say? Genteel poverty amid excess."

"Stow it, Eja. I can hear those wheels turning. This is not some English country house mystery. We're five miles from the heart of Boston, for God's sake."

I beamed the practiced smile of the submissive hausfrau. Occasionally, I dabbled in womanly arts just for fun. Deming was not deceived.

"Stop screwing with me, Eja. I mean it. I know your tricks." He hustled me along the path to an enormous walnut door and pressed the buzzer.

When the door opened, I gasped.

There stood the perfect replica of an English butler in full livery, straight from the pen of Dorothy Sayers or Christie herself. His elegant posture accentuated a whippet-thin frame coupled with a look of unassailable dignity. He was an ageless relic of the good life, with unremarkable features and a thin-lipped smile. If his name was Bunter, I'd lose all self-control.

"Evening, Carlisle." Deming nodded toward me. "This is Ms. Kane."

Carlisle bowed and led us down a long hallway filled with ancestral portraits. I made that assumption based on the prominent Exley nose sported by each subject. The males could carry it off, but a large proboscis was less attractive on the females.

"They're in the parlor," Carlisle said. "Except for Mr. Horton. He's in his study."

"Take me to him," Deming said. "Ms. Kane will join the other guests."

The last thing I wanted was to be trapped in a confined space with Heather Exley and company. However, in the spirit of pre-connubial bliss, I said nothing.

"See you later, darling." Deming's voice held a hint of triumph.

"Of course, Twinkle Toes."

I STOOD IN THE doorway, observing the group and admiring my surroundings. The parlor was actually comprised of twin rooms divided by a concealed pocket door. Elaborate wood moldings, offset by a sprightly selection of French pieces in lemon and red, were anchored by a phenomenal Aubusson carpet. Tasteful accessories were sprinkled among more utilitarian items; antiques coexisted with modern art. Whatever her personal failings, Heather made one hell of a decorator. Either that, or she had the good sense to hire a pro.

She was not much of a hostess, however. Most of the dozen or so partygoers were engrossed in conversations or cackling with alcohol-fueled hilarity. Heather stared me down, turned her head, and dismissed me as she would an errant serf. Only when Anika waved from the far end of the room did Mrs. Exley stir.

Her impeccable attire was a vivid contrast to her manners. Heather wore a column of shimmering white silk with long, graceful sleeves and a scalloped hem.

"I've seen you at the dojo," Heather said, her voice a breathy whisper. "Eartha, Erma, something like that. I'm hopeless when it comes to names." She extended a slim hand bedecked with diamonds.

"Actually, it's Eja Kane." My smile oozed synthetic charm as I lowered my voice and shook her hand. "We share the same sifu instructor—Justin Ming."

Heather's lovely eyes widened, and her skin lost its bloom. When I touched her arm, she grimaced. "I don't understand."

I recalled Deming's assessment of her as a dim bulb. Oh yes. Before I succeeded in leveling our hostess, Anika glided our way in a swish of satin. Unlike more timid souls, Mrs. Bolin Swann had chosen a fiery orange frock that bared her shoulders. Her uber-hot hubby was at her side.

"Have you two met?" Anika asked, putting her arm around me. "Eja will soon be my daughter, Heather, although she's been part of our family for years."

"We were just discussing that," I said. "Anika is my workout buddy at Shaolin City. She also trains with Justin Ming."

Heather clutched her throat and coughed.

"May I get you a drink?" Bolin asked. "Perrier or something stronger?"

Her eyelashes fluttered as she played the coquette. "That's so gallant of you, Bolin. It must be allergies." She seized his arm and headed for the bar, leaving Anika and I alone and bemused.

"What in the world did you say to her?" Anika asked.

I shrugged. "Not much. I think her guilty conscience went into overdrive. Remember, I saw that tiff between her and Phaedra Jones."

Anika patted my arm. "Well, don't worry. I chatted her up about fashion and decorating, her favorite topics. Believe it or not, she really knows her stuff. Anyhow, we're meeting for lunch on Monday. Care to join us?"

My grin enveloped her like London fog. "Count on it."

Chapter Nine

SOMEONE TAPPED MY shoulder as I stood at the bar sipping wine. I spun around, startled by an apparition from my past. Ames Exley, the younger, cuter, brother of Horty grabbed me in a tight, decidedly friendly bear hug and squeezed.

"Eja Kane! How come you still look like a coed?"

I dismissed the flattery, although it warmed me more than I cared to admit. Ames himself showed a touch of Dorian Gray in his lean, lithe body and curly brown hair. Like the graduate student of yore, his perfect teeth framed a wry, disarming smile that never reached his eyes.

"So, Ms. Eja, you're a prize winning author, and all I can say is wow! The rest of us talked a good game, but you delivered."

I felt the flush move up my neck and creep across my cheeks. "Do you still write? As I recall, you were keen on finishing a screenplay—sort of a Henry David Hwang concoction."

Ames waved his arms. "Quite some memory you've got. Actually, I haven't written anything in years. No time."

My patience had been rewarded. This was the opening I had hoped for. "So. What keeps you busy?"

He flashed that grin again. "Let me buy you lunch, and I'll fill you in. But be warned, it's rather dreary. Typical family saga. You know the drill."

"Great." I handed him my card, but before we made arrangements, a strong arm gripped my waist.

"There you are," Deming said, giving me a squeeze. "Thanks for keeping my fiancée company, Ames. She does tend to get lonely."

"Deming Swann—too long, buddy." Ames exchanged one of those male bonding moves. "I forgot. You're the lucky guy who snagged the prize." He shook his head. "Last I heard, you were pursuing every debutante on the East Coast. Glad you finally got some sense."

Deming showed his stoic side, but I paid a price for it. His arms gripped me in a vise that had more tension than passion. "We'll make sure to send you a wedding invitation and a front row seat to the christening."

"Whoa! I had no idea. Congratulations, man. You too, Eja."

"He's joking, Ames. We are getting married, but the christening is years away."

The moment was salvaged by the arrival of a petite woman with undistinguished features and a knot of mousey brown hair. By the way she deferred to Ames, I assumed that this was the impoverished cousin who survived on family sufferance. Portia Amory Shaw wore classic Brahmin apparel that had seen better days. Her dun-colored twinset was enlivened by a circle pin and a single strand of pearls. The matching tweed skirt and kitten heels were so dowdy that I glowed like a supermodel in comparison.

"We haven't been introduced," I said. "I'm Eja Kane."

She blinked and mumbled something unintelligible. Despite the humble act, I decided that Portia was sly, not shy. It was something in those watery blue eyes, a sharp intelligence masking a hint of malevolence.

"Nice to meet you," she said, extending a slightly limp hand. "I've read your books."

Like most writers, I'm a glutton for praise, no matter what the source. "Really? Are you a mystery fan?"

Portia shrugged diffidently. "Not really. I prefer serious literature, but your books were already in our library."

Ames jumped in to salve my ego. "I confess, Eja. I'm an unabashed fan. The others have to fight me for your books. Perhaps you'd consider signing them for me."

"Careful, Ames," Deming said, squeezing my arm. "You'll give her a swelled head. Eja's won some national competitions, you know."

I counted way past ten, hoping in vain to remain calm. For two cents, maybe less, I would kick mousey Ms. Shaw across the room. "Sure. I'll gladly sign them whenever you like."

Ames crooked his finger. "Mind if we steal away to the library, Dem? I'm sure Portia has some legal questions she's dying to ask you."

He led me across the hallway to a magnificent walnut-paneled room packed floor to ceiling with books. "Here." He pointed to an imposing partners desk with gilt mounts. "Sit down and get comfortable."

True to his word, Ames produced hard copies of all five of my books. "Try this pen," he said, thrusting an elaborate lacquered instrument my way.

"Wow. This pen is really special. Italian, isn't it?"

"German, actually." Ames beamed foolishly. "It's a Pelikan Toledo, gold nib and all. I collect fine writing instruments. Sort of a hobby. This one is new, and I can't think of a better use for it." He sat opposite me at the other partner's space.

I inscribed each copy with a personal message that might be meaningful to Ames. Knowing Deming, our time together was growing short, and I had to maximize the opportunity.

"I spoke with an old Brown classmate of ours just yesterday," I said. "Fleur Pixley. You must remember her."

His reaction surprised me. Ames grew pale, and he leaned back as if I had struck him. "Fleur? Oh, yes. Redhead with an overbite. Always hanging around Deming as I recall."

"That's the one. She's an executive with the FTC now, you know. Some bigwig in charge of fraud and Ponzi schemes. Stuff like that. Isn't it weird how everyone settles into a different profession? In college, we all seemed destined for academic careers."

"Not me," Ames said ruefully. "I yearned to be a cross between Eugene O'Neill and Arthur Miller. Silly dream."

I summoned my small store of feminine wiles. "All dreams sound silly in daylight, but it's never too late to start. What's keeping you busy these days?"

Ames leaned over and lowered his voice. "Family. I ride herd on Horton, you know, do my bit with the family trust, or try to. Our mother was a do-gooder in the best sense of the word. That trust meant a lot to her."

"I have no head for business," I said. "Just managing the paperwork and regulations must be difficult. Not to mention the taxes. Ugh!"

That ignited a spark in his eyes, as Ames embellished the topic. "Such drama you wouldn't believe. I swear that money causes more feuds than religion, especially when one person controls everything." He tented his hands in prayer. "There are so many needy causes, Eja. Those of us who have been blessed have great responsibilities."

The link between Fleur Pixley, the FTC, and the Exley trust grew clearer. The anonymous tipster might well be sitting on the other side of the partners desk, beaming his pious smile. Before I reacted, the door burst open, disgorging Horton Exley and my fiancé.

"Portia said you two came this way. What's going on here, Ames?" Horty glowered. "We have guests, you know." He glanced at me and gave a brisk nod. Deming flashed a triumphant grin my way but said nothing.

"Chill, big brother," Ames said. "Eja and I were reminiscing, and I lost track of time." He stacked my books into a neat pile and pushed back his chair. "Guess I better go earn my keep. Thanks, Eja. That trip to the past was fun."

His genial tone was negated by the murderous look in his eyes. Deming caught it, but Horton seemed oblivious to his brother's moods. Perhaps he didn't notice. Maybe he just didn't care.

"I think I'll get something to eat," I said. "You fellows can have your privacy."

My real plan had nothing to do with food. I zeroed in on the slight form of Portia Amory Shaw languishing in a corner like yesterday's wallflower. Be kind, I chided myself. Maybe the woman is shy or socially awkward. A sharp inner voice told me to trust my instincts. Ms. Shaw was a stealth bitch who bore watching.

I plucked a lemon tart from a tray, took a bite, and pasted a friendly grin on my face. "This is sinfully delicious, don't you agree? Worth every calorie."

Portia curled her lip in a semi-sneer. "I avoid desserts. They're bad for you."

"So many things are," I agreed. "Sometimes, one just has to take a risk and go for it."

She shrugged and gave me a mile-high stare. "I suppose."

I took a deep breath and soldiered on. Portia had the social skills of a mollusk, but I had tenacity on my side. Everyone has an ego, even a drab specimen like her. The trick was finding the right key to unlock it. Writers are paid to fabricate things, so I had no problem with a little white lie.

"Ames mentioned that you help out with the foundation. Indispensible, he called you."

Portia's eyes brightened immediately. "He did? I do my best, of course, but others help out as well. I'm an accountant by trade. A CPA."

Why was I not surprised? The woman probably had a calculator for a heart. That explained her diffident manner and bland attire. Accountants see life as one great balance sheet with debits and credits queuing up in the ledger. Their creativity is predictably low. After all, creative accounting lands one in the pokey.

"Wow! Numbers are not my thing, and I'm in awe of anyone who can master them. Deming minored in finance, and he's always lecturing me about precision." I shook my head. "Boring!"

I had found the key to Portia Amory Shaw. The drab household retainer was transformed into a fiery champion of fiscal prudence. With her face flushed with emotion, Portia wagged a finger my way.

"Oh, no, Eja. Think what the world would be like without accountants. Chaos, that's what. We are the guardians of stability and order. Why, I could tell you stories that would chill your blood. Checks and balances. They're essential, but not everyone agrees with that. Putting too much control in one person's hands leads to disaster. Ames agrees with me. He minored in accounting, you know."

We both paused as Heather breezed past us like an errant sprite on a mission.

I lowered my voice to a conspiratorial level. "Poor Heather. That woman's murder must have really shaken her."

Portia leaned forward, suddenly eager to swap girl talk. "*That woman* was a menace. Phaedra Jones—even the name sounds trashy. Up to no good, I knew that from the first."

"Surely she didn't come to the house," I said. "After all, there are limits."

Portia sneered. "No. She hung around the foundation, though. Posing as a financial wizard, can you believe it? Blathering about gold. Horton mooned over her like a love-struck teenager."

Her voice suddenly trailed off as if she were a wind-up toy whose battery was spent. The reason soon became evident. Heather Exley had sidled up behind me, and by the look on her face, she wasn't happy. She stood, hands on hips, her Botoxed brow straining mightily to frown.

"You're needed in the kitchen, Portia. Help Carlisle supervise the caterers."

Without another word, Portia marched toward the exit with the sharp, stiff gait of a marionette. The triumphant gleam in Heather's eyes was unsettling yet strangely appropriate. I'd seen that look the night she fought with Phaedra Jones, the spectre of a foul inner core that obscured her classic beauty. Lowbrow Barbie doll she might be, but Heather Elliot Exley had a mile-wide mean streak.

"I hope she wasn't bothering you," Heather said. "One tries to be kind, but sometimes . . ."

"Oh, certainly not," I lied. "We were just chatting about books. By the way, Heather, I never expressed my condolences to you."

The look she gave me was even more blank than normal. "I don't understand."

"About your friend. Phaedra Jones. I saw you two at the dojo and could tell you were close."

Heather hissed a reply and turned on her heel. "You are misinformed. I hardly knew the woman."

I stared after her, startled anew by the depth of her venom. When Deming joined me I was considering the possibility that Phaedra's murder might be a simple case of vengeful spouse syndrome. Heather Exley relished the perks of the Exley name even as she lusted after Justin Ming. If threatened, she might lash out to protect her interests.

"There you are," Deming said, stroking my arm. "Winning friends again, I see. Heather's face was a veritable thundercloud. What did you say to her?"

I threw my hands up in the air and played innocent. "She's kind of a flake. Who knows?"

"Come along then. I have a little pre-wedding surprise for you." Deming raised his eyebrows suggestively.

I'm a sucker for any gift large or small. My parents seldom indulged me, so that made any present extra special. "Where is it?"

"Calm down, my girl." Deming showed his lawyer's face. "You have to earn it."

"Earn what?" Anika asked. "How about joining us for dinner, you two? I'm starving."

"Good idea," Deming said. "Let's find our hosts and say goodbye." He did a quick survey of the room and sighed. "Hmm. Seems like they flew the coop."

I spotted Ames and flagged him down. "Thanks for inviting us. Everything was lovely."

This time, his smile seemed genuine. "I enjoyed our chat. It reminded me of happier times. Okay if I call you for lunch? Don't want Deming to get the wrong idea and mess me up. He's some kind of martial arts master as I recall."

"I trust Eja's judgment," Deming said, pointing to my engagement ring.

Anika looped her arm in Bolin's and laughed. "You children. Always cutting up. Please tell Heather that I look forward to our luncheon date."

After Bolin shook hands with Ames, they led the way out the door. I was anxious to leave, partially because of my present, but mostly so that we could all compare notes. I'd noticed Bolin chatting up several investment bankers, while Anika charmed the rest of the crowd. No one had mentioned the Exley trust, not directly, but both Ames and Portia had dropped hints that all was not well. They might be malcontents, or they might have insider information about Horty's misdeeds. Either way, the cocktail party had been a gold mine of information. I giggled at the unintentional pun and what it portended.

Deming galloped toward the Porsche while I trailed along behind acting nonchalant. He wanted me to beg, and I refused—that would set a dangerous precedent for married life. After he opened the door and kissed my cheek, I felt my resistance ebb. I'm not made of steel. Who can resist a strong, gorgeous man with a tender side?

"Guess," he said, as he turned on the engine. "You'll never figure it out in a million years."

"Okay. Earrings or some other kind of jewelry."

His derisive snort answered that. "Not even close. Besides, whenever I give you jewelry you always say it's too expensive. Here's a hint. This is something you can touch but not wear."

Action was called for unless I was prepared to play twenty questions.

"If you tell me, I'll share what I found out from Ames and Portia, plus my observations about Lady Macbeth." I crossed my arms and hung tough. "It involves your client."

Deming knew when to fold. "Reach under your seat," he said. "You can unwrap it now, but for God's sake be careful. It's valuable."

I felt like a kid at Christmas tearing into a present. It was beautifully done up in silver paper with an exquisite bow. That didn't keep me from shredding the thing in ten seconds flat.

"Careful, Eja, careful." Deming couldn't hide his smile as I uncovered my prize—a first edition of Chandler's opus, *The Big Sleep*, in original dust jacket.

I stroked the cover reverently, terrified of ripping it. "It's from Bauman Rare Books. You must have paid a mint for this thing."

"It can be returned if you don't want it. Dad knows the owner."

"Don't want it! Are you kidding? Raymond Chandler is my hero, an American original. Thank you, Deming. It's perfect. I'll keep it on my desk for inspiration."

His eyes glowed at my reaction. "Better put in on your bookshelf. If Cato ruins it, I swear I'll pulverize that mutt."

I leaned across the seat and kissed him. "I love you. For so many reasons."

Our lips met in a tender touch that spoke volumes. Deming drew me close and whispered, "I waited a long time for you, Ms. Eja Kane, and I will never let you go. Understand?"

I shivered, barely able to speak. "Absolutely."

Chapter Ten

AS THE PORSCHE zipped toward Newbury Street, I shared my impressions of the evening. The news didn't faze Deming one bit. In fact, he summarily dismissed it.

"Big deal," he said. "Let's analyze what you learned. Ames is envious of his brother. Nothing new there. Story as old as Cain and Abel."

"As I recall, that didn't turn out so well." I can hold a grudge with the best of them, and Deming was teetering on the brink of disaster. He knew how much detective work meant to me and refused to acknowledge my small triumphs.

"Number two." Like most lawyers, Deming loved the sound of his own voice and lived to argue. "This business about Portia is slightly more interesting. Who knew that mousey little thing was a CPA? She's my candidate for deep throat, the viper in the nest, so to speak."

"She loathes Heather. That much was clear when she was treated like a scullery maid."

"Don't dramatize, Eja. Portia was probably eager to help." Deming made a sharp turn and swung into his parents' driveway. "You haven't heard my news yet. Horty wrote a check to reimburse the foundation, subject to one condition. No disclosure about his mistake and no nonsense with the Feds about penalties and interest."

"Sounds good," I said, "except for one thing."

Deming sighed. "What now."

"There's the little matter of Lieutenant Euphemia Bates and murder. Does she know about this five million dollar *mistake?* Seems to me it's an excellent motive for murder. Horton is obsessive about his reputation. What if Phaedra was blackmailing him?"

I could see the wheels turning in Deming's brilliant mind. Euphemia Bates was a worthy adversary who would never let the Exley name stand in the way of solving a murder.

"Forget about it," Deming growled. "I'm Horton's lawyer, not a police officer. I won't volunteer anything against my client's interests."

He switched off the engine and grunted. "I'll mention it to Pam, of course."

Ugh! Just when I started to feel mellow, he brings up Pamela Schwartz. I quickly changed the subject. "How far did you go with Fleur?" I asked. "She might get into trouble with her bosses, you know. They're very conservative."

Deming dismissed my concern with a wave of his arm. "Above all, they are a business, and like any other business a closed case is a big win. Besides, penalties are negotiable." He smirked. "And I, my love, am one hell of a negotiator."

That set me back awhile and strengthened my desire to see Fleur Pixley, my old college chum. We might relive old times or have a serious chat about the future. She was goal oriented, focused, and aggressive. Whatever her game, if it concerned Deming, she'd met her match in me.

"Stop daydreaming, Eja. I'm starving." Deming opened my door and rolled his eyes. "Remember. Say nothing about that check. Confidentiality and all." He towed me toward the front door, where Po awaited us. "I hope they've got some snacks ready," he said. "Horty must be economizing. Didn't have anything worth eating."

Anika and Bolin were in the dining room, sipping Pellegrino. "Come on in, son," Bolin said. "Don't keep Eja just standing there."

"We were dissecting the party." Anika winked as she said it. "Your dad found out more than I did."

"Not really," Bolin said, "but several of the guys had also been approached by Phaedra. At social events and fundraisers. You know the drill. Her pitch was pretty slick, I'll have to admit."

Anika giggled. "Phaedra was pretty slick too. She knew how to maneuver men."

Deming curled his lip in an excellent imitation of a villain. "Wait a minute, Dad. Those guys are all in the upper money brackets. They must have tons of financial advisors who would smell a rat right away."

"That was the beauty of the plan," Bolin said. "Phaedra flattered them, flirted with them, and told them they were way smarter than their stodgy advisors. And . . ." His eyes sparkled, "she had a partner."

"What?" I cried. This was totally unexpected, but it made sense. Phaedra had been a "fixer," but she needed someone else to close the deal, someone who might react badly if she ruined his scheme.

Deming forgot his hunger. He glanced at his watch and rushed from the room clutching his cell phone. Horton Exley had some explaining to do, especially if he forgot to mention a third party.

Euphemia Bates would blow her stack.

"Oh, dear," Anika said. "That boy will have an ulcer before he's forty." She lowered her voice. "I learned a few things tonight myself."

Bolin glanced at his wife with such pride that I choked up. It was a rare and beautiful thing to witness.

"Okay, here it is." Anika gave a deep, throaty laugh. "Several of the ladies were well-acquainted with Phaedra Jones, or women like her. Those vultures always hang around powerful men hoping to snare them." Anika locked eyes with Bolin, making it clear that she had no such worries. "They were relieved when she made a play for Horton Exley."

"Kind of mean, isn't it? After all, Horton has a family too." Bolin winced.

"I'm afraid Heather isn't well-liked," Anika said. "I'm not sure why."

I thought of several reasons, starting with the fact that Heather was a Grade A bitch. In fairness, I had to admit that her beauty was probably another barrier.

"So they know about Horty's affair?" I asked. "Interesting."

Anika sat silently for a moment, sipping her Pellegrino. "There's more. I think they know about Heather's affair too."

"Really?" Bolin shifted in his chair as if gossip made him uncomfortable. "What makes you say that?"

"No one mentioned it directly, but there were several comments about exercise regimens and some coy references to trainers." Anika showed her dimples. "In fact, one of them asked Heather if she recommended Justin Ming."

If Euphemia Bates cornered anyone in Heather's circle, it wouldn't take long for that tidbit to surface. I spent a pleasant moment fantasizing about Heather the jailbird, stripped of designer duds, her skin chafed by rough prison jumpsuits. Trouble was, even in that scenario, Heather Exley still looked beautiful.

I dished about my chats with Ames and Portia, especially the family feud that afflicted the Exleys. "Doesn't seem related to the murder," I said. "Portia resents Heather, and Ames and Horton have a sibling rivalry going on."

Bolin pursed his lips, as if he were reluctant to speak. "You might consider one other possibility. If Horton's mismanagement were made public, he'd be removed as principal trustee of the foundation. That would benefit Ames."

"Not just Ames." I flashed back to my chat with Portia. "Portia would be right there steering the ship. The chance to show up Horton and Heather—she'd love it. She complained to me about inadequate checks and balances right after we met."

"But she seems so shy," Anika said, "like a spectre at the feast. The family treats her rather badly, you know."

"Shy my foot," I said. "Unless I'm totally off base, Portia is sly, the type who would skulk around and find secrets."

Just then, Deming breezed into the room, eyes blazing. "I couldn't get Horty on the phone," he fumed. "Maybe the party was too much for him." Deming was a curious case in contrasts—blank and unreadable at times, or volcanic, especially when he started cracking his knuckles.

"Stop that, son." Anika's voice was as soothing as cool water in a mountain stream. She filled a plate with smoked salmon and shrimp and handed it to him. "Now relax and eat this before you do anything else. I insist."

Bolin hugged his wife. "You heard her, Dem. Always a mother."

Deming wiped off his Mr. Sulky Pout face and sat down. "I don't know why I bother anymore. Some clients are more trouble than they're worth."

Before treading into dangerous waters, I took a deep breath. Unfortunately, Deming glimpsed my expression and pounced. Sad but true, I have a lousy poker face. "Something bothering you, Eja? I gather you don't agree."

"Forgive me, but isn't Horty exactly the kind of client who needs a good attorney? That is what you guys *do*, isn't it?"

Bolin's laughter rang out. "She's got you, son. Protecting our clients comes first. Never get in a verbal tussle with a writer. At least one as good as Eja."

I watched them, father and son, alike yet so different. They shared the same dreamboat genes, but inhabited very different psyches. Deming's passion was tempered by Bolin's seismic sense of calm—fire and ice warring within two brilliant minds and two exceptionally fit bodies.

Deming crumpled his napkin and jumped up. "I've got to go. No telling what Horty is up to."

"Wait a minute. I'll go with you." I dismissed his protests without a thought. "Hey. You may need a woman's touch."

He waved his arms in surrender, knowing that any further argument was useless. I trotted behind Deming as he swept past Po and out the door.

"YOU STAY IN THE car," Deming told me when we reached the Exley estate. "Things might get rough."

"Dream on," I said. "You seem to forget that I carry pepper spray."

"Great. I'll probably be the first casualty." He stepped over to my door, undid my seatbelt, and helped me alight. "At least don't say anything. This won't take long if Horty has a brain in his patrician skull."

Suddenly, Deming thrust his arm out crossing guard style. "Wait a minute. What are police cars doing here?" He pointed toward two commonplace vehicles that littered the Exley's side driveway. "They're unmarked, but that doesn't mean anything."

"Maybe they belong to guests who are down on their luck. Or perhaps this crowd likes to go slumming."

Deming's glare suggested that he didn't appreciate my humor. "I better go in and find out," he said. "Let's hope Horty kept his mouth shut."

At that moment, the front door opened, disgorging Euphemia Bates, her sergeant, and the Exleys. Horton was protesting vigorously and waving his arms, but Heather looked dazed, more Stepford wife than socialite.

"Call Pam," Deming whispered. "I have her on speed dial." He quickened his pace and headed toward his client.

I followed instructions and summoned my least favorite female to the scene. Naturally Pamela griped when I said that Deming wasn't there.

"You're sure this is urgent," she asked. "I have plans tonight."

I fought and won a battle for self-control. After all, the first Shaolin law bade me to love fellow disciples. "Deming was fairly insistent, Pam, but it's up to you. I should mention though that Horton Exley and his wife just got into a squad car."

"What? I'm on my way. Have Dem text me with the location."

I took a long, deep breath. Deming humped that harlot for two years, but that was no reason to overreact. We were both accomplished women with much to offer. Pamela Schwartz was tall, toothsome, and blond; I was short, curvy, and brunette. Why should that activate my insecurity? After all, I was his fiancée, and she was merely his colleague. Plus, I have a superior sense of humor. Men always choose that when selecting a mate. That happy talk might have worked except for one thing: I'd seen Pamela Schwartz in a bikini, and the sight still haunted me.

Meanwhile, activity outside the house intensified. Euphemia Bates, looking like a svelte, sexy messenger of doom, swept into her car and was whisked away. Deming marched toward me, followed by an apoplectic Horton Exley.

"Did you call her?" Deming grunted.

I nodded and gave him Poison Pam's message and his phone.

"You've got to do something," Horty wailed. "She's innocent."

"Who?" I asked.

Horton's glare was bright enough to cause blindness. "My wife, of course. They think she murdered Phaedra."

That news staggered me. I had suspicions, plenty of questions, and absolutely no answers. Admittedly, Heather was the type of narcissist who could kill to protect her interests. She had three compelling motives to do so, but for some reason, I doubted it.

"Eja, did you hear me?" Deming touched my arm. "I've got to get Horton downtown. Call Po, and he'll take you home."

"Don't worry," a deep voice said. Ames Exley appeared out of nowhere wearing his bespoke suit and a sly smile. "I'll see her home safe and sound. It will be my pleasure."

He didn't like it, but Deming had little choice. His brow was knitted into a thundercloud, but he nodded briskly. "See that you do." Then he and his client jumped into the Porsche and roared away.

Ames dangled his car keys in front of me and pointed toward the garage. "This has been one hell of a night. Thank God we don't have any neighbors nearby. Exleys simply don't get hauled away by the authorities." He grinned. "We make a killing in the market, not the dojo."

He loped into the garage, never noticing my tepid response to his feeble joke. I recalled that Ames had always been self-absorbed. It was one of the reasons why we'd never connected in college.

"Come on, Eja," he called. "I won't bite." Ames helped me into his mammoth vehicle, a nondescript black Surburban with no running board.

"Surprised you, I bet. Pure function, nothing fancy. We haul lots of people around for charities and such, so a behemoth like this makes sense."

The intensity of his stare unnerved me for a moment, until I reminded myself that this was a man I had known for years. Correction.

This was a man I knew years ago.

Ames plugged in his iPhone and fired up the Surburban's monster engine. Classic country music blared out, songs I knew by heart. After humming along to Crystal Gayle, Charlie Rich, and Kenny Rogers, I was finally able to relax.

"Everything okay now?" Ames asked. "You might think our entire family is a bunch of loonies, but the Exley foundation does a lot of good. You should get to know us, Eja."

"Thanks. Maybe I will." He made a few deft turns and followed my directions. Soon we were at the entryway to the Tudor.

Sometimes enthusiasm outstrips my common sense. Before I could say "bad idea," Ames Exley was ensconced in my living room, sipping cognac. I know nothing about fine liquor, but Deming is an oenophile who insists on stocking the liquor cabinet. Based on the approving nods from my guest, Deming was right on target.

I sat on the opposite side of the room, holding Cato. Fortunately, the little devil behaved reasonably well. He ignored Ames and focused on licking my ears.

"This is some place, Eja. Maybe I should have stuck with writing."

I skipped my self-deprecating tale about inheriting the co-op and its contents. Ames was a bit too slick and calculating for my taste. Let him think I was a superstar.

"So how did you and Deming get together?" he asked. "I thought you married someone else."

No need to rehash my ill-fated marriage. I shrugged and gave Ames a bland smile. "It was just meant to be, I suppose. You're the interesting one. How come a catch like you is still on the market?"

"Just lucky," Ames said. "After watching my brother and his wife, I'm rather jaded about connubial bliss. My cousin's situation was just as bad, and now this drama tonight. It's absurd, of course." He took another sip of cognac. "Heather is insulated from life. She doesn't care enough about anything, including her sons, to commit murder. Only one thing motivates that woman—Heather Elliot Exley."

Having seen her at the dojo, I had a very different opinion. Heather breathed fire when anyone approached Justin Ming, and her reaction to Phaedra had been volcanic.

"It's none of my business, but I saw her arguing with Phaedra at the dojo. It got pretty heated."

Ames raised his eyebrows. "Really? How odd."

I anointed myself with eau d' innocence and continued. "It was very awkward, believe me. I didn't know either of them, yet I was trapped there."

Unfortunately, Ames remembered my tricks from long ago.

"Bet you made the most of it, though. You once gave an impassioned speech about the value of eavesdropping to a writer. What in the world were they fighting about?"

I filled his snifter with more cognac.

"It didn't make much sense. Heather was shouting something about bullion. Phaedra was fending her off and sneering." I shrugged. "You know, Portia mentioned something this evening about Phaedra posing as an investment guru. Maybe that's where this bullion thing fits in."

Ames leaned his head back and laughed. "You are some detective, Ms. Kane. I suspect that Heather considered her a rival and warned her off. My brother was quite taken with Phaedra, you see."

I contrasted the two women—Heather, the ice princess, and dark, sinewy Phaedra. Horton wouldn't be the first man to seek a wife's comfort and a lover's passion. That made him the ultimate patsy and a prime target for blackmail. After all, Exleys simply didn't get divorced.

"So," Ames said, "you mentioned something about Fleur Pixley. If you get together, let me know. I'd love to join you."

"Okay, but are you up to handling two hot women at once?"

"I can manage," Ames said with a wink. "At one time, I was very fond of Fleur, but all she could see was Deming. He ignored her of course." He twisted his cufflink and adjusted his jacket. "Come to think of it, you're not his type either. Dem pursued those prom queen debs, the ones who always looked camera-ready. Strange how things work out."

He was right, but those comments still stung. No pep talks, book tours, or wolf whistles could ever eradicate my self-doubt. One look at Deming Swann made my heart quake and my innards roil with insecurity. If he walked out my door someday and never returned, it wouldn't surprise me. In some sick way I would even feel vindicated. Keeping pace with the Swanns was no easy task for a simple soul like me.

Ames walked over and pinched my cheek. "Hey, cheer up. I was only teasing. Like I said before, Dem got lucky when he found you. You always were the smartest kid in the room."

My phone buzzed before I responded. Deming has an uncanny radar about other men and is seldom shy about asking questions.

"I'm home safe and sound," I said. "Okay. Ames is here with me."

I handed the receiver to Ames and shrugged. "He wants to speak to you."

After a brief exchange, Ames hung up. No more snarky grin; his face was somber as he squeezed my hand and prepared to leave.

"Is everything okay?" I asked. "It's still early if you want another drink."

He shook his head. "Thanks, anyway. I should be there when Horton gets home. By the way, Dem said he'll be here soon."

"Sure you don't want to stay?"

Ames grinned. "Nope. Clearly a case of three's a crowd."

Chapter Eleven

DEMING DIDN'T SAY much that night. When Cato and I returned from our jaunt around the Common, I found him collapsed on the couch, snoring lustily. I tucked the cashmere throw over him, set the security alarm, and headed for my bedroom with Cato in tow.

Sometime during the night, Deming crawled in beside me, his arms cosseting me with a lover's sweet embrace. I snuggled close to him, drifting into a deep, dreamless sleep until sunlight streamed through the window shades. Deming was still snoozing, looking as innocent as any lawyer can ever hope to. A thick curtain of black hair masked his eyes, and I saw through the linen sheet that he was totally nude. Who needs caffeine with that visual to stimulate you? I sprang from my bed ready to seize the day.

After attending to Cato, I grabbed some espresso and got down to business. My makeup routine is simple, but it takes work to tame those irrepressible curls. Glamorous I'm not. I strive for a wholesome look seasoned with a dollop of sex appeal. Think girl next door with plenty of attitude.

Fortunately, when Deming stumbled into the kitchen, he was too preoccupied with his client's woes to interrogate me. He knew that something was brewing, but time and artifice were on my side.

"What are you up to today?" he asked, narrowing his eyes. "You have that look."

"Calm down, Perry Mason. Save your suspicions for the courtroom." I gave him espresso and a kiss. "By the way, what happened last night? Did Mia Bates eviscerate poor Horty, or did he tough it out?"

Deming curled his lip and inhaled caffeine. "Leave it alone, Eja. Things are still fluid, and I don't want you interfering."

"Okay. Just tell me this. Did they arrest Heather? I might have to testify, you know. Mia never misses a trick."

"Testify? There's no trial yet. There hasn't even been an arrest."

I patted his cheek. "Thank you, Counselor. That's just what I wanted to know."

He was still huffing impotently when he stalked out the door bound for a conference with Pamela Schwartz.

I ARRANGED A lunch date with Fleur Pixley at the Parker House restaurant, a historical spot not far from her office. Call me traditional, but I love the ambience and the learned spirits that inhabit the hotel. I waited for her, supposing the antics of the Saturday Club, where Ralph Waldo Emerson, Nathaniel Hawthorne, and even Charles Dickens had supped, argued, and spread their magic. Forget about Parker House rolls and Boston cream pie. The hotel's literary legacy shone brighter than the Waterford chandelier or intricate woodwork. It captivated me, thrusting me into a writer's paradise of long-forgotten lore. So much so that I ignored Fleur Pixley until she drew up her chair and rapped me on the knuckles.

"Wake up, Eja Kane. You haven't changed one bit. Still lost in another world."

Fleur hadn't changed much either. Her pixie cut, freckles, and turned-up nose were a vivid contrast to the sober navy suit that covered her tiny frame. Her college nickname, Pert Pixley, was a moniker that even such grown-up attire couldn't mask.

"I just can't picture you as a handmaiden of the establishment," I said. "At least I stayed true to myself. You defected to the Dark Side, big time."

Fleur's grin widened. "Bet your sweet ass. I enjoy fighting for the red, white, and blue. Sure beats consorting with criminals. Ask Dem about that."

I ignored her jab and buried my nose in the menu. After debating the calorie count, I opted for virtue over appetite. Caesar salad with dressing on the side would fill me up even though I longed to plunge face down into fried chicken and lemon meringue pie.

"I read a few of your books," Fleur said. "Believe it or not, I really liked them."

Left-handed compliments activate my fighting spirit. Fortunately I've learned to control my temper. Otherwise that glass of Chablis might have found a home in Fleur's bony lap.

"I'm not surprised that you liked my work. Why would I be? Most readers do."

Fleur held up her hand, affecting innocence. "Whoa. No harm, no foul. It's just that I don't read much fiction. My life is one dusty tome after another. Financial instruments—what could be more boring? I know every bad CPA joke ever made. That's why when Dem phoned, I jumped at the chance to see him."

My hand tightened on that wine glass, but I managed a sympathetic nod. "It's fun to revisit the past."

Fleur bent forward. "You know, I had a terrible crush on him in college. Totally unrequited, I must say."

We exchanged smiles.

"He's more gorgeous than ever," Fleur gushed. "Aren't you the lucky one?"

My muscles ached from smiling and nodding, but I soldiered on.

"You know, I barely remembered Horton Exley," Fleur said. "Not until Dem brought up his name. Naturally, I can't discuss particulars with you. Confidentiality, you know."

"Absolutely. Besides, his brother was our classmate. Ames. You must remember him. He had a major crush on you."

Fleur brightened. "No kidding? I told Dem that I might have to recuse myself from the entire mess. I know his wife. Horton's, I mean. I'm the treasurer for the Back Bay Garden Club, and Heather is the chief fund-raiser. We're not friends or anything. Heather isn't the type to have BFFs, if you know what I mean. Certainly not female ones. I would have looked into the whole bullion mess myself, but with all the connections, it was better to delegate it to my assistant." She shuddered. "Gold! I'm only interested in getting a little band on my ring finger."

"Ames is still unattached," I said. "He told me someone is out to get his brother. Anonymous tips to the authorities. Bad business."

Her smile was sly. "Actually, it wouldn't have been such a big deal as long as no one was raiding the cookie jar. Embarrassing maybe, but not criminal. I'm surprised that Horton Exley would fall for something so contrived."

"In some circles, scandal is criminal," I said, "and reputation is everything."

Fleur shrugged. "Dem handled it. God, he is brilliant. Rich, gorgeous, and smart—you won the trifecta, Ms. Eja."

I ignored the panegyric. After all, who could argue with the truth?

"You must face this situation every day in your business," I said. "What kind of person makes her living that way? The criminal, I mean. It's so sordid."

"It does take a jaded individual, someone who gets off on deceiving others. You know the type: a cold bitter person who thinks he's smarter than anyone else." Fleur chewed her scrod and thought about it. "Occasionally a whistleblower, someone with a conscience, comes forth and spills the beans. Lots of these foundations have huge pots of money to play with. Easy enough to tempt someone, especially when a middle-aged man who thinks with his zipper is in charge."

I leaned forward, genuinely curious. "Don't they vet these schemes? After all, that kind of fuss could destroy lives and reputations."

"That's the point. Con artists find the mark's weak spot and exploit it. A guy who grew up in his father's shadow wants to excel on his own. A slick piece of work would flatter him, play to his ego. You know how that is with a man like that."

"Like Horton Exley, you mean."

"You're fishing for information," Fleur said. "Don't tell me you plan to write a book about it?"

I laughed. "No way. I just wanted to understand. Human nature and all that. I find it fascinating. I read everything when the Madoff scheme came undone."

Fleur eyed me with the steely gaze of a hanging judge. "Well, for the record, our job is to verify the information, not investigate the tipster. If things go south, we'll get an injunction to stop the bleeding." She shrugged. "You won't believe the kind of schemes that reasonably intelligent people fall for. These con artists are very smart, brilliant about human nature, actually."

"I hear those gold commercials every night," I said. "Hard to take them seriously."

"Ah, yes. Gold. Most of them are legitimate," Fleur said, "but they create just the window a con artist needs to ply his trade."

I was curious, so I took a risk. "How could anyone believe Phaedra Jones? The woman even looked sleazy. I'm sure her financial acumen was limited to the size of a man's wallet, or possibly something else."

Fleur waved her arms and smirked. "Now you're starting to get it. These people are geniuses at finding out what you want and giving it to you, even for one brief moment. We call it 'affinity fraud.'"

"What does that mean? It's like a foreign language."

She always was a show-off. I counted on that when we scheduled our lunch.

"It's simple, Eja. They usually find victims with similar needs and backgrounds—same social strata or religious beliefs. Anything that works. Then they use that to build an emotional bond."

I got an *aha* moment. Phaedra Jones sought out rich, spoiled men who were hungry for sex and adventure. She flattered them, serviced them, and picked their pockets. It had worked like a charm, until she fell for Justin Ming. Then things had gone haywire.

Fleur signaled for the check and gathered her things. When I pulled out my wallet, she shook her head. "Nope. My treat. That way I can't be accused of anything."

"Bribes must come cheaply these days," I said.

She raised her eyebrows. "You got that right."

WHEN I GOT HOME, a surprise awaited me. Officer Jennings, the Opie look-alike and aide-de-camp to Euphemia Bates, was waiting in the lobby trying to look inconspicuous. Between blushes, he informed me that Lieutenant Bates wanted to see me. Immediately.

"Why?" I asked.

"The lieutenant will tell you, Ms. Kane." Opie grinned. "Don't shoot the messenger."

I could think of a hundred reasons not to go and only one reason to comply—curiosity. Deming would burst a blood vessel either way. I sent him a text and made a quick call to Anika.

"Mia Bates summoned me," I whispered. "Is Bolin around?"

"Still at work," she said. "Don't worry. I'll meet you there."

There was no sense explaining that I wanted an attorney, not a co-conspirator. Besides, Anika's advice was every bit as sound as any lawyer's. I hopped into the unmarked sedan for the brief ride to police headquarters, praying all the time that Deming would ignore my text. If he hadn't clammed up last night, I'd be better prepared for this encounter. Euphemia Bates was up to something, and I had to know what it was.

She was waiting for me in her office, looking as guileless as a six foot tall, gun-toting police lieutenant could ever hope to. Although I admired Mia's bottle-green pantsuit, especially the jeweled belt encircling her waist, I kept that to myself. Bolin's words rang in my ears—don't lie, don't volunteer anything.

"Ms. Kane. Thank you for stopping by." Mia's raven eyes probed me like a truth detector. "Sorry to disrupt your day." She was lying through her teeth, and we both knew it. After offering me coffee or tea, she got down to business.

"I re-read your statement this morning and have some questions. I'm sure you can clear them up right away. Mr. Deming Swann has already contacted me about this *Dim Mak* business. You'll need to make a further statement about that, of course."

I buttoned my lip as Mia thumbed through a sheaf of papers. Silence is an effective weapon that most cops love to use. They say it makes even a strong man crack sooner or later. Meanwhile, I spent my time devising plot lines for my next mystery. The murderer looked awfully similar to Euphemia Bates, and the victim resembled Officer Opie.

Mia put aside the file and looked my way. "I saw you at the Exley house last night, so you must know what happened."

"Not really," I said. "Deming never filled me in."

Mia spread her arms in the universal sign about obdurate men. It was a bonding moment that I ignored. "What do you know about Heather Exley?" she asked.

"Hardly anything. The woman is either incredibly rude or moronic. We've barely exchanged five sentences."

"But you socialized with the Exleys," Mia said. "Surely that means something."

A tap on her door signaled the arrival of Anika Swann. My pal and future mother-in-law sailed in as determined as the Maid of Orleans girded for battle. She nodded at Mia and joined me on the sofa.

"Welcome, Mrs. Swann. Perhaps you can help us." The lieutenant kept her voice low, as if we were girlfriends swapping stories. I almost forgot about Officer Opie taking notes in the corner and the shoulder holster that Mia wore.

"Of course," Anika said. "I'll be glad to help." She fixed luminous hazel eyes on Mia. "Do we need our attorney, or is this off the record?"

"For now, most of this is just background. If we amend your statements, you might want to confer with counsel." Mia donned oversize reading glasses and scanned the file once more. "Let's see. You both saw Mrs. Exley and the victim together in your class. Is that right?"

We nodded like swaying tops.

"Okay. Now, I want you to describe this quarrel between Mrs. Exley and Ms. Jones. Give as much detail as possible."

"I never saw the quarrel," Anika said. "That was Eja."

"May I see my previous statement?" I asked. "That should jog my memory."

She didn't like it, but Mia complied. She handed both of us our formal statements.

I quickly scanned the documents noting buzz words like "vicious quarrel" and "pointed talons." From a writer's perspective my statement was brilliant. A defense attorney might not agree.

"Okay," I said. "Ask away."

Mia ignored the sarcasm and beamed good will my way. "You mentioned 'bullion' as something Mrs. Exley said. What was that about?"

"I don't know. Frankly, I was too busy watching the fur fly, so to speak."

She nodded, pretending to believe me. "Does the term bullion jog your memory, Mrs. Swann?"

Anika tilted her head. "It has to do with money. Stocks, mines, nuggets. All that boring financial talk. You know."

That earned her an appreciative smile from Euphemia Bates. "I'm asking because apparently our victim dabbled in the shady side of the gold bullion market."

"No kidding?" I said, trying for the wide-eyed ingénue look. By Mia's reaction, I realized that my act was rather rusty. Innocence constantly wars with my snarky side and loses every time.

"Money is an emotional issue," Mia said, "even to those with plenty of it. No one enjoys being snookered." She crossed long shapely legs and gave me the evil eye. "What do you know about the Exleys and a gold bullion confidence scheme? Remember, Eja. We're talking about murder here."

I hesitated, allowing Anika to throw me a life preserver.

"I'm not friends with Heather," Anika said, "but my husband and I were very close to the elder Exleys, Horton's parents. Fine people, Lieutenant. Absolute rocks. I refuse to believe that Horton Exley is capable of violence."

"Anyone is capable of violence under the right circumstances," Mia said. "What about his wife?"

I added my two cents. "Well, she certainly mixed it up with Phaedra that night. But in my opinion, money had nothing to do with it."

"Oh?" Mia infused more meaning into that one syllable than I ever thought possible. No wonder Deming lectured me about volunteering. "You mentioned Justin Ming. Mrs. Exley was interested in him, was she?"

"All the women flirted with him, Lieutenant." Anika's eyes gleamed. "Except Eja and me, of course. But even I admit that he is a charmer."

"Hmm. What's your opinion, Ms. Kane?"

I had no allegiance to Justin Ming, serial philanderer. If Mia wanted gossip, I'd give it to her. I cleared my throat. "Sifu Ming told me that

Phaedra was in love with him."

"Really?" Mia's one word mania grated on my nerves. "You do have a way of burrowing in and getting information. Tell me. Did Ming reciprocate her feelings?"

"He said not. Of course, I have no way of validating that."

"Interesting."

Before Mia continued the inquisition, a firm knock on the door announced the arrival of legal counsel. Deming strode into the room, briefcase in hand, wearing a mask of civility that deceived no one.

"Ah. Here they are." He managed a cold, tight smile that dripped icicles. "You're not charging my fiancée and mother with anything, are you, Lieutenant?"

Mia was all affability. "Certainly not. Ms. Kane clarified her recollection about the decedent's final words, and they were kind enough to help me sort out some points in their statements. Most helpful."

Deming clutched the handle of his briefcase in a death grip. "Fine. Then you'll have to excuse us. We have a social engagement this evening that we can't miss."

"Of course." She stood up and shook our hands, very much Lieutenant Euphemia Bates now. "Thank you so much, ladies. I'll be in touch."

As we filed out the door, Mia fired a parting shot. "By the way, Eja. I'm afraid we can't return your jacket after all." She shook her head. "A shame. It really was quite lovely."

I avoided Deming's eyes and fell headlong into her trap. "How come?"

"Oh. Didn't I mention it? The blood on your jacket matched the DNA of a person of interest."

Deming grasped my elbow and guided me out the door. Unfortunately, he left his mother unattended.

"Who is that, Lieutenant?" Anika asked.

"Why, Heather Exley, of course."

Chapter Twelve

DEMING RETREATED into sulky silence until we reached his car. Had Anika not been there, he would have unleashed a string of invectives. As it was, he pressed his lips together and hissed through gritted teeth.

"What were you thinking of, Eja? I told you to stay out of this."

I also have a temper, but I'm a superior tactician. Instead of arguing I smiled sweetly and climbed into the backseat. "So you did."

"Well?" Deming cracked his knuckles.

Anika placed her hand on his shoulder and squeezed. "Children, please. Eja didn't have much choice, Dem, and I joined her to provide support. Let's go home and discuss this with your father. Police are everywhere."

He grunted, but as usual, Anika stopped her querulous son in his tracks. He gunned the Porsche's engine and reached the Swann manse in record time.

"I can't stay for chitchat," he grumbled. "I'm meeting Pam for a conference. And I'll speak to Dad later." There was a glint of triumph in those hazel eyes when he said her name. Instead of reacting, I turned to Anika.

"Are we still on for our exercise class tonight?"

"Absolutely. See you at six." Anika hugged her son, blew me a kiss, and glided to her front door.

I scrambled into the front seat and faced my sulky spouse to be. "Can you drop me home, or shall I call a cab?"

Instead of lecturing me, Deming took my hand and gently kissed each finger. "I'm sorry I was grumpy," he said. "There's no excuse for my behavior."

If he expected me to comfort him, Deming was disappointed. I squeezed his arm and said nothing.

"Don't go back to that dojo, Eja. Please."

"Why not?"

He sighed, finger-combing his thick black mane. "Something about that place creeps me out. Justin Ming is dangerous, not to mention a womanizer. I sense it."

"Hey, don't worry. It's only exercise. Besides, your mom will be with me. What could happen?"

That earned me an eye roll and a brisk, derisive snort. Before Deming catalogued every one of my misadventures with Anika, I stopped him cold.

"Euphemia Bates knows something about that bullion scheme," I said. "We didn't tell her anything, but she made it pretty clear. I wonder how many other victims Phaedra Jones snookered?"

"She's playing you, Eja. Christ! You and Mom are such amateurs."

I have the patience of the Biblical Mrs. Job. That comes in handy when dealing with a petulant lawyer.

"Perhaps," I said, "but you should know that I sicced her on Justin Ming, not your clients. That should give you some breathing space, at least for a while."

The look on his face was something akin to admiration. "That's clever. Very clever. Naturally, she'll figure it out soon enough, but it does muddy the water." He swept up Commonwealth Avenue and deposited me at the door of the Tudor. I avoided a lecture by giving him a quick peck on the cheek and skipping past the doorman.

"Eja, wait!" Deming was right behind me. "I'll stop by this evening after dinner. It might be late though." His eyes telegraphed a message that hiked my adrenalin to the sky.

I stood on tiptoe and kissed his ear. "Not a problem, Counselor. You're worth waiting for."

SHAOLIN CITY LOOKED untouched by tragedy. Without crime scene tape, patrol cars, and police seals, the dojo had an oddly festive air. Anika and I filed in for our private session behind a chattering group of students who were was focused on kung fu, not murder.

To my surprise, we were greeted by the master himself. Avery Moore bowed to us and shared a gentle smile. His manner was gracious, but something was definitely amiss. Then it struck me: the taint of violence had stained this peaceful refuge and in the process diminished the man who loved it.

"Ladies, I will be your instructor tonight. A poor substitute for Sifu Ming, I know."

I tried to be subtle, but curiosity overwhelmed me. "Where is

Justin? Not ill, I hope."

The master waved his hands. "No, no. Nothing like that. He is leading our beginners class tonight."

Was the studly sifu avoiding me? His disclosures hadn't seemed to trouble him one bit, but that might be misleading. Perhaps Justin Ming had more to hide than an occasional dalliance with his students.

Fortunately, Anika used her superpowers to intercede. "My condolences, Master, on the loss of your pupil. I know all your students are family."

Why hadn't I thought of that? The indirect approach can sometimes yield better results than a frontal assault, especially in the murky world of kung fu. Chalk that up to lessons learned.

He hesitated, and for a moment I thought he might weep. Then Avery Moore patted Anika's shoulder and urged us into the practice room where he led a ruthless regimen of stretches, thrusts, punches, and defensive maneuvers. Although I am decades younger than either Anika or the master, you would never know it. I wheezed and gasped while they appeared unaffected by sixty minutes of sheer torture.

"You did fine, Eja," Anika said. The woman was an expert fibber, capable of ladling up faux praise at a moment's notice. "Think of the calories that we burned!"

"Both of you made excellent progress," said Master Moore. "Each student improves at her own pace."

I noticed on the bulletin board that Shaolin City had doubled the class offerings and expanded its repertoire to more exotic offerings like Tiger Claw, Straight Sword, and Kung Fu Forms.

"You must be busy," I said, "with all those new classes. How can you handle the workload?"

Avery Moore plucked the sleeve of his uniform and straightened it. The gentleness briefly left his eyes as he gave me a hard stare. "Very observant, Ms. Kane. No wonder your detective stories are so popular."

Anika, my champion and publicist, had to comment. "Isn't she marvelous? Eja's plots are incredible, Master, and she's solved real crimes as well."

"A rare talent," he said, "but potentially dangerous. Take care, Ms. Kane. After our recent tragedy, I fear for the future." He nodded to us and vanished into a side exit.

"Master Moore has changed since the murder," Anika said, as we exited the dojo. "What do you make of it?"

"Money," I said. "Bet you anything that the dojo needs a cash infusion. Justin hinted around about that when he was at my place."

Anika bit her lip as she thought the problem through. "Bolin could find out in an hour. He's an absolute wizard when it comes to financial things. I hate to get him involved, though. Scruples—he has more than he needs at times."

If Bolin Swann found any information, he'd feel honor-bound to share it with both Deming and Euphemia Bates, and that might start a firestorm. My financial acumen was limited, but I knew someone with mad money skills.

"How about asking a CPA for help?" I said. "As a favor. Nothing serious."

"Sounds fine to me," Anika said. "Who?"

"We actually have two choices—Fleur Pixley or Portia Amory Shaw. They both have the right credentials and may know something about the murder as well. We'll say it's a business venture between the two of us that we want to keep from Bolin and Deming."

Anika thought about it and nodded. "That might not be too far off. I've been looking for a something to invest in. Nothing elaborate, just something that's my own."

I tried to tread carefully. "How would Bolin feel about that?"

Her face lit up like a roman candle. "Oh, Eja. Bolin is the most supportive husband ever. He would give me anything, but I want some success on my own terms. You understand."

"Absolutely. It's about self-respect. That's something my writing has always given me, even though I don't make much money from it."

Anika hugged me. "You are such a comfort, just like Cecilia. I was afraid to hope that you and Dem would get together." Her eyes filled. "Selfish of me, I know, but you two were always perfect for each other and too stubborn to admit it."

As usual, she was right. Deming and I squabbled bitterly from preschool through university. He squired around one snooty socialite after another, and I married a fellow writer. Neither plan worked out until CeCe's murder awakened our feelings, forging a union of two passionate, strong-willed people who loved each other. The rest was history, imperfect and fraught with conflict.

"Hey, I almost forgot. Is lunch with Heather still on tomorrow, or will she be brown-bagging it at the city lockup?"

Anika swatted my hand. "You nut. We're meeting her at the Four Seasons, one o'clock sharp. Be prepared to talk clothes and makeup.

Anything else will be wasted breath. Poor child, she's the type to get lost playing peekaboo."

That was the consensus about Heather Exley, but I wasn't so sure. Many beautiful women used the "dumb blonde" prejudice as a tool to lower expectations and do as they pleased. If Heather had murdered her competitor, she was wise to act like a dimwit. She had already perfected the blank stare and redefined the concept of helplessness.

"Deming wouldn't discuss the DNA match," I said, "but surely Heather is the prime suspect. I wonder where that blood came from?"

Anika pointed toward the Bentley and waved me in. Po had performed another miracle by finding a parking space directly in front of Shaolin City.

"That's no mystery, Eja. Remember how thin that blood was? Nose bleed. When the twins were young, CeCe was always getting them. Then Deming went through his tough guy phase and got into fights." She sighed. "It's a wonder that boy has such a perfect profile."

I leaned back and speculated, cradled in that incredibly soft leather. "Let's ask her how it happened tomorrow. I figure she and Phaedra mixed it up again, and Heather got bopped in the nose. You do it, Anika. No one ever suspects you of anything."

She winked, mindful of Po's long ears. "No problem. I'll see you tomorrow."

OUR EXERCISE SESSION had left me wired. I prowled around my living room, too antsy to write, think, or sleep. To compound matters, Cato patrolled the perimeter, emitting a constant low growl that stretched my nerves to the breaking point. No one was at the door. I felt confident of that after peering into the peephole several times. Nevertheless, when the phone rang, I jumped like a scalded pup.

"You sound funny," Deming said. "What's wrong?"

"Nothing. Just my imagination."

He knew better than to ask anything more. "Hey. I can't make it over tonight. We're still slugging it out in the conference room with no signs of progress."

That conjured up lurid mental images of Deming Bjorn Swann and Pamela Schwartz entwined like perfect pretzels. I resisted temptation and refused comment.

"So. How were things at the dojo? I hope you kept your distance from Justin Ming?"

"Of course," I said. "Barely noticed him." I'm the chatty type, so silence is the nuclear option, retrieved from my arsenal as a weapon of last resort.

"You understand what I'm up against, don't you?" Deming asked after an awkward pause.

"Perfectly. I'll talk to you tomorrow."

Before hanging up, Deming lowered his voice and whispered into the phone, "Love you, Eja. Always have, always will."

BEFORE JOINING ANIKA the next day, I telephoned Fleur Pixley, my former college chum. "Are you up for some adventure?" I teased. "I can promise a hefty reward."

Fleur wasn't buying my sprightly act. She immediately demanded details. "Cut the crap, Eja. What do you want, and why involve me?"

"My oh my. You've become a total cynic." I paused. "It's no big deal, only one hour of your accounting skills. Normal consulting rates would apply, of course."

"I repeat. Why me? This doesn't involve that gold scam, I hope."

After I summarized my proposal, Fleur calmed down. "So. Let me see if I've got this right. You and Mrs. Swann are hatching a scheme—"

"Business venture, please."

"Okay. A business venture to buy some failing kung fu parlor without involving Bolin Swann or Deming. Is that about it?" She must have been a hanging judge in a previous life. Her voice was grim, as if she were pronouncing sentence.

Frankly, it annoyed me. "Forget it, Fleur. We'll go elsewhere."

"No, wait just a moment. Is this the same dojo where that murder happened last week?"

My heart sunk. Fleur was a lot sharper than I recalled. She had a suspicious nature that was very unbecoming for a public servant. On the other hand, duplicity is hardwired into my genes, so I had no problem responding.

"Right you are," I gushed. "We figure this is the perfect time to make an offer. Revenues have to be down after a scandal like that. If the owners knew that Bolin Swann was involved, the price would skyrocket. That's why we prefer anonymity."

Oddly enough, my explanation made sense. Fleur paused, and before we hung up, she agreed to consider the proposition.

I spent the rest of the morning attending to Cato and choosing an appropriate outfit for a Four Seasons fashion fest. I settled on a red Escada suit that showcased my best assets. The garment was form-fitting and made me feel saucy, stylish but not slutty. Deming was especially fond of it.

My home is only two blocks from the hotel—two long, excruciating blocks when you're wearing stilettos. By the time I limped into the Bristol Lounge, Anika and Heather were already seated, enjoying their wine.

"Eja, we were worried," Anika said. She wore an elegant peach pantsuit that accentuated her creamy complexion. Heather was model-slim in a black skirted suit straight from the pages of *Vogue*.

Apparently, Anika had launched a full charm offensive, and Heather was lapping it up like cream.

"Isn't she stunning, Eja? As you can see, Heather has a direct line to all the New York fashion houses." Anika sipped sparingly as she spoke. "Perhaps she can include us on her next shopping trip. After all, you need a new jacket."

Fashion talk bored me silly, but I immediately took my cue and heaved a big sigh. "Lieutenant Bates said I'll never get that jacket back. Not in this lifetime anyway. What a pain."

Heather awakened from her stupor long enough to blink. "Really? Why not?"

"Oh, you know, dear," Anika said. "Nosebleeds are so difficult to deal with, and Eja got your blood all over her sleeve." She patted my arm. "Not to worry. We'll find you something even nicer, Eja. My treat."

"My blood?" Heather said. She was either an Oscar-caliber actress or totally befuddled by the conversation. "I don't understand."

"You and Phaedra must have mixed it up again in the locker room," I said. "My sleeve got messed up when Anika and I found her body."

Heather sat motionless with her mouth agape. "But I never even saw her that night. After my session with Sifu Ming, my nose started bleeding. I thought I'd mopped it all up."

I spent a few seconds imagining the gymnastics that led to her nose-bleed. Justin Ming was certainly agile enough to cause a girl's blood to boil, and Heather was thoroughly engaged, body and soul. One false move or elbow jab could easily inflict injury.

Anika wore her most maternal look. "I'm so sorry. I just assumed that your attorney had already discussed it with you. Lieutenant Bates told us about it yesterday. Don't you worry one bit. Your legal team will handle it."

A wave of color swept over Heather's cheeks. "Yes. Pamela Schwartz and your son take good care of me."

Anika and I locked eyes, signaling that the time was right for some real girl talk.

"What was the story with this Phaedra Jones?" I asked. "She seemed so hostile."

Anika nodded. "Some women are very competitive. It's a shame really."

I leaned closer to Heather. "Lieutenant Bates had the lowdown on her. She said Phaedra was a con woman. Can you believe it?"

Heather curled her lip. "You bet. She zeroed in on any man with money, even Master Moore. Justin told me she made a real pest of herself."

"Surely Master Moore doesn't have money," Anika said. "Running a dojo is expensive."

I smirked. "Phaedra's interest in Justin Ming doesn't surprise me, though. That man is a sexual magnet. Women seem to flock his way."

Her reaction was right on target. Heather drummed her fingers on the table and set her patrician jaw. "I'm not supposed to discuss it," she said. "Pamela said so."

"Of course," I said, patting her hand. "Besides, Justin told me that Phaedra was in love with him. Can you believe it? No surprise. I'm certain that he shut her down right away."

Heather drained her water glass. She clutched her chest, slumped in her seat, and went limp.

"Oh, no," I cried. "Should I call a doctor?"

Medical emergencies terrify me. Instead of helping, I dithered. My contribution was ineffectually chafing Heather's wrists and rubbing her forehead with a damp napkin.

Anika stayed cucumber cool. "Don't panic, Eja. I have just the thing." She plucked a vial of smelling salts from her Birkin bag, leaned across the seat, and waved them under Heather's nose. "There. That should do it."

Chapter Thirteen

I WATCHED TRANSFIXED as Heather Exley rapidly came to her senses. Her recovery made me question whether the entire drama had been yet another bid for attention. Anika winked at me as she gave Heather a second dose of sal volatile. Anika was a marvel! How many society matrons carry smelling salts in their Birkin bags?

"How in the world . . ." I asked.

Anika laughed. "That came in handy when the twins were little. Wait 'til you're a mother, Eja. You'll understand."

I felt the heat rising to my cheeks and looked away to avoid embarrassment. Meanwhile Heather blinked her big blue eyes and spoke in a tremulous voice. She seemed far more interested in her wayward lover than her own ailments. "Is it true about Justin and Phaedra? He told me she was only his student."

I shrugged and feigned indifference. "So many women are lonely. She was probably fixated and threw herself at him. Everyone's a stalker these days. It often happens with male authority figures, and you must admit, Justin is a babe."

Heather's agitation was obvious. Her perfectly manicured fingers shook as she took a sip of wine. "He told me he loved me, and I believed him. I would have given him anything."

How many times had I heard that familiar tune from credulous women? Oddly enough, I'd pegged Heather as too calculating to fall for a line as old as Adam and Eve. Instead of steamy, sweaty sex, the lady wanted old-fashioned romance and exclusivity. Go figure.

Anika didn't miss a step. She gripped Heather's arm in a gesture of female solidarity.

"How much money did you loan him?" she asked. "We've all been there, Heather. Don't feel ashamed."

Her flawless makeup never faltered, even as a fat tear trickled down Heather's cheek. "Not much. Justin needed investors. He plans to start his own dojo, you see, and the down payment was more than he'd planned for."

"Perfectly understandable," Anika fibbed. "Eja and I want a business opportunity too. It's important for a woman to assert her independence, don't you agree?"

I summoned my sweetest smile. "How much was Justin asking?"

Her whispered response was almost inaudible. "Fifty thousand. He had a lot of expenses. Renovation and such."

How many generous patrons had forked over a similar sum? No wonder the sexy sifu was so confident. Between thrusts and embraces, he managed to pick more than a few pockets. In many ways, he was no different than Phaedra herself. Both profited from the weakness and neediness of others.

Heather plucked a mirror from her purse and dabbed her eyes. "I have to leave," she said. "Please don't tell Horton about this."

"Of course not," Anika said. "Po can drive you home, Heather. You still look pale."

"No. Please. I have my car here."

Heather did look unwell, but I saw an opportunity to connect with Portia Amory Shaw without appearing too obvious.

"No problem," I said. "You can ride with Po while Anika and I follow behind in your car. That way we won't take any chances."

Anika placed a water glass on some bills and herded us out the door to the Bentley. "Where did you park your car, dear?" she asked.

"The valet has it." After handing me her receipt, Heather sunk into the Bentley's sumptuous seats. She was either faking or genuinely distressed, but I couldn't tell which.

"Take Mrs. Exley home, please," Anika told Po. "We'll follow right behind you."

The valet snapped to attention and in short order delivered Heather's car. It suited her, a striking Jaguar convertible that oozed money and class. I don't own a car, and my skill at navigating in city traffic verges on dangerous. I had no desire to mar the custom paint or dent the pristine exterior of a work of art.

"I'll drive, if you don't mind." Anika's eyes sparkled. "I love Jaguars, in fact, for the longest time I nursed an old XKE along." She sighed. "A beautiful beast but trouble, like so many gorgeous creatures."

As we belted ourselves in, I said, "*Beauty is its own excuse for being.*' Remember?"

"Ah, Emerson," Anika said. "How like a Boston boy to appreciate nature. You know, I quoted that to Bolin every time the XKE broke down. Finally, he just shook his head and made me get something more reliable. You know how he is about safety."

Anika had a reckless streak that confounded her husband and horrified her son. That's why we made such a daunting duo—although Deming had another less flattering term for our partnership.

She stepped on the accelerator and made that jungle cat roar. By ignoring several vulgar hand signals and bleating horns from other drivers, Anika eased into traffic and headed toward Belmont.

"Did you buy that fainting act?" I asked. "Surely Heather knew what Justin Ming was up to? She's a prime suspect in my book. I think her pride took a shellacking when she realized that her body and her money were being used. Besides, what were she and Phaedra fighting about if not that?"

Anika shrugged. "Love is blind, as they say, and lust is doubly so. She was very convincing about that blood though, don't you think? I watched her reaction, and she was clearly shocked."

"Maybe she's a sociopath," I said. "Supposedly they pass lie detector tests with flying colors. That would make it fairly easy to fool us."

Anika beamed her Mona Lisa smile my way. "Didn't you ever fib to your mother, Eja? Even a little."

I dredged my memory banks for guilty secrets. My parents were both academics, philosophy professors who believed in abstractions and syllogisms rather than conventional child rearing. They were rationalists who forbade me almost nothing. As a result, I was a studious little prig who rarely strayed from the straight and narrow. Things changed when I hooked up with Cecilia Swann and her dark twin, but even then my mother regarded my antics with amused tolerance. In short, I had no need to lie.

"Eja—are you okay?" Anika swerved onto Storrow Drive and stepped on the gas.

"Sorry. I was pondering your question."

"No matter. My point was that most children fib to their mothers quite often, and that gives one a sixth sense about lying. Bolin always says that I have a truth detector in my brain. That's why I believe Heather."

"Loaning a man money is bad business," I said. "Your body, maybe, but never let them into your purse. More great advice from the Bard."

Anika laughed and executed a sudden U-turn into the Exley driveway. "Here we are. Po is already here. Heather probably went upstairs."

I locked eyes with Anika. "We really should check on Heather. Don't you agree?"

She parked the Jag and hopped out. "Sure. It's only polite. If Portia is around, we can say hello."

We hadn't discussed my encounter with Fleur yet. Even though she hadn't rejected our proposal outright, I was having second thoughts. Even in college Fleur loved to keep one dangling until the last possible moment. She was heavily into power plays, especially when they involved other females. All things considered, Portia might be an easier target. She fit every stereotype of the dull-as-dishwater accountant more enamored of debits than desire. Yet I recalled the malicious gleam in her eyes when Phaedra's name was mentioned. That suggested that Portia, the down and out family retainer, might be ready for adventure.

Anika greeted Carlisle and asked for Ms. Shaw. As a well-trained servant, the butler wouldn't think of questioning Mrs. Bolin Swann or her motives. He gave me the fisheye.

We were ushered into a small parlor furnished exclusively with sofas and chairs in various patterns of chintz. In another era, ladies would have fanned themselves, exchanged confidences, and received their visitors in such a space.

"What a surprise!"

It was impossible to tell how Portia Amory Shaw meant that remark. As usual she was clothed in a shapeless shift that gave new meaning to the term nondescript.

Anika recovered quickly. "We didn't want to intrude, but since Mrs. Exley got ill during lunch, we thought you should know. She probably wouldn't mention it otherwise."

"You're joking," Portia said. "Heather loves drama. She feeds off it."

"Not like those of us who work for a living," I said. "We don't have that luxury."

She gazed at me, surprise mingled with a healthy dollop of respect. "Exactly."

"Speaking of work," Anika said. "Eja and I have a proposition to make. It presumes that you don't mind doing financial analysis."

"And that you can keep it to yourself," I added. "This matter is confidential. Just the three of us."

Portia's dour features brightened. "Oh, I can keep a secret. Believe me."

We spent the next twenty minutes outlining our fantasy takeover of Shaolin City and her role in the process. As Anika embellished, her enthusiasm grew to the point that even I got excited.

"This is our project, understand. No men allowed. Eja and I will be the primary investors, and the current staff will manage the property."

Portia put on her CPA hat and nodded. "You'll want to form a sub-chapter S Corp. All the small businesses do that. But let me get this straight—exactly what do you want from me?"

"An assessment of the financial health of the business and the owner." I paused. "And here's the tricky part. You have to do it without tipping off Master Moore."

A frown knitted Portia's brow as her green eyeshade descended. "Master Moore?"

Anika nodded solemnly. "Master Avery Moore. He's the owner, a venerable martial arts master and respected teacher."

"Gee, I don't know. That's pretty tough these days with privacy laws."

"Surely there are public records, filings and such that anyone can access. Don't you run credit checks through the foundation?" I rummaged in my purse and found the information packet that all Shaolin City clients received. "Here. This might help you."

I could tell that Portia was intrigued. The poor woman's life was probably so dull that any respite was welcome. When Anika mentioned a suitable fee, I knew that we had her hooked.

"Let me poke around on the Internet," Portia said. "I might be able to help you."

Anika rose and made our excuses. "I'm afraid we have to run. Please contact me or Eja if you learn anything."

We congratulated ourselves on a successful venture, dissecting our day in hushed whispers. After stopping at my place to pick up Cato, we headed for the Swann homestead feeling triumphant and a bit cocky. After all, our detective work had yielded some important clues. Heather's explanation of the blood bore some scrutiny, but it seemed genuine as did her shock at the relationship between Phaedra and Justin Ming. If true, someone else murdered Phaedra, someone who had access to the locker room, or was bold enough to risk being discovered in a fairly public place. That narrowed the field but shed a blinding spotlight on spurned lover Horton Exley and the nefarious Justin Ming.

Instead of plaudits, an unpleasant surprise awaited us the moment we reached Swannland. Bolin, Deming, and a redheaded quisling with a pixie cut were huddled over the library table plotting our doom. I assessed the situation the moment I saw Fleur Pixley. That traitorous minx had revealed our scheme to the last person on earth I hoped to involve. Anticipation is usually my strong point, but I'd forgotten just how desperate Fleur was to curry favor with Deming. So much for female solidarity—sisterhood, be damned!

"A party! What a surprise." Anika strolled up to Fleur and hugged her. "It's wonderful to see you again."

Anika's poise in the face of danger gave me courage. I resisted the urge to bolt, stared straight at Deming, and plastered a smile on my face. Cato proved his allegiance by baring his fangs and lunging at Fleur.

"He's not good with strangers," I said. "Such a protective little cuss."

Bolin, ever the gentleman, greeted us and offered refreshments. His eyes twinkled with a bemused expression that said nothing surprised him anymore. Unfortunately, Deming was less understanding. He grunted, sipped his scotch, and hunkered down, never moving a muscle.

"Fleur called Dem after you went out today," Bolin said. "It seemed like a good idea to get together and catch up on things, particularly since, as usual, you ladies are way ahead of the rest of us."

Deming eased into the conversation like a hungry shark on the prowl. "What else is new," he fumed. "I thought you were a writer, Eja, not an investor. Imagine my surprise when Fleur mentioned your new interest."

"She's my partner," Anika said. "Lots of people diversify. It makes financial sense."

"Besides," I said with all the sweetness I could muster, "we're exploring options. Everything is tentative, and we assumed our dealings with Fleur were confidential."

Even the most brazen hussy can feel shame. Fleur's fair Irish skin turned beet red as she absorbed our scorn. "I felt obliged to read Dem in on everything. After all, his client is involved."

"Really? We discussed a business proposition, nothing that concerned the Exley family. Their name never even came up in conversation." Rage boiled up within me the more I considered her treachery. "I'm very disappointed in you, Fleur."

Anika chimed in, polite but pointed. "Me too. As it turns out, you don't have to worry. Eja and I have made other arrangements. That probably is best for us all." She stood, indicating in the classiest way possible that the discussion was over, and Fleur was no longer welcome in her home.

Bolin shook Fleur's hand and thanked her for her concern. "Nice to see you again, Fleur. Good luck with your future plans." He nodded to Deming and walked over to join his wife. "Dem will see you home."

Once again, I felt like an alien in the splendid realm of Swannland. Between Fleur's treachery and Deming's arrogance, there was no place for a midlist mystery writer with an inquiring mind and an independent streak.

Deming stalked out the door without even turning my way. I almost wept, but pride and a compulsion to avoid pity kept my eyes dry. I patted Cato's head and put on my great big Brownie smile. "It's getting late. I'd better head on home."

"Wait, Eja." Anika sensed my pain. "Why not stay for dinner. I'm sure Dem will be back soon."

"No, thanks. I'll go home and do some writing. It's my therapy when I need to think."

"We'll speak tomorrow," Anika said. "Don't worry. Everything will be fine."

I wasn't so sure, but good manners demanded an upbeat response. After flashing a plucky grin, I prepared to leave.

"Oh, Eja, one more thing. Will you be at our exercise session tomorrow?" Anika bit her lip. "I'm not sure. Maybe . . ."

"I'll be there," I said. "Wouldn't miss it for the world. But if you're busy, don't worry. I'll tackle the group class instead."

Bolin walked to my side and squeezed my hand. "Come on. I'll walk you to the car."

His presence was comforting, even when he said nothing. Bolin Swann projected warmth, self-assurance, and strength, just the prescription I needed at that moment.

"Forgive him, Eja. Ever since Cecilia died, Deming has been terrified that he'll lose someone else. He feels helpless, and that overwhelms him. If Dem had his way, he'd wrap up you and his mother and never let you go."

I took a deep breath. "He's angry all the time, Bolin, and I can't live that way."

"Not angry, just vulnerable. A control freak. I know my son, Eja, and he loves you more than you could ever realize. Always has, even as a kid."

"Maybe we're not right for each other. I'll never be a compliant wife."

Bolin chuckled. "I know all about that. Anika has an independent streak a mile wide. It took some time for me to accept it. Swann men are hardheaded."

I shrugged and reached for my iPhone. "More time, huh? I promise to try."

"You don't need a cab," Bolin said. "Let Po drive you. I insist." Anger was easy to rebuff, but kindness broke me down. He nodded to Po, opened the passenger side door, and patted my shoulder.

"Give him another chance, Eja. Please." Bolin's dark eyes gleamed. "Anika depends on you so much, and I already think of you as my daughter."

The cool wind brushed my face, making me shiver. I stood on tiptoe and kissed Bolin's cheek. "You've both been wonderful to me." I paused. "But Deming has to come to terms with things before it's too late."

Chapter Fourteen

DEMING DIDN'T CALL that night. Perhaps he was snuggled in Fleur's arms, granting that harridan's every wish. I thought of the parallels between Anika's Jaguar XKE and her own son, both sexy, fractious beasts meting out pleasure with pain. That described Deming as much as a slinky auto. Should I keep agonizing every time our relationship broke down or make a clean break? The conundrum weighed me down, banishing all hope of restful sleep.

I loved Deming and accepted him with all his foibles. Unfortunately, he viewed me as a work in progress, fresh clay to mold and manipulate to his specifications. We had battled since childhood about our differences. At one time I considered them strengths, but now I wasn't so sure.

Cato had no patience with my struggles. He prescribed exercise and vigorous ball tosses as the answer to almost everything. Come to think of it, the little devil had a point. After tramping about the Common with him, I felt invigorated and curiously optimistic. When my telephone rang, I answered it without even checking caller ID.

"Eja? Sorry I missed you yesterday." Ames Exley's distinctive Brahmin voice enunciated every syllable as if his life depended on it.

"Oh, yes. Just a temporary health scare. How are you?"

He paused. "Hungry. How about joining me for lunch at the Seaport Hotel? At Tamo, the restaurant. I guess I should have made that clear, although . . ."

"Today?" Last minute invitations were always chancy propositions. I wondered how many women before me had turned him down. On the other hand, memories of the restaurant's tuna sliders and chicken fingers made me salivate. I ignored the part about the hotel.

Ames laughed. "You got me. I'm playing hooky. Escaped my big brother's clutches just a minute ago and wanted to have some fun. C'mon. My treat. Are you game?"

"Sure. I can be there by noon, if that works."

"See you then."

Ames rang off, leaving me with mixed emotions and a faint glow of triumph. A date with an attractive man might be just the tonic I needed. Deming Swann could sulk in silence as far as I was concerned.

When the phone rang again, I saw his name and chose the better part of valor. I simply stiffened my spine and ignored Deming's call. He never left messages, no need to. My heart and brain were attuned to the special ring tone that he had. Besides, I had some prep work to do. No time for platitudes and angst-laced conversations. Eja Kane was on a mission.

I chose conservative garb in case Ames actually had designs on my virtue. No one could fault the cashmere sheath, snappy red jacket, and Ferragamos that I wore. They were prim, with subtle well-bred Brit touches. Stylish but austere, just like my mindset.

Nightmarish lunch hour traffic kept my cab driver swearing and me wondering. I arrived at Tamo on the stroke of noon, rather like Cinderella fleeing the ball. Despite the crowd, Ames had already snagged a seat. He waved merrily, beckoning me to join his front row table.

"How nice you look," Ames said, kissing my hand. "Already dressing for success, I see."

"Since when do you kiss hands?" I asked. "On overload from some Parisian jaunt?"

He gave me that measured Exley sneer before remembering our purpose. "Alas, no. My excursions are confined to this fair city until the mess with the foundation is sorted out."

"Oh?" Being coy is a stretch for me. I'm no coquette.

"I'm sure Deming told you all about it." Ames watched my reaction like a cat at a mouse hole.

"You obviously don't know Deming. He's tighter than a vault when a client's concerned. Horton mentioned the bullion scam himself."

Ames shook his head as he scanned the menu. "Foolishness. My brother threw away millions just to play house with that slut. I could have gotten her for free."

My jaw dropped, making me gape like the village idiot. "Phaedra came on to you?"

"Is that so unbelievable?" He sounded rather testy, as if I'd questioned his charm. Ames sipped a martini as we placed our order. "Sure you don't want something stronger? Wine or maybe a cosmo?"

"No, thanks."

He leaned forward, simulating a leer. "Not pregnant, are you, Eja?"

I glared at him. "What's wrong with you? Maybe you should discuss it with Deming if you're so intrigued by our sex life."

Ames threw up his hands. "Whoa. No harm, no foul. I'm in a mood. The Exleys are prisoners of primogeniture, thanks to my father's will. I'm a thirty-five-year-old man who's beholden to his older brother for money, while Horton blows five mil on a hooker, and that idiot wife of his drags our family's name through the mud." He took a healthy slug of liquor and continued. "He thought he was so clever. Like no one else was smart enough to find that vault he rented. Fool's gold for a rich fool. How appropriate."

My patience with young Mr. Exley was wearing thin. "So get a job. Make your own way. That's what Deming did."

He snorted. "Deming Swann, the paragon. How many women did he have along the way, Ms. Kane?"

I yawned. "Ancient history."

The gleam in his eyes bordered on evil. "Are you so sure? Some habits die hard."

He wanted a reaction, hoped to wound me by mentioning the very thing I feared most. It gnawed at the edges of my mind, forcing me to confront a painful question. Was I pretty enough to satisfy Deming, or merely safe and comfortable like an old shoe?

I shrugged. "Who knows? Anyhow, Horton repaid the foundation with interest. That should satisfy the cops if they check it out."

Luckily, the arrival of our lunch forestalled further conflict. I tucked into those tuna sliders, giving every succulent morsel the attention it deserved. Ames seemed more interested in a liquid lunch. He toyed with his salad, pushing spinach leaves around the plate.

"He probably killed her, you know." He spoke in that too loud, boozy tone.

I narrowed my eyes. "Lower your voice. Do you know what you're saying?"

He made no attempt to be civil. "Exleys are used to getting what they want. We always have, just like the Swanns. You wouldn't understand that, Eja."

I put on my party smile and remained silent.

Ames squeezed my hand. "No offense intended."

"None taken. Have you any proof that Horton murdered Phaedra?"

He shook his head. "Not take-it-into-court proof, but I know my brother. He was wild about that woman. In love. The day he found out about the gold scam, he aged ten years."

"Euphemia Bates is a bottom-line cop. She demands proof. Besides, Heather had motive too. Plenty of it. Take it from me, sharing a man is a recipe for disaster." I banished an image in my mind's eye of Fleur Pixley, Pamela Schwartz, and Deming—a frolicking ménage à trois.

As Ames signaled for another drink, he balled his hands into tight fists. His anger was raw and palpable, quite unlike the polished frat boy I used to know. Had we been alone, I might have been frightened. Instead, I decided to test something Bolin had mentioned.

"You'd be the winner if Horton was arrested," I said. "Isn't there some type of morality clause in the foundation's charter?"

His skin turned fushia from either drink or rage. I voted for door number one.

"You always were a know-it-all," Ames hissed, "writing your turgid prose and predictable plots."

"Guilty on both counts." My smile was sweetness personified. "Now answer my question, unless you're afraid to."

He took a deep breath and sputtered a response. "Yes, I would take control of the foundation. Why not? Horton is a figurehead who doesn't do anything except control the purse strings. Portia and I do all the real work without a word of thanks from him. Heather won't even answer the phones. They're both worthless, and that goes double for my bratty nephews."

Sometimes I forget just how vulnerable I would be in a physical confrontation. I forged ahead, determined to milk Ames Exley for every drop of information. "I've heard nothing but supposition and whining from a jealous younger brother. Why would either Heather or Horton kill Phaedra? Convince me."

Ames jabbed his finger in my face. "I'll tell you why. Horton planned to divorce his wife and marry that harlot. I heard them screaming at each other the night before the murder. Heather threw a vase at him too—a valuable Ming dynasty piece."

He sank back in the chair, sipping his liquid lunch. That outburst had deflated him as surely as a punctured tire. I was no longer frightened. He disgusted me.

"Thanks for lunch, Ames," I said, sliding from my seat. "Take care of yourself."

"Eja, wait." He stared at me with bloodshot eyes. "I'm so sorry. Don't tell Dem. Please."

I shook my head. "Relax. He'll never hear it from me."

I WAS TROUBLED by Ames. His boozy assertions raised more issues than they solved. Both Horton and Heather had excellent reasons for murdering Phaedra Jones. Horton, that prim and proper Bostonian, had risked his money, reputation, and marriage for the sultry vixen. She had swindled him out of millions and broken his heart while pining for the muscled arms of Justin Ming. If Horty realized that, he might strike out at her. Scions of privileged families don't share well.

Heather was a different proposition—spoiled, selfish, and mesmerized by the charms of Justin Ming. Although she was no intellectual, when it came to getting her own way, she was cagier than most.

I walked the twelve blocks to my home, dodging traffic and brooding all the way. Conflict makes me weary, so instead of working, I stretched out with Cato at my feet for a brief nap. My dreams were immediate and violent. Heather Exley starred as a homicidal wife on a tear. Her startling blue eyes were so vivid and her smile so smug that my shrieks awakened Cato.

Then I remembered. Phaedra was suffocated with a kung fu move that Heather was probably quite proficient at. After all, she had threatened the victim on the night before her murder. I was a witness to that.

Cato gave me the canine eye roll and licked his lips. He took mealtime very seriously and had unpleasant ways of reinforcing his will. After attending to his needs, I jumped in the shower and prepared for a night at Shaolin City.

When the phone rang, I forgot my grievances and grabbed for it.

"Everything okay, Eja? You sound out of breath." Anika never missed a trick. Perhaps she sensed the disappointment in my voice.

"I'm on my way to the dojo," I said. "I'll give you a full report this evening."

"Be careful, and don't take any chances." Anika paused. "Portia called today with an update. Based on his credit reports, she says Master Moore is loaded. No delinquencies or outstanding balances on credit cards. I guess we were way off base."

I considered the threadbare carpets and manic expansion of class offerings. "I wonder. There's something going on at Shaolin City besides the obvious. Lots of intrigue."

Anika hesitated. "Have you spoken with Dem?"

"Nope."

"Bolin told me about your discussion," Anika said. "Hang in there, Eja. Please. My son would be lost without you, and so would I."

YEARS OF CATHOLIC schooling made me punctual to a fault. I zipped into the classroom with minutes to spare, joining the other acolytes in their warm-up routines. Oddly enough I enjoyed the mindless ritual of stretching and bending. It cleared away the cobwebs and gave me clarity. My progress had been painfully slow but steady. I could now execute basic maneuvers without inviting ridicule from my peers. Besides, Shaolin Law number eight forbade bullying.

As class progressed, I grew even mellower, keeping my focus despite the presence of Justin Ming. The sexy sifu was everywhere, offering guidance, meting out praise, and showcasing his perfectly toned torso. When he reached me, Justin lowered his voice and angled his body away from the others.

"Good work, Ms. Kane. Your progress continues." His words were fine, but his tone suggested something more sinister.

Fortune favors the brave, so the saying goes. Although I'm suspicious about bromides and slick solutions to thorny problems, I confronted Justin head on. "Thank you, Sifu. You honor me." I beamed a specious smile his way.

"Some moves may prove dangerous," he said. "We encourage our students to be cautious. To avoid injury."

I bowed my head. "Wise counsel, indeed. Too bad Phaedra wasn't cautious."

He clenched his jaw and spit out a response. "Why is Phaedra your concern? You didn't even know her."

It was a fair question, one that I'd wrestled with myself. My meddling had plagued Deming and led to our most recent spat. There was no easy answer for someone like me who made her living devising plot twists and solving fictional crimes. My secret was shameful but true—I enjoyed the intellectual challenge of a real murder.

"I found her body. That makes her my concern." I crossed my arms and faced him. "Tell me. Did Phaedra give you money like the rest of your clients?"

Justin Ming flinched. "You've been busy I see. Invading my privacy." He guided me through one of the more complex sets, gripping my arm so tightly that I yelped.

"Heather spoke with us. I know all about your new dojo." I broke free and moved back a step. "Or was that another charade?"

Suddenly, Sifu Ming relaxed, gifting me with a dimpled grin. "I love all my pupils, even challenging ones like you, Ms. Kane. It's the Shaolin way." He dismissed me with a nod and glided over to the opposite side of the room.

When class ended, I headed for the exit, avoiding the locker room with all its ghoulish memories. In the shadows, I saw an obstacle—Master Moore standing between freedom and me.

"A steam shower will soothe your muscles, Ms. Kane." His lustrous green eyes had a feline quality—clear and glowing.

My heart pounded as if it might leap from my chest. I had no reason to fear this man, yet I did. Perhaps it was guilt that pumped adrenalin through my veins, spiking my fight or flight response. "Thank you, Master. I will do so at home." I clutched the doorknob with ice-cold fingers, but he was there before me.

"All students are family here," he said. "Each of you is my child."

"Even Phaedra Jones?" I asked, as fear emboldened me. Despite his pious ways, Avery Moore was still human and susceptible to feminine wiles. Had Phaedra snared the master in her web?

"Shaolin Laws are neither punitive nor restrictive," he said, "but sometimes we must ask a follower to leave. Harmony is essential to our way of life."

I did a quick review of the Ten Commandments, Shaolin style. By my count, Phaedra had violated at least three of them, including two of the biggies. Justin Ming wasn't far behind.

"Did you ask Phaedra to leave the dojo?"

Avery Moore's opaque expression was impossible to read. He had obviously aced Inscrutability 101 at Shaolin school.

"Are you happy here, Ms. Kane? There are other paths to the Moral Way."

Annoyance supplanted my fear. This guy wanted to kick me out of his dojo! How fair was that? Anger surged through me as I gave the master a veiled glance of my own.

"There is much I can learn from you, Master. I seek the goal of joyful living."

Duplicity is not my strength, but I'm a fast learner. Channelling Anika's technique was more productive than direct confrontation. The results pleased me.

The master pursed his lips before responding. "Our laws transcend race and culture, Ms. Kane. My African ancestors would embrace our precepts as readily as yours. But those who break our laws reject spiritual cultivation. They must go elsewhere."

"Murder is never a solution," I said, staring straight at him.

The master nodded. "Quite right. Unjustly taking life is a grave of-fense."

I clasped my hands behind my back to quell their shaking. "I must leave now, Master. Please let me pass."

He patted my shoulder and moved out of the way. "Of course."

I plunged out the door and turned left, head down, arms pumping. Someone was following me. I felt it. Home was only blocks away, but my legs felt stiff and leaden. The only hope was the canister of pepper spray nestled in my backpack.

I rounded the corner onto Newbury Street, pausing to breathe and reach for my weapon. Suddenly, strong arms snaked around me, pulling me into a tight embrace. I should have been terrified, but the faint scent of Royal-Oud gave him away.

"I missed you," Deming said, brushing his lips against my cheek. "Do you forgive me?"

Chapter Fifteen

SELF-RESTRAINT WAS never my strong suit. A wiser woman would have played it cool and let him stew. Instead, I stood on tiptoe, pressed against his soft alpaca sports jacket, hugging him with all my might.

"Someone was following me," I said. "I could feel it."

Deming looked around and shrugged. "Nobody's there, so don't worry about it. I'll watch over you. Always." He brushed his lips over mine and whispered, "We need to talk. Let's go home."

I was scarcely a figure of romance with my damp wushu clothes and sweat-soaked curls. "I need to clean up," I said, averting my face. "You ambushed me."

Deming lifted up my chin, forcing me to meet his eyes. "You're beautiful just as you are, Eja. Don't you know that?" He gently kissed my eyelids and forehead. "Lovely."

That moment was so intimate, so tender, that I melted.

We walked briskly across the Common hand in hand, past star-struck lovers, empty Swan Boats, and earnest pet owners. The sky was overcast, but the glimmer in his eyes was enough for me.

We didn't say much while we cuddled on my living room sofa. I forgot every gripe and grievance the moment that he kissed me. A tide of emotion swept away pain, flooding my heart with unimaginable joy. Deming softly murmured my name, saying that he loved only me.

Before long my wushu garb was history, a crumpled heap that formed a nest for Cato. Deming pulled the cashmere throw over us as we lay skin on skin, savoring each touch.

"Did your dad speak with you?" I asked afterwards.

He nodded. "Mother too. They lectured me as if I were a teenager. I already felt bad, but they rubbed salt on the wounds."

I tugged at his thick black hair and drew him closer. "You know me better than anyone. I'm curious, nosey even. That probably won't change even if I try."

He twisted the signet ring on his left hand. "I never dreamed that I might actually lose you. It was so unthinkable that I panicked."

Was dashing Deming Swann actually mortal? I chuckled at that odd, delicious notion. His arms tightened around me, and he dozed off before discussing Phaedra's murder. Eventually, I was able to loosen his grip and slip out to contact Anika.

"I can't believe you found all that out," she said. "But what does it mean?"

That was indeed the puzzler. My efforts had yielded suppositions, possibilities, and suspicions but no solid proof.

"Who knows?" I said. "We're back where we started from. Phaedra burned the candle on both ends, that's for sure. Between her love affairs and gold swindles, she was one busy bee."

Anika stayed silent for a moment. "Maybe we should let it go, Eja. Lieutenant Bates can handle things. It really isn't our concern. I should never have involved you."

"Fair enough. I thought you felt obligated to Horty's parents, and trust me, both he and his lovely wife are prime candidates for the noose."

"Massachusetts doesn't have a death penalty," Anika said.

"Artistic license. Prison would be the same thing."

"What if Horton did it, and we proved it? I'm sure it was an accident." Anika's voice trailed off. "We'd have to turn him in."

"True. And I'd hate to see Ames come out on top. He's turned into a major creep."

Anika's years on the catwalk made her a model of composure. She waited until the last moment to ask me about her son. "Did Dem find you?" she asked. "I don't mean to pry."

"He's in the living room, and all is well." I lowered my voice. "Our private session is still on for tomorrow. Interested?"

"I'll be there," Anika said. "No harm in a little exercise."

I'M NOT JULIA CHILD, but I have a specialty that never fails. While Deming slumbered on, I whipped up a spinach quiche and sliced some strawberries. By nine o'clock he was dressed, showered, and ravenously hungry.

"Yum!" he said, as he inhaled the quiche. "My favorite."

A man with a full stomach is easy to manage. Between bites of food, he listened carefully to my exploits, pausing occasionally to ask very lawyerly questions. I was encouraged when he dove in for more quiche instead of bristling with rage.

"You've been busy, I see." He tried to look stern but failed. Spinach will do that to a man. "Maybe you should join me tomorrow night when Horty and I have dinner."

"Really? I'd love to. Will Heather be there?"

Deming winced. "Not likely. Those duelling affairs put a monkey wrench in their marriage, at least temporarily. I'm going straight from work, so you'll have to meet us there. L'Espalier at eight."

"Wow!" I said. "Pretty pricey, isn't it?"

L'Espalier is Boston's premier French restaurant renown for exquisite fare and posh surroundings. I've always felt like an interloper there, terrified that some snooty server might unmask me as a child of Socialists and send me packing.

"Horty insists," Deming said. "Absolutely loves the tasting menu. Besides, cut him some slack. He's still in mourning since Locke-Ober closed."

I swallowed my misgivings and gave Deming a big thumbs up. In my world, restaurant closings weren't a tragedy. There could be a big upside to our dinner date, especially if Horton Exley loosened up and became vulnerable after sampling the wine selection. High time to confront him with the truth.

"Follow my lead tomorrow night," Deming warned. "You can ask him anything you want, but let me set the stage."

"No problem." I was too busy considering hair and dress options to quibble.

Deming is hard to fool. He gave me the gimlet eye but wisely said no more.

"Any word from Euphemia Bates?" I asked. "I thought we'd hear from her by now."

Deming stalled for time by cracking his knuckles. He does it every time he evades an issue. "I'm not quite sure, but Pam's on the case, and you know how tenacious she is."

That was one word for it. I took the high road and broached another subject. "What's the latest from Fleur Pixley? Any guesses about Phaedra's partner?"

Deming reached across the table and took my hand. His eyes twinkled as he sucked my fingers one by one. "You're full of questions, Ms. Kane. Fair is fair. I have one for you too."

"Okay."

"Shouldn't we turn in early tonight? Tomorrow is a very busy day."

I SPENT THE NEXT morning outlining my new book, a mystery featuring murder, greed, and gold with a Shaolin twist. Finding the victim was a cinch until I considered the many casualties of greedy ghouls like Phaedra. Those caught in her scam were victims as surely as Phaedra's crumpled corpse in the dojo. There were no winners in this story, just a long parade of losers with compelling motives.

At two p.m., I galloped out the door headed for Shaolin City. To my surprise, an unannounced visitor waited in the lobby. Heather Exley popped up the moment she spied me and strode my way. She was clad in head-to-toe black, like the angel of death or harbinger of doom. Come to think of it, I'd never seen the woman in bright clothing.

"Heather! What a surprise. I was just heading out." I slowed my pace and glared at Jaime, our concierge, first line of defense and major wimp.

"You're going to the dojo," Heather said. "I'll join you."

We trotted up Newbury Street to Boylston, maintaining a healthy pace that left me winded. To disguise my problem and gasp some oxygen, I pretended to window shop at La Perla. Heather quickly put a stop to that.

"Don't bother looking," she said. "They don't have your size."

Now I truly was out of breath. Outrage, not exercise, fuelled my gasps.

She shrugged. "I shop there all the time. They don't have anything past a D cup."

I bit my tongue and changed the subject. "Not to be rude, Heather, but Anika and I have a private lesson," I said. "With Justin Ming."

Heather reeled back as if I had walloped her, and her poreless complexion lost all its color. It suddenly occurred to me that Heather had been dipping into the Botox bin and was very likely a BFF of other injectables. Although she was at least ten years my senior, the ravages of time had passed her by: no laugh lines, errant wrinkles, or age spots. I was officially jealous as hell!

"A private lesson," she gasped. "I thought you were happy with Deming? And Anika has Bolin Swann. What more could she want?"

I finally caught her drift. To Heather, "private lesson" was synonymous with only one thing. That's why payback was so sweet.

"Well, you know what they say. Variety is the spice of life, and I think we can agree that Justin has plenty of life in him. Spice too."

It was surreal, standing frozen in place, with Boston's self-absorbed upper crust strolling by us. When Heather reached into her Kelly bag and produced a gun, the tension kicked up a notch. My knowledge of firearms is strictly theoretical, based on research, not practice. Heather's gun was small, pearl-handled, and lethal looking. In the manicured hands of a madwoman, it terrified me.

"What is that thing?" I asked. My voice held steady, and I was proud of that.

She cackled, a surprisingly vulgar sound for such a fine lady. "A double-barreled pearl-handled derringer. It's a showpiece."

"Well, put the damn thing away. You might hurt someone."

Another scoff by Heather. "Not someone, Eja, *you*. Leave Justin alone, or you'll regret it. This is a warning."

I thought of my bravest fictional creation and how she'd handle this mess. Crying or fainting was not an option. Upper class scorn was called for. Of course in novels, I'm in charge and can spare my heroine. Real life is more complicated.

I launched a verbal assault. "You threatened Phaedra that way. I heard you, and Lieutenant Bates probably knows too."

Heather opened her mouth to speak, but no sound came out. That gave me the opening I sought. With a show of bravado I imitated the Exley sneer, strolled away, and crossed the road heading toward Newbury Street. I hoped that my leisurely pace would rattle Heather. There was also the possibility that she would panic and fire a bullet into my back. Fortune favored me this time. The sudden appearance of a police cruiser prompted Mrs. Horton Exley to lower her weapon and flee to the nearest cab.

By the time I reached Shaolin City, my hands were shaking, and I felt uncomfortably familiar with my breakfast. Talk about life imitating fiction—I'd just been threatened by an unhinged, gun-toting socialite stalker! That kind of incident was fodder for my novels, not my life. Besides, pricey lingerie stores have strict behavioral standards for their clientele. If Heather had drilled me with her derringer, I'm positive that her days at La Perla would have ended. That penalty alone might deter a fanatical fashionista from committing murder.

The sight of Anika emerging from the Bentley elevated my spirits, as did the thought that Po was close at hand. My future mother-in-law was daisy-bright in a yellow two-piece number complemented by her perfect French braid. No wonder Bolin Swann doted on his wife. She made elegance seem so easy.

"Eja! You look positively shaken," she said. "What's wrong? Nothing about Dem, I hope."

I shared my Heather story, embellishing my courage under fire just the teensiest bit.

"The woman's a maniac," Anika said. "She must be stopped."

For safety's sake, we scurried inside the dojo and headed for the locker room. Oddly enough, the murder scene felt safer today than the streets of Boston.

"Will you tell Deming?" Anika asked. "Someone has to know."

"How about telling Euphemia Bates? If Heather pulls a gun on me, she might have canceled Phaedra Jones as well. Her motive was far stronger there."

Anika mulled it over as she stepped into the changing room. "They cleaned this place up rather nicely, wouldn't you say? No blood drops anywhere."

Suddenly it hit me. Since Heather was so handy with a gun, why hadn't she shot her rival? *Dim Mak*, the death touch, was a much trickier proposition, and there were no guarantees that a beginner like Heather could strike the right pressure point. Phaedra was fit and ruthless. She could defend herself in a fair fight with a woman, but not against a gun.

"Get the lead out," Anika said. "Our session starts in three minutes."

I scrambled into the changing room, shed my clothing, and donned the humble garb of a Shaolin wannabe. Call me delusional, but since starting my training, I felt fit and more self-confident. Not ready for prime time, but closer, less self-conscious. In five more months, I might glide down that aisle after all.

"She's not hiding somewhere, is she?" I peeked out from behind the curtain, hoping history would not repeat itself.

"Of course not, Eja." Anika said. "She's probably in her psychologist's office, crying her eyes out. Heather goes from high to low without the elevator, if you get my drift."

"She's bipolar?"

"Not at all," Anika said, as we walked toward our classroom. "Everyone claims some malady these days to excuse bad behavior. Believe me. I've known Heather Exley for twenty years, and she's as sane as both of us. Not crazy, just spoiled and egocentric."

I respected Anika's opinion and her unerring way of cutting to the chase.

"You don't think she did it?" I asked as we entered our practice room.

"She's certainly capable of it, but not in a fit of rage. Heather plans things out."

I flipped the switch in the room and saw a dark figure huddled on the floor with his head down. "Shit," I cried, "another corpse!"

Immediately, the figure came to life, and Justin Ming leapt to his feet. "Don't worry, Ms. Kane," he said. "I was only meditating. I believe you've had enough shocks for one day."

He didn't explain—he didn't have to. Justin Ming was all business as he led us through stretches, basic forms, and some self-defense moves. Anika had no problem with acting the warrior princess. I was less successful, but Justin awarded me a great big A for effort.

"Keep trying," he said. "You'll eventually meet your goals." Our eyes locked until he broke the stare and looked away. The sexy sifu was a complex man with a devious mind. From my observation, his affection for Avery Moore was genuine, but everything else was an elegant façade. Why then would Justin desert his mentor and devastate the Shaolin City family? He had a pretty sweet arrangement going as it was.

"When will we learn more aggressive patterns?" I asked him. "You know, the real fighting moves."

Amusement spread over Sifu Ming's face from the upturned corners of his full lips to those dimpled cheeks. "Are you in danger, Ms. Kane?"

"Life itself is perilous, Sifu." I pasted an enigmatic smile on my face that rivaled anything he himself could offer.

Anika sized up the situation and immediately jumped in. "What about *Dim Mak*? Will we learn that?"

Justin held out his arms, palms up. "Ladies, we guide students toward enlightenment, not mayhem. Surely you realize that."

"My husband and son have fighting skills, Sifu. Do you exclude women?"

He bristled. "Certainly not, but students must first progress through various stages of training. Combat is totally different. Some of our female disciples are versed in all techniques. They are veteran practitioners of kung fu, not novices like Ms. Kane."

"You taught Heather that stuff," I said. "She told me so."

Justin Ming reeled back as if I had struck him. "Absolutely not," he stammered. "Mrs. Exley never learned that here. Her husband is a longtime student of the master, but I cannot comment on his skills." He narrowed his eyes, no longer the affable object of lust and laughter. "Perhaps you should consult the master about this."

As we prepared to leave, I flashed a saucy grin guaranteed to irritate the hell out of Justin Ming. "Thanks for the suggestion. I just might do that."

Chapter Sixteen

TONIGHT'S OUR DINNER with Horty," I told Anika. "Time to find out the truth. No more stalling."

"Focus on this gold scam. I don't believe sex had anything to do with it." She clucked her tongue. "No matter how besotted he was, Horton is still an Exley. Their behavior and thought patterns haven't changed since the Mayflower landed. With old-line Bostonians it all comes down to money."

I checked the time as soon as I got home. With a pinch of luck, I might reach Fleur Pixley before she left work. That former friend owed me big time, and her guilty conscience might nag her into shedding some light on Phaedra and her gold-digging ways.

It took persistence and several chats with her underlings before I penetrated the federal bureaucracy. No doubt after her recent bout of treachery, Fleur consigned me to the no fly list. Man-stealing traitors are usually quite adept at the runaround, but tenacious writers have limitless patience and very little shame. After ten minutes of excuses and evasions, Ms. Pixley got on the line.

"Eja! Sorry for the misunderstanding. My assistant is dreadfully protective of my time." Fleur used that high-pitched, singsong voice that indicates a guilty conscience or a throat malady. "Now, how can I help you?"

Good thing I'm a disciplined person. Otherwise I might have suggested a permanent dirt nap. "Hey, Fleur," I said. "Thanks for taking my call. Listen—I could use a quick tutorial on the gold scam Phaedra used. Think you can help?"

That suspicious nature surfaced again. Fleur hesitated and asked, "Why? What's going on?"

"Nothing. I'm having dinner with Horton and wanted to impress him. That's all."

"Will Deming be there?"

That was the Fleur I'd always known—obsessed, obnoxious, and totally tone deaf.

"Naturally," I said. "I never let him out of my sight. So. Can you help me?"

She growled something unintelligible and answered, "It's simple, Eja. Anyone can master it. Fueled by greed and a dollop of stupidity. In Horton's case, it was sex. Whatever Phaedra gave him, that boy couldn't get enough. The perfect mark."

"Okay." Patience may be a virtue, but it's hard on the nerves. "I've read the FTC brochures about investment gold. Here's my question. Would Phaedra need a partner, or could she go it alone?"

Fleur thought about that for a moment. "If it were gold stocks, no problem, but considering the numbers we're talking about, she had to have help. Some shill, her partner, fabricated those faux gold bars and arranged delivery. I've seen the product Horton got, and it looked genuine. Remarkably good."

"Maybe Phaedra got greedy, and her partner struck back."

A long, low chuckle flowed over the line. The sound had a sharp, metallic quality that ticked me off. "Still trying to solve it, aren't you? What about your business venture? Aren't you and your mother-in-law interested in that dojo?"

"We have many interests, Fleur. You know how families are. I can hardly keep up with the Swanns."

After exchanging a few more pleasantries, I rang off, primed and ready to rock and roll. Horton Exley had some explaining to do.

Like most men, Deming appreciates beautiful women. Scratch that. During his storied sweep of debutantes, Deming prowled the East Coast like a hungry shark on a tear. His tastes and appetites were the stuff of legend. That upped the ante for me and generated plenty of rash-inducing angst every time a big occasion arose.

I tamed my curls, applied makeup, and slipped into a slinky, deeply discounted Valentino sheath that I'd snagged for a song. It was red—Bordeaux actually—and made me feel like a femme fatale. Irene Adler to Deming's Holmes. No snooty server at L'Espalier could harm me now!

Another time, I might have welcomed a brisk walk down Boylston Street to the restaurant. The route passed plenty of tempting shops in addition to the typical human distractions. Tonight I chose a cab. No sweaty drama or wounded feet for me. Not this time. I stopped at the Mandarin Oriental, crossed the street, and made my entrance.

Horty had already claimed our table and was busy inhaling a martini. Not for the first time, I wondered whether he was nervous or a confirmed boozer.

"Eja! You look incredible." He was obviously stunned. I welcome compliments, but in this instance, the sentiment verged on insult.

"Thanks. I wonder where Deming is?"

Horty dismissed me with a wave of his patrician arm. "Dem called. He'll be a few minutes late. Some business with Lieutenant Bates." He grumbled sotto voce, "That woman is a menace. No respect for the dinner hour."

At his insistence, I ordered a cosmopolitan. After a timid sip, I ladled on some charm. "Maybe you'll clarify something for me while we're waiting. I never can get this stuff straight."

Marriage to Heather had conditioned him to befuddled females. Horton launched a patient pout my way and nodded. "Of course. Anything to help."

My smile was flawless, my words concise. "Who was Phaedra's partner? In the gold business, I mean."

Horty downed his martini and signaled for a refill. Before answering, he gave me the full Exley sneer. "Pardon me. Why do you ask?"

Girlish innocence sometimes works for me. Not with Deming—he's wise to my tricks—but Horton is far less astute. "Oh," I said. "You asked me to find the murderer, so I just assumed . . ."

"The murderer—yes, yes. I guess it can't hurt to discuss things. The truth is, I never met Phaedra's partner. Her associate, she called him." Horty shrugged. "Come to think of it, I'm not even sure it was a man. Phaedra never gave a name, just said she had to be discreet."

"Oh?" I gave him the big-eyed look. "Why was that?"

Horton flushed. "To keep anyone else from horning in on below market prices. The gold game is very competitive, Eja. Caution is the watchword."

After losing five million dollars in a honey trap, he lectured me about caution. The Exley arrogance was on full display. Fortunately, I have neither excess cash nor a trusting heart. Con men give me a wide berth.

I persisted, jabbing away at Horton's complacency. "It's something to consider, you know, especially if Phaedra double-crossed her partner. That spells motive, and right now, you and Heather need all the suspects you can scare up."

His eyes opened wide, and his mouth former a perfect O. "But I'm innocent. We're both innocent. One of those hooligans must have killed her."

"Hooligans?"

"You know," Horton sputtered, "those kung fu people. Isn't that what killed her? Some death chop?"

Now I understood. Horton planned to use the SODDI defense—some other dude did it. Whether it was a Hail Mary play or a brilliant ploy by Pamela Schwartz, things would get very interesting very quickly. When Euphemia Bates dismantled the Exleys, I hoped to have a front row seat.

"But, Horton," I said in my most winsome voice, "you know all about *Dim Mak*. I'm sure Master Moore taught you how to do it. Heather may have learned it too. She's a diligent student and certainly knows her way around guns."

He clutched his throat and gasped. "Guns? What are you talking about?"

"Don't answer that," commanded a stern voice. "Say nothing."

Pamela Schwartz, accompanied by Deming, stood behind her client, grasping his chair. "This isn't an inquisition, Eja. Buzz off. My client has nothing to add."

Despite her sour disposition, Pam Schwartz had the total package—blond bob, perfect makeup, and eye-popping body. Too bad she was the bitch from Hell.

Deming sat beside me and kissed my cheek. "You look like an angel, Eja," he whispered in my ear. "Too bad, you're such a devil."

Horton Exley remembered his manners and stood until Pam was seated. "Good thing we haven't ordered yet. I recommend the tasting menu." His dark mood had been lifted by the arrival of his lawyers. He was jovial now, ready to share gastronomical tips.

"We worked late, and Pam agreed to join us," Deming said. "I knew you wouldn't mind."

My smile was sweetness personified. "The more the merrier. Horton and I were discussing weapons."

"So we heard," Deming said. "What's this gun stuff about? Phaedra wasn't shot, you know."

"Just small talk," I lied. "Wiling away the time."

"Well, change the subject," Pam hissed. "The walls have ears, you know."

There are worse clichés, although I couldn't think of one offhand. I revised my mental outline and substituted Pamela Schwartz for the victim in my next novel. Crimes against the English language deserve the death penalty.

"How was your session at the dojo?" Deming asked. "Did you and Mother behave?"

Pamela Schwartz eyed me like a raptor sizing up dinner. Her long, varnished talons tapped the table.

"We observed every Shaolin Law," I said. "Like perfect acolytes. Of course, we're only beginners. I had no idea that Horton and Master Moore even knew each other. Small world."

Deming exchanged uneasy glances with Pam. They realized how incriminating such an admission was. Horton Forbes Exley had a working knowledge of the dojo. That strengthened his opportunity to kill Phaedra and pop her into the utility closet. Between lust and lucre, he had motive aplenty.

"Avery Moore was my sifu for several years," Horton said. "A deeply spiritual man. No head for business, but an old soul."

"I'll bet you learned fast," I gushed. "You're probably a black belt or something."

Pam saw the danger signs, but Horty responded before she could stop him.

"You flatter me, Eja. I'm rusty now, but at one time, I was pretty damn good at martial arts, if I do say so. Ames was even better." He turned to Deming. "You and Bolin dabble in that too, don't you, Dem?"

By focusing on the menu, I masked my reaction. Both Deming and Bolin did more than dabble. They were competitive martial artists, serious practitioners who honed their lethal skills. Blowhards like Horton hadn't a clue.

After we selected our entrees, Pam motioned to her client. "I need a few minutes of your time. Let's step out into the bar." Her tone left no room for argument, and after a momentary rebellion, Horty excused himself and followed his attorney.

"What's the story?" I asked Deming. "I'll never make any headway with her here. He asked for my help, didn't he?"

I expected a spate of knuckle cracking, but to my surprise Deming hung tough. "It's complicated," he said. "Pam got an offer from the DA—voluntary manslaughter. Heat of passion. You know the drill. She has to present it to Horton, even though I doubt that he'll accept."

"But why? They haven't even arrested him yet or charged him. Plus, I don't think he did it. Heather is a better suspect."

I folded my arms and glared at my fiancé. He looked devastatingly handsome in his navy suit and crisp white shirt. I resisted the impulse to grab his Hermes tie and kiss him senseless.

"Hold on," Deming said. "It's only exploratory. Pam and the DA go way back, and they like to nip these scandals in the bud whenever they can. Let's face it—Phaedra wouldn't make a very sympathetic victim. The taxpayers of Massachusetts would applaud the action."

"Listen to this." I shared my run-in with pistol-packing Heather, the terror of Boston's upper crust. "That woman is unhinged when it comes to Justin Ming. She'd wring Phaedra's neck like a stewing chicken. Count on it."

Deming raised his eyebrows. "Hmm. Vivid imagery, Ms. Kane. You should be a writer." He checked the room for eavesdroppers and leaned over. "My money is on Justin Ming. If Phaedra caused problems, he'd handle it. That guy bothers me."

"I didn't even realize that you knew him."

He shrugged. "Dad and I ran into him at some competitions. Martial Arts stuff. Ming has an ego that won't quit, and if a woman dumped him, he might snap. Hold on. Here they come. Act normal."

By the look on Pamela's face, things had not gone well. Her mouth was set in a firm, mean line, and her forehead muscles made a valiant though unsuccessful effort to scowl. Another testament to the awesome power of Botox!

"I have to get back to the office," she said. "Please excuse me."

"What a shame," I said, sweet as pie. "Won't you get hungry?"

Lawyers always want the last word. Pam pivoted, eyeing my curves with naked scorn. "Starvation has its benefits. Try it some time." She cleared the room in three angry strides and never looked back.

Horton was oblivious to everything but his meal. He huddled with the sommelier, debating the finer points of each wine in the tasting menu. His expertise impressed me, but Deming merely grunted.

"Don't let Pam get to you," he said. "She plays rough when things don't go her way."

"She meant every word she said. Bitch."

He took my hand and kissed it. "Pam's envious, darling."

"Of me?" I was genuinely shocked. "She's got everything. Brains, beauty, success."

"So do you. But you have someone who loves you and Pam doesn't."

Our eyes met, and for a moment, we were in our own little world. I forgot about Horty, L'Espalier, and murder. All I saw was Deming.

"Hey, you two," Horty said. "Ready to eat?" He pointed to the viands gracing our table. They were typically French—elegant, portion controlled, and beautifully presented. Screw Pamela Schwartz and her nasty ways; I was starving.

After his third glass of wine, Horty grew more voluble. There was no time for delicacy, so I moved in for the kill.

"What was Phaedra like?" I asked. "You knew her so well, and you cared about her."

He hesitated, reached for his handkerchief, and dabbed at his eyes. "She's hard to describe—a mass of contradictions, like most of us, I guess. Harsh, but incredibly sweet too. Beauty and sex appeal were tools to her. Phaedra grew up poor, I mean dirt poor. She vowed she would never be that way again. Hard work and brains pulled her out of the cesspool. I admired that."

"She had ethical problems, Horty. Massive fraud hurts lots of people. It probably caused her murder too." Deming's handsome face looked grim. "The way we clear your name is by finding an alternative. The real murderer."

"I felt alive whenever I was with her," Horty whispered. "I loved her."

"She betrayed you," I said gently. "That must have hurt."

If he confessed right now, it wouldn't have surprised me.

Blue Exley eyes stared coldly at me. "You're wrong. Tell her, Dem. Phaedra thought that gold was real. She planned to confront her partner."

This was no time for delicacy. I plunged headlong into a cauldron of emotion. "What about Justin Ming? Weren't they involved?"

"Who told you that?" he asked. "She was his student. Nothing more. Men always pursued Phaedra, but she never gave them a second look."

"Forgive me. I was misinformed. You know how people love to gossip."

My response was reasonable enough, although Horton obviously didn't think so. He swilled another glass of wine and made an ungentlemanly burp. "For your information, Ms. Kane, Phaedra agreed to marry me on the night before she died."

I scoured my memory banks, recalling each detail of that doorway tryst. Horton, prisoner of lust, had been so welded to Phaedra that he hadn't noticed anything. Perhaps I wasn't the only passer-by who got an eyeful. Thoughts of Heather Exley and Justin Ming made me wonder.

"What about Heather?" I asked. "She must have noticed something."

He laughed, a sharp, guttural sound with no mirth in it. "My wife hasn't noticed me for years, unless she needs the checkbook. Peaceful coexistence, détente. That's how most marriages end up. As long as she got a juicy settlement, she wouldn't murder Phaedra or any other woman." His eyes narrowed into malevolent slits. "Your turn will come. Just wait and see."

Chapter Seventeen

WE BUNDLED HORTON Exley into the Porsche and headed for Brookline. Deming had forced his tipsy client to relinquish the car keys, promising to sort everything out in the morning. Before long, raucous snores wafted from the back seat as Horton drifted into dreamland. I leaned back in the glove leather seat, closed my eyes, and inhaled the sounds of Chris Botti's golden trumpet.

"It isn't true, you know." Deming put his arm around me and pulled me close. "Horton's take on marriage, I mean. Just look at my parents. They still act like honeymooners after all these years."

I laughed, thinking of the passion between Bolin and Anika and the openness with which they displayed it. A stark contrast to the Exleys.

"We'll never be that way," Deming said. "Not if I have any say so."

"No détente for us," I said. "I'd prefer the nuclear option to cold war." I watched his perfect profile, marveling at my good fortune.

"Good thing," he said. "By the way, once we get Horton sorted out, I've got a surprise for you, and it's not what you're thinking, cheeky girl."

Bemused speculation kept me entertained all the way to Brookline. When we arrived at our destination, Merry Meadow was ablaze with lights like a mini-Versailles. We sailed through the gate and parked next to the entryway where Carlisle awaited us. I stayed in the car, snuggled under Deming's Burberry while the two men carefully maneuvered Horton up the steps and into the house.

Deming didn't linger. He soon loped out the door, dangling a strange-looking key.

"Hey, wake up. Time for your surprise."

I blinked as he turned on the powerful interior lights. "A key?"

"Not just any key," Deming said. "Keys to the Kingdom, or something like that. Come on. You and I are going to see Aladdin's cave."

AT FIRST BLUSH, Sumo-Tek, the robotic storage vault, looked rather ordinary, more futuristic prison than opulent cave. It nestled so anonymously on the Route 128 corridor that I'd passed it many times without a second glance. Except for the gated entryway, it was an unremarkable space, a windowless, faceless dance with obscurity.

Deming stopped at an outdoor kiosk and input a pin number. An unseen, all-knowing system identified him and directed us to a private staging area inside the hulking structure. After swiping an identity card, he submitted to a biometric scan.

"This is creepy." I shivered. "Futuristic nonsense. Besides, how come it acknowledged you? I thought this was Horty's secret place."

"We made arrangements following Phaedra's murder. After all, I am his attorney."

"Now what?" I asked. "Will some disembodied voice summon us?"

He made a brusque comment and ignored me. Suddenly, an unseen metal hand unloaded a self-storage pod in front of us. It was large, at least five feet by ten feet, and looked heavy.

"What does a gold bar go for these days?" I asked.

Deming wrinkled his brow. "A kilo bar is roughly $45,000 in today's market. That means that Phaedra delivered over one hundred of those babies. No easy task for a woman alone."

He nodded when I mentioned Phaedra's partner. Horton had already discussed that with Deming as well as his theory that Phaedra herself had been duped.

"Too bad your client couldn't play with hotels or high-end autos like a good little scion. Harder to lose sight of or falsify."

"Just be patient," Deming said. "This place will pique your imagination. The selling point is robotics. Untouched by human hands." He opened the module with Horton's electronic key. "I'm sure you get the implication."

A child of ten could understand. This high-tech setup demolished Horty's tale of thwarted virtue. Phaedra Jones knew about the fraud—she had to. No one could slip into this facility and spin gold into iron, not even Rumpelstiltskin.

"She and her partner conned Horton," Deming said. "Look inside." He pointed to the hundred or so faux gold bars that were neatly stacked in the module. "No one could substitute these babies for the original. As the Great Detective said, when you eliminate all other factors the one that remains is the solution."

"I love a man who quotes Conan Doyle," I said, blowing him a kiss. "So sexy. Has Lieutenant Bates been over this?"

Deming's lips twitched in a ghost of a smile. "Count on it. Her crew tested every one of those kilo bars. All phony. By the way, Euphemia Bates reached the same conclusion that we just did. Either Phaedra conned Horton, or her partner deceived Phaedra. Since she has a rather extensive police record under her real name, I trust the first explanation."

"Darn," I said. "You mean her name wasn't Phaedra? I love that name."

"You are such a romantic," Deming said. "Her real name was Enid. Enid Jones."

"No wonder she turned to crime," I said. "Classic case of parental indifference."

"I'll bear that in mind when we have kids," Deming said, pinching my cheek.

He followed directions, pressing the touch screen to his left. We watched as the door closed, and the robotic system retrieved and stored the module. Only then did the exit door open, allowing us to escape.

I held my breath until we were back on the highway, speeding toward Back Bay. The cloying, claustrophobic air of Sumo-Tek had drained my energy and left me shaken. The joyless, depersonalized future was here, and it was sobering.

"Where do we go from here, partner?" I asked. "How do we find Phaedra's confederate?"

Deming gripped the steering wheel and said nothing. He shot me a look that melded outrage with chagrin. "There's no more 'we' in this, Eja. Lucky thing you weren't murdered by that crazy bitch Heather. Do I have to remind you that this is reality, not one of your manuscripts? You and my mom are permanently benched."

I knew better than to argue. It was far easier to ignore Deming's lectures and plow ahead. "Horton lives in a dream world," I said. "He's absolutely useless. The person that absconded with five million bucks must have left an audit trail. Find him—or her—and you'll nab the murderer."

Deming swore under his breath as he swung into the driveway of my condo and parked the Panamera. He ignored my comments as easily as I did his, a trade-off that suited us both.

"Come along, Nancy Drew," he said. "Your dog awaits you."

Cato! I tried not to leave the little rascal unattended for more than a few hours. He has a vindictive streak five miles wide and no compunction about showing it. I strolled up the driveway and into the lobby, two strides ahead of Deming. In a stirring example of vigilance, the concierge waved us through without glancing up from his iPad. "Are you staying the night," I asked Deming, "or does Pamela need you?"

He pushed the elevator button and stared down at me. "I might be persuaded to stay for the right inducement."

I fanned myself and batted my eyelashes in Scarlett O'Hara fashion. The effort was spectacularly unsuccessful.

Deming finger-combed his thick hair and sighed. "You should ramp up your seduction techniques."

"Really?" As we exited on two, I undid my dress and stepped half-naked into the hallway. My very proper fiancé gulped and ran after me like a man on fire.

"For God's sake, Eja, someone might see you."

"Just what I'm hoping for, big boy." I sashayed to my doorstep and hesitated. "Did you send me flowers?" I asked, seeing a box from one of Boston's premier florists.

"Nope. Must be one of your many admirers. Should I be jealous?"

I ripped open the box and gasped. "Maybe not."

My gift was no love offering—it contained a dozen decapitated black roses. A plain white card amplified the message. *Deadheads*, it read. Someone had sent me a clear and unambiguous threat that sent chills from my head to toes.

"Step aside," Deming said. "Is there a message?"

My voice sounded strange, even to my ears. "Oh, yeah. They call this kind of pruning 'deadheading.' It eliminates problem stems but doesn't do much for the roses."

Needless to say, Deming stayed at my side for the balance of the night. Cato got an abbreviated nightly stroll, although both of us stayed on high alert. Our attempts to quiz the concierge were wasted words. He checked his log, pointed to the flower delivery at 8 p.m., and shrugged helplessly.

"Look at your security tapes," Deming growled. "Ms. Kane could be in danger."

I shook my head and whispered, "Forget it. This guy is new and hasn't the foggiest notion what you're talking about. We'll tackle Jaime tomorrow. He's supposed to be up on this stuff."

"I pay him enough," Deming said. "That guy should be right on top of it."

That made no sense. "What do you mean? You pay Jaime?"

Deming pulled me to him and kissed my forehead. "Yep. Call it insurance, bribery—I don't care. That little whelp gets a sizable bonus to keep you extra safe. I'm not taking any chances. Not with your life. It's precious to me."

"I'M GOING TO SEE Lieutenant Bates," I said the next morning. "She needs to know about those flowers and Heather Exley too."

Deming had the look of a man suffused with deep sleep and great sex. He sipped his espresso with only one eye open. "Be careful what you say. Remember, Horton is my client. Heather has arranged other counsel, but she's still family. That makes things tricky."

"Not for me," I said. "Besides, your mother will be there, and you know how tactful she is."

He rolled his eyes and gulped more latte. "We'll be lucky if they don't charge both of you. By the way, I'll deal with Jaime this morning. Remind him of our arrangement."

"Don't scare him. He's afraid of you." I'd seen Jaime cringe when the imperious Mr. Swann strode his way. Deming had a habit of prowling a room like a hungry tiger stalking prey. Not comfortable for the tethered goat.

"One more thing, I spoke with my dad last night about those roses." Deming's nostrils flared. "We'll contact the florist today. Swann Industries has a corporate account with the firm."

"That's client information," I said. "Isn't it confidential?"

He shook his head as if I were a simpleton. "They're business people, Eja. Think about it. Besides, Dad can be very persuasive, especially when his family's at risk."

I patted his cheek and was out the door before he could stop me. Fortunately, the red Mercedes with Anika at the wheel was parked at the curb, ready for action. She waved merrily at me and flung open the passenger side door.

"Come on! We don't want to keep Euphemia waiting." Anika defined elegance in a trim, tailored pantsuit. I chose the safe road by wearing a nondescript beige suit designed to avoid attention.

"Does Dem know what we're up to?" Anika asked. "I'm so glad he was with you last night. Creeps who send dead flowers are nasty customers." She peered into the flower box and shuddered. "Terrible waste of roses."

Anika pulled into a parking lot adjacent to Roxbury Community College. Boston police headquarters sprawled across Tremont Street, an uninvited guest or strong sentinel, depending on your point of view. The futuristic design was jarring to me, inconsistent with the historical landscapes that made Boston unique. I'd been here a number of times, but familiarity brought me no comfort. I was an alien in a harsh, efficient universe where death was a constant visitor.

We entered through the middle door, cleared security, and stated our business to the desk sergeant, a sharp-eyed veteran with an Old Testament face. He verified our appointment and grunted as if life held few surprises.

As the elevator sped to her floor, I reviewed my presentations for the lieutenant. I admired Mia Bates, but she intimidated me. My moist palms attested to that. She was always courteous and professional, even when she knew I was hiding something. Maybe that was the answer—the wisdom and cynicism radiating from her cop's eyes activated every inch of my guilty conscience.

"Are you okay?" Anika asked. "You really have to report this before things escalate."

I nodded, licking desert dry lips. "She'll wonder why I'm the target. Remember, we were warned about getting involved."

Anika shrugged. "So what. Euphemia knows you. She never thought you'd do what she said anyway." She strolled off the elevator and into the lion's den without any hesitation.

Several detectives were in the bullpen, hunched over their computers or flipping through case files. They said nothing, yet I knew by their expressions that they didn't miss a thing.

"Help you, ladies?" asked a tall, swarthy man with a lanyard dangling from his neck. He raised his eyebrows when we said we were expected and pointed toward Mia's office. Perhaps I wasn't the only one in awe of the lieutenant.

As soon as we entered, she looked up and left her desk to greet us. Euphemia Bates was a long, lean column of teal wearing an ensemble only ectomorphs can manage. A hint of turquoise shadowed her lids, giving her the regal look of a potentate. She motioned toward the sofa and sat directly opposite us.

"Tell me what happened," she said. "Quite frankly, at this point, we're still collecting evidence."

I gulped and launched into a fairly coherent account of yesterday's excitement. Anika supplemented my comments with her own observations.

"You're saying that Heather Exley threatened you with a gun?" Mia bit her lip and turned her head to the side as if to suppress laughter. "It seems so out of character."

"Right on Boylston Street," I said. "It had pearl handles. A derringer, I think."

"In front of La Perla. Can you believe how brazen she was?" Anika, a devotee of fine French intimate apparel, was outraged by such desecration.

"Shocking," Mia said. "Did she confess to Phaedra's murder while she was waving that gun?"

"Not really. She seemed more focused on separating me from Justin Ming. She's crazy about him."

"Besotted," Anika added. "The woman even lent him money. That's bad business."

Mia nodded at that. "I hear you. No good comes from mixing love and money." She leaned forward and stirred her mug of tea. "Didn't you tell me that Phaedra was also in love with this Ming?"

"That's his story," I said, "but I don't doubt it. He has that impact on women."

Anika nodded sagely. "My son affected women the same way, but he wanted only Eja." She leaned across the couch and patted my arm.

Mia Bates looked up from her iPad. "What about the flowers? I presume these are the ones." She opened the box with a pencil tip and stared. "Hmm. Is this Mrs. Exley's work too?"

I paused and gave that question some thought. "No. Heather wouldn't waste the money. Besides, I think she's too dense to devise something that cool."

"Cool, is it?" Mia's jaw clenched tighter than a vault. "The message is rather pointed, Eja. You've been rattling someone's cage, and that could be dangerous. I'll have the lab look at this, but I doubt that we'll find anything other than the florist and delivery guy's prints."

"Bolin's checking out the florist," Anika said. "He and Dem are doing that personally."

A momentary cloud flitted over Mia's face. "Oh, joy. Someone else doing my job. Guess we public servants need all the help we can get."

Mia was distracted, and I saw an opportunity. "Have you found Phaedra's partner yet? She had to have one. Those gold bars were heavy."

Her eyes narrowed into fiery slits. "Seems like you went on an excursion, Ms. Kane."

"Deming has permission," I said. "Isn't Sumo-Tek the creepiest place ever?"

She ignored my comment and stared at her tablet. "Tell me again. I'm still puzzled. Why are you involved in the murder of someone you didn't even know or like?"

Anika ran interference. "After all, we discovered her body, Lieutenant. That makes it personal."

I felt the heat of Mia's anger and blurted out my reason.

"It haunts me—her eyes and the way she grabbed my hand. She was counting on me to avenge her, and I can't let it go."

Chapter Eighteen

OUR MEETING WITH Euphemia Bates sapped my spirit. After Anika dropped me off, I vowed to forget murder and focus on my writing—at least for a few hours.

Jaime intercepted me the moment I entered the lobby. His sad puppy dog eyes confirmed that Deming Swann had cuffed him around or worse, threatened his wallet.

"Oh, Ms. Kane, I hope you'll forgive me." Jaime elevated obsequity to an art form with half bows and fulsome smiles. "I promise to do better."

"Fine, Jaime, no problem. Just hold my deliveries and keep them for me at the front desk." I recalled Heather's ambush of the prior day. "And for goodness sake, don't let anyone lurk in the lobby without being announced."

He nodded vigorously enough to cause whiplash. "Understood. A lady stopped by this morning, but I told her she couldn't stay."

My antennae rose to full length. "The blond lady from yesterday—Mrs. Exley?"

The concierge struggled to craft a tactful response. "No. This lady was . . . older."

After coaxing a description from him, I realized that my visitor was Portia Amory Shaw. Even in Boston, weathered twinsets and sturdy brogues were a rarity worth noting. Portia had cornered the market on those get-ups.

"She left a note." Jaime bustled off to his desk and retrieved it.

Portia's message was concise, almost brusque. "I have new information on the dojo. Call if you're still interested."

There went my good intentions. I immediately called Portia and invited her to my place for tea.

"Make it something stronger, and I'll be there," she said. "Is five o'clock too late?"

"Not at all." That gave me plenty of time to strategize and assemble some snacks before she arrived. "You have my address, so I guess we're all set."

Portia paused. "Yes. Ames told me where you live. I happened to be in the neighborhood this morning, so I took a chance and stopped by."

"Not a problem. See you later."

I sat at my computer shivering. It was preposterous, a residue of last night's flower delivery and unwanted attention from the Exley clan. It was time to tread a new path.

I explored the Shaolin Way of meditation and positive thoughts instead of gnawing on the negative until my mind exploded. I sat cross-legged on the floor, closed my eyes, and focused. To my surprise, Master Moore's suggestions actually worked. A sense of well-being filled my mind, clearing away the cobwebs and night terrors. Shakespeare had said it best as he did most things. I refused to die many deaths by cowering in my room waiting for the end.

When Deming called an hour later, I was the soul of composure.

"How did it go with the lieutenant?" he asked. "I presume you're not under house arrest or awaiting indictment."

"Very droll. How was your date with flower power?"

His voice dropped, a warning that all was not well. "Don't overreact, Eja."

Meditation was forgotten as my blood pressure soared. "Okay."

"The flowers were ordered by phone and the money messengered over. Things were busy, and the receptionist didn't recall much."

"I expected that order to stand out. Deadheaded roses can't be that common."

Deming gave a man-sized sigh. "Believe it or not, they are. Mostly at Halloween, but other times too. Devotees of Jerry Garcia and now the Goth influence."

"Oh. Lieutenant Bates told me to be careful. She seemed rather concerned."

Deming's cool façade started to crack. "Just stay home today, Eja. Please. I forbid you . . . that is, I beg you not to go to that dojo. I'll come over later and stay the night."

That cheered me up as nothing else could. I decided not to muddy the waters by mentioning my date with Portia. Maybe I was skating on ethical thin ice, but by adhering to the letter if not the spirit of my promise, I kept Deming satisfied and relatively calm. I didn't even have to cross my fingers.

"Fine. Okay. Except for walking Cato, I'll stay here all day."

He whispered into the phone so quietly that I almost missed it. "I love you, Eja Kane. Never forget that."

THE OUTLINE FOR my next novel beckoned, and for the first time since Phaedra's murder, I felt energized. Three hours hunched over my computer left my back and shoulder muscles begging for mercy, but the results were worth every niggling ache. I produced a character outline and two solid opening chapters of *Dojo Death,* a work that closely paralleled reality. Naturally the names were changed—not to protect the innocent, but to indemnify me from pesky lawsuits. I hadn't identified the killer either, but that could be deferred until subsequent chapters. It was easy to devise any number of motives for murdering Phaedra Jones or Prudence Brown, the pseudonym that I invented for her. In my novels, lust and lucre figured prominently just as they do in real life. Phaedra or Enid was a big-time overachiever in both areas.

I attended to Cato, freshened up, and arranged a tray of smoked salmon and assorted cheeses on the coffee table. Most women nibbled canapés rather than chowing down like guys. Despite the ubiquitous twinset and brogues, I gambled that Portia would follow the same path as her glitzier sisters. No need to pile on the carbs.

When Jaime announced her arrival, I put a leash on Cato and plastered a smile on my lips. Portia wasn't the most engaging visitor I could think of, but my mother instilled in me the mantra of a true lady: always pamper your guests.

Imagine my chagrin when the door opened to two visitors rather than one. No dull attire for my CPA friend—Portia Amory Shaw had morphed from grey moth to butterfly. Shorn of her usual duds and fortified with a dab of makeup, she flirted with the outer fringes of glamour. The little black dress was unpretentious, but it suited her, and those trademark pearls looked totally at home nestled on her cleavage. *Cleavage!* Who knew?

The bonus guest was the real shocker. Ames Exley, clad in black designer jeans, T-shirt, and jacket slid in behind her thrusting a box of Godiva chocolates my way.

"Sweets for the sweet, or something equally banal," he said. "I tagged along without Portia's permission. She's far too well-bred to approve."

Something in those Exley eyes cautioned me. Their intensity was at odds with his breezy banter and hammy grin. For once, I applauded when Cato launched into his snarling, macho routine. It comforted me and caused Ames to step back.

"Please sit down," I said, "and help yourselves to some snacks." I opened the chocolates and added them to the other treats. "Portia and I had business to transact, but that can wait. A handsome man is always welcome. Besides, Deming will be here later, and then we'll have two hot guys to drool over."

The cousins exchanged a brief side-glance, as if some plan had been disrupted. I settled Cato down and played hostess.

"What have you two been up to?" I asked. "Everything okay at the foundation?"

Ames poured a scotch on the rocks and eased into the leather wingchair. "Ah . . . superb. Isn't this place fantastic, Portia? Much better than that mausoleum we live in." He pointed to the logs crackling in the fireplace. "Just perfect."

"You look different, Ames. I've never seen you so casual, even during college." I pointed at his black T-shirt with its colorful Uncle Sam logo. "Very nifty."

Ames shrugged off my praise. "It's vintage. My uncle was a real music freak."

Portia sat on the edge of her seat and fumbled with her purse. "Forgive my curiosity, Eja, but have you heard anything else? About the murder, I mean."

I spritzed on some eau d' innocence and shook my head. "Nope. No one tells me anything."

"Oh, come now. You're far too modest. Weren't you with Euphemia Bates just this morning? A little birdie told me that." Ames bared every one of his excellent teeth in a Cheshire grin. "Heather's ears were burning after you finished. Bet you Daddy's going to take her derringer away."

"We didn't discuss the murder," I said. "Anika and I had other business with her."

He dismissed me with a scornful snort. "I understand Deming took you on the deluxe tour of Horty's gold empire. Impressive, isn't it?" Ames curled his lip. "Too bad it isn't worth a damn dime."

I smiled, gave him the big-eyed look, and said nothing. Ames obviously had an agenda. Why not let him pursue it.

"That Sumo-Tek is really something," he said. "The automated future."

Portia shuddered. "It's so sterile. Like a sci-fi movie."

I stood and poured myself a Pellegrino. "I'm surprised you two know about it. Horty said it was a big secret."

"You'd be surprised what we know, dear Eja." Ames rose and stepped toward me, causing Cato to growl. "Wow. That mutt really doesn't like me, does he?"

"He's the cautious type," I said. "Very protective."

Unlike her aggressive cousin, Portia was a bundle of nerves. Her left eye blinked incessantly and she constantly moistened her lips. "Phaedra Jones was a bad person who got what she deserved. She seduced men and then she robbed them. Horty wasn't her only victim, you know."

Ames walked over and stood behind her chair. "Come on, Cuz, give poor Enid a break." When his cell phone buzzed, he looked at the caller ID and rolled his eyes. "Speaking of the devil. It's Horty. Mind if I take this call?"

"Not at all," I said. "Go into the kitchen if you need privacy."

As soon as he left, Portia motioned to me. "I forgot to mention this before. Avery Moore has gotten regular payments exceeding a half million dollars over the past year. That's what keeps the dojo afloat." Her voice was low, almost a whisper. "I managed to trace the source." She blushed. "A friend of mine is a banker. Anyway, they all came from a single payer."

I heard the low rumble of Ames' voice as he prowled about the kitchen. "Who was it?" I asked. Now I was excited, leaning forward to catch her every word.

"You probably won't believe it. I know I was shocked." Portia paused. "The money came from Justin Ming. Every penny of it."

That bit of news left me gobsmacked. It also altered my view of Sifu Ming, despoiler of women and serial gold digger. Was he scheming to take over the dojo or propping up his master's dream? With great effort, I closed my gaping mouth and responded.

"Well, so much for Shaolin City. Anika and I won't subsidize a failing business. Frankly, I'm surprised that Justin had that kind of money."

Portia cocked her head to one side. "Really? Phaedra probably had a partner. You said so yourself. She would have done anything to please Justin Ming. When that type of woman falls hard she has no sense."

The malicious gleam in her eyes transformed Portia from mild-mannered accountant to gleeful conspirator. I drew back and stroked Cato's fur, trying to make sense of things. Was Justin Ming the unknown partner in crime? He was certainly strong enough to hoist those gold bars and clever enough to target potential marks. His motive was easy to imagine—greed and need, the two biggies of crime.

But murder was another issue entirely. According to Euphemia Bates, Justin had no history of violence. Marriage-minded women were probably a common occurrence in his life, and he was wily enough to elude them without resorting to murder. Why eliminate Phaedra and risk a murder charge?

Ames sauntered back into the room, sporting a snarky grin. "Miss me, ladies?"

"Were you gone?" I asked. "I hadn't noticed."

"You always were a smart-ass, Eja. Life with the Swanns hasn't changed that."

Portia gasped. "Ames! Manners."

"Maybe Eja can solve the murder and save Horton. That's what she really wants." Ames sneered. "Why talk with the cops when we've got our own Sherlock Holmes right here?"

I took a deep breath and killed him with kindness. "Actually, I pattern myself after the female sleuths. Amelia Peabody or Kinsey Millhone will do nicely. Miss Marple is a bit long in the tooth for me, though."

Neither one of my guests was a mystery buff. They both shot puzzled looks my way and gaped.

"Forgive me, Eja. That was rude." Ames took a healthy slug of his drink. "Tension has been mounting lately, and I haven't been myself. I've finally come to a decision. It wasn't easy, but I've decided to move on."

"Move on? You mean, leave Boston?"

"Leave the family business and strike out on my own. I'm following your advice, Eja. Remember? You told me to pattern myself after Deming. I've decided to join a law practice in the city."

"He's moving out of the house too," Portia said. "We both are."

"Together?" I gasped.

I couldn't blame Ames for snarling at me. Manners had gone out the window long ago. "Of course not," he said. "Don't be absurd. We're both professionals with great credentials. Doors will open for us." He drained the scotch and leapt to his feet.

"Come along, Portia, Eja is a busy woman. So much to do, so little time." The words were fine, but his tone was faintly menacing. "Where's your fiancé, by the way? Writing briefs with Pamela?"

"Right here, Ames. Is there something you want to tell me?"

Deming walked through the door dressed in corporate avenger garb. His lips brushed my cheek as he stood next to me—legs apart—in a wushu stance.

"Nothing. Never mind. I didn't mean anything." Ames motioned to Portia. "Come on, Cousin. Time to disappear."

Portia reached out and touched my arm. "Thanks, Eja. I'll be in touch."

They hustled out the door without saying a word.

"WHAT THE HELL was going on?" Deming asked. "I thought you promised to lay low, not throw a party. And how come you left the door unlocked?"

"You said don't leave the house and I didn't. Portia was okay, but Ames was creepier than usual. As for the door . . . that was just a lucky accident." I stood on tiptoe and kissed him. "Who knew that my personal superhero would rescue me?"

Deming glowered at me, playing the heavy parent. "Ames certainly looked odd. Who wears a Grateful Dead shirt during dinner hour in Boston?"

Something clicked in my mind as he spoke. "Repeat what you just said."

He locked luscious hazel eyes on mine. "His T-shirt. Classic Grateful Dead. Vintage, too, by the looks of it. Didn't you see the skull design?"

I realized with a grim finality what that meant. My tormenter, the sender of dead black roses, had been in my home enjoying my liquor and planning God knows what. According to Horty, Ames was also versed in the martial arts, just like Phaedra's killer.

"I've been so dense," I said. "How could I have missed it? Freaks who follow the Grateful Dead are called Dead Heads just like those decapitated roses. Ames came here to taunt me. Probably expected me to faint or cower. Bastard! No wonder he got a strange look when he found out you were coming over." I threw my arms around Deming and hugged him. "Thank you."

"Hey, what's this all about?" He gently stroked my hair and whispered, "Remember the song? I'm the one who watches over you, Ms. Kane, and I always will be. Forever."

We walked hand in hand into the bedroom, undressed, and held each other close. For a while I lay in his arms feeling safe and cherished, a world away from murder and malice. Then without warning, I started shaking.

"That does it," Deming said. "You're going to stay with my parents until this whole mess is over."

I thought of the comfort and safety of the Swann mansion with the ever-vigilant Po standing guard. It was tempting. Too tempting. I salvaged my dignity and fought through my fear.

"I can't do that. If I let a creep like Ames disrupt my life, then he wins. I need to concentrate on my writing and live normally. Besides, I have Cato here to protect me."

Deming snorted, using vivid scatological terms to express his opinion. "Okay. Here's the compromise. I'm moving in here until things settle down. Okay?"

I showered him with fevered kisses and the promise of much more. By the time we finished our discussion, both of us were in agreement. Even Cato was reconciled to our new living arrangements.

Chapter Nineteen

ANIKA AND BOLIN joined us for breakfast the next morning. Like all good guests they came bearing gifts—a picnic hamper of international goodies prepared by Po. Even Deming stopped grousing long enough to wolf down crabmeat quiche, *Dou Jiang*, and smorgas, tributes to the native countries of both of his parents.

Left to my own devices, I would have plunged facedown into these delicacies. Fortunately, wisdom prevailed, and I followed Anika's lead, taking modest amounts of each dish. Bolin and Deming showed no such restraint. They piled on the carbs, as though fat deposits were a curse reserved for females only.

After a civilized interval, we sipped espresso and discussed murder. I summarized last evening's cocktail chatter, aided by Deming's withering asides and snide observations about Ames Exley.

"Wait a minute," Anika said. "You mean he sent you those flowers? That's monstrous!"

Bolin frowned as he evaluated the situation. "My question is why? What did Eja say or do that provoked him?" He turned to his wife. "You were part and parcel of it all. He might try to harm you too." A look of tenderness passed between them. It was enough to make a romantic out of a confirmed skeptic.

"I told them, Dad. Eja is confined to quarters until this thing is resolved." Deming hesitated when he saw the expression on my face. "In any event, she needs to be extra careful. That's why I'm moving in."

Bolin gave his son a thumbs up. "Great idea. I'll tell Po to be especially vigilant. No more hikes up Boylston to that dojo, ladies. He'll drive you if you insist on going."

I ignored Deming's scowl and fed Cato a few tidbits under the table. Vigilance makes watchdogs burn up the calories.

"Looks like we need to reevaluate Justin Ming," I said. "He's sort of a Robin Hood figure, taking from the over-privileged and donating to his master. I wonder if Avery Moore even realizes what's going on?"

"Don't count on it," Deming said. "According to Horton, this

Moore character is unworldly. No head for business."

Anika squeezed her husband's arm. "We may be safer at Shaolin City than on Beacon Hill, as long as Eja avoids Heather."

Bolin locked eyes with his son the moment he heard Heather's name. "I hope you spoke to Horton about that, Dem. Heather needs counseling before she harms someone."

Deming's reaction bordered on surly. "Right, Dad. Heather is Pam's client, so she's handling things. Thanks to Mom and Eja, Lieutenant Bates called them down to headquarters today. Pam isn't happy at all."

Normally I bite my tongue to stifle ill-advised comments. Today I chomped down on a Danish instead. The sweet treat took the sting out of Deming's words and made me feel fine. Pamela Schwartz's happiness was the least of my worries.

"I still don't understand it," Anika said. "What got Ames Exley involved in this? He was always a sweet boy when his parents were alive. Now you say he's moving out and leaving the foundation."

"His cousin manages the accounting functions," Deming said. "She'll be hard to replace. I'm not exactly sure what Ames does there other than trot around looking important."

I wondered more about the root of all evil—money. Ames and Portia would soon be without jobs or a place to live. Boston's stratospheric housing costs and surplus of lawyers made life a very dicey proposition—unless, of course, one had a nest egg of five million untaxed dollars.

"Wake up, Eja," Anika chided. "You're dreaming."

"Not dreaming, thinking. Maybe Horty's been right all along. What if Phaedra tried to go straight and was deceived by her partner, a slick number named Ames Exley?" I recalled the smug expression on his face when he called me Sherlock.

Bolin leaned forward, his eyes wary and intense. "You think he's the murderer?"

"Oh, no, Bolin," Anika cried. "I refuse to believe that."

I wasn't captive to fond childhood memories of Ames. During our days at Brown, he was considered a dilettante and a major prick. But murder was a giant leap into the ninth circle even for an Exley.

"It's possible," I admitted. "If Phaedra threatened him, he might lash out. According to Horty, Ames had martial arts training. Some kind of black belt."

Deming exchanged amused glances with his father. "You remember them, Dad. Always competing, never winning. I doubt that either one has the guts to commit murder. Exleys never dirty their hands."

We chewed on that thought while digesting our breakfast. Bolin and Deming left for work shortly afterwards, leaving Anika and me a few minutes of privacy.

"Our lesson is still scheduled for three o'clock," I said, flexing my muscles. "Are you going?"

Anika nodded. "Wouldn't miss it, especially after ingesting all these calories. We'll pick you up at two thirty." She shrugged. "Marriage is compromise, Eja. It's no big deal if Po drives us."

There were a hundred objections I could raise and only one sensible solution.

"Not a problem. Besides, it's kind of cool, having a bodyguard."

MY ATTEMPTS TO write were doomed that afternoon. Instead of producing prose, I saw a kaleidoscope of sounds and faces linked to Phaedra Jones. A braver person would have told Euphemia Bates of her suspicions. I cursed my cowardice and did nothing. Cops demand proof, and all I had were assumptions and unsupported conclusions. No arrests had been made, and according to Deming, none were imminent. Mia Bates would flay me alive for wasting her time and poking into police business.

My cell phone buzzed as I prepared to meet Anika. No caller ID necessary—the velvety baritone on the other end was unique.

"Ms. Kane," said Justin Ming. "Will you be at class this afternoon?"

"Absolutely," I replied. "I'm looking forward to it. Remember, time is running out."

He stayed silent for a moment, as if he were considering his next move. "Of course."

"Who will teach us tonight?"

"The master sends his regrets. I am his unworthy replacement."

"Excellent. There are so many things I want to ask you."

The air was thick with innuendo and an undercurrent of menace. I vowed to puncture the aura surrounding Justin Ming with a few well-placed barbs. The man was a living, breathing study in cant, a trickster of the highest order. One way or another I would find a way to crack that smug exterior.

After we hung up, I gave Cato an abbreviated turn around the Common and then sprinted out the lobby to join Anika. True to form, Po assisted me into the car with a curt nod and a remote semi-smile. My tactics never changed. I chattered nonsensically to him, hoping to provoke a reaction. As usual, he was far too wily to grunt, grimace, or give the game away.

Anika gave me a hug and immediately joined in speculating about sexy Sifu Ming and his motives.

"Maybe the master isn't so holy," she said. "What if he's blackmailing Justin? The dojo is Avery's whole life. The Shaolin Way is his vocation, not a job. Some men would do anything to preserve that even when it violates everything they stand for."

"Some women too. Who knows what Phaedra had in mind? Maybe she was blackmailing Justin. Not the best basis for marriage, but effective." I closed my eyes, thinking of Deming, who would risk everything to protect me. How lucky was I?

To my surprise, the exterior Shaolin City was virtually deserted. The normal hubbub had been replaced by a veil of silence that sent a shiver up my spine. Before Anika could speak, Po hopped out of the car and surveyed the terrain. The whole charade resembled theater of the absurd, but oddly enough, I found it comforting.

Anika clutched my arm. "Don't mind him, Eja. Bolin's word is law to Po. Believe me, nothing will harm us on his watch."

When Justin Ming appeared at the door, he spoke with Po and waved us in. There was nothing suspicious in his manner, nothing that accounted for the sudden spasm of panic that gripped me.

"Come on, Eja. He's ready." Anika leapt out of the Bentley without waiting for Po. She exited as gracefully as a gazelle whereas I lumbered out grizzly fashion.

Sifu Ming held the door open and waved us into Shaolin City. "We had to cancel most classes today, ladies, but don't be alarmed. Electrical problems. Fortunately, the practice room can still accommodate our private clients."

"Shall we reschedule?" Anika asked.

"Not at all. In fact, I suggest we try a new area today. Do you feel adventurous?" His dreamy eyes focused on me, issuing either a challenge or a warning.

"I'm up for it," Anika said. "What do you have in mind?"

Justin flashed his enigmatic smile. "You have progressed beyond our basic program, Mrs. Swann. I prescribe the Dragon form. It builds upon the cardiovascular workout, adding self-defense techniques." He cocked his head to one side, letting a lock of thick black hair obscure his face. "Interested?"

"Absolutely," Anika said. "I'll change and stow my things in the locker room. Coming, Eja?"

"I'll be okay if you'll take my bag with you. Don't worry."

Justin Ming folded his arms, studying me with bemused tolerance.

"What about me?" I asked, expecting the worst. "I've learned a lot too."

He glanced down at me. "You alone can best gauge your progress, Ms. Kane. Have you found what you were looking for at our dojo?"

I should have been terrified, but I wasn't. Justin Ming didn't frighten me even though he could snap me like a twig or use that *Dim Mak* maneuver. Seduction was his go-to trick, but I was impervious to those charms.

"I've learned a good deal," I said. "There are some answers I don't have, but I'll get there eventually."

"Tenacity must be tempered by caution," he said. "Overconfidence can be dangerous." He bowed and turned aside as though waiting for my next move.

I took one step toward Justin Ming. "Phaedra had a partner, you know. Someone strong who helped her move those gold bars."

He pivoted, his expression blank and unreadable. "Why tell me?"

"You admitted that you two were close." I stepped sideways, praying that Anika was on her way. "You have plenty of cash to throw around—enough to subsidize this dojo."

Justin Ming clenched his fists, his expression no longer impassive. "Stay out of my business, Ms. Kane. I did not kill Phaedra. That's all you need to know."

"Half a million dollars—that's quite an investment for a silent partner. Maybe Master Moore can clear things up."

I expected anger, but he surprised me. Justin Ming closed his eyes and hung his head. "Please. Don't do that. The master knows nothing about the money. I handle our financial affairs, and I promise you that money had nothing to do with Phaedra's gold scheme. It would humiliate him if he found out."

"But why?" A wiser woman would have stopped while she was still breathing, but I couldn't help myself.

Justin spoke through gritted teeth. "I told you about my clients—their generosity. That's how I am able to help."

He saw the doubt in my eyes. "Money is unimportant, but the dojo means everything to me. Master Moore saved my life. I was drowning when he found me. He gave me purpose, a moral compass, and something to believe in. He is my father."

I had much to consider but was fraught with indecision, mesmerized by the vein throbbing in his forehead. Justin Ming inspired fear and admiration in equal parts. He was certainly capable of violence—but his claim of innocence rang true.

"Know this, Eja Kane. I will do anything to protect my master and Shaolin City. Anything." He took a step toward me, flexing his hands as he did so.

I tried to scream, but I couldn't. Instead, I relived those horrible nightmares everyone has faced—paralyzed vocal chords, immobilized legs—I had them all.

"Sorry I took so long." Anika bounded into the room ready to exercise. "Dem called, Eja. He'll pick us up after class." Despite the angelic expression, a spark in her hazel eyes told me that she knew what was going on.

"Time for our conditioning drills," Justin said. He commenced thirty minutes of sheer torture designed to hone flexibility and endurance. No wonder he didn't harm me. Why bother when his exercise regimen would do the trick?

Because of her ability, Anika was promoted to doing kung fu forms, a higher-level use of hand, knee, elbow, and foot techniques. I was relegated to basic exercise routines.

"You may start with the Dragon form," Justin told her, "an introduction to effective self-defense." Anika was an apt pupil who soon won her sifu's praise. "Excellent, Mrs. Swann. You'll be doing Tiger form before you know it."

Justin spent some time educating us on the revered place of the Dragon form in kung fu lore, especially its dedication to protecting the master. He stared pointedly at me as he extolled the virtues of such loyalty.

I'm no clock-watcher, but I stole several glances at my watch during the session, wondering if I could stave off collapse.

Our hour expired before I did, but not by much. As we limped toward the locker room, I observed two men locked in heated conversation. One was Master Avery Moore, but the other was a shocker. Why was Ames Exley skulking around the dojo?

They stopped as soon as they saw us. Avery nodded and turned away, but Ames stood there frozen in time and space.

"What a surprise," Anika said. "Are you a student here?"

Ames tried to recover, shrugging and turning on the charm machine. Although duplicity was hardwired into his genes, his eyes gave him away. They had the panicked look of a man tumbling toward an approaching train. Ames flinched when he saw me, despite his show of bravado.

"Eja Kane, you pop up everywhere these days." His words were friendly, but not his tone.

Justin Ming stood behind us, quietly assessing the situation. He said nothing, but his imposing presence made Ames squirm.

"May I assist you?" he asked. "Master Moore has other commitments."

"Nah, it was nothing. Just business."

Justin stepped forward. "I conduct all the dojo's business. The master is our spiritual guide." He opened a side door that led to his office and herded Ames through it. "Excuse me, ladies," he said.

Anika and I exchanged puzzled looks and headed for the locker room. I immediately hit the showers, making a valiant effort to scrub away doubts and primp for my fiancé. Shaolin City had enough drama for a soap opera, but Ames Exley's role was a mystery. I didn't share Anika's fondness for him. Still, I couldn't cast him as a murderer. Not yet.

"What was that all about?" Anika asked. "Maybe Ames is a student here."

"I don't think so. Something important gave the master a major meltdown. You saw him—he was livid. That violates at least two of the Shaolin Laws, maybe three."

We tiptoed down the corridor and out the door without meeting anyone else. Deming was waiting for us, leaning against the Porsche with his arms folded. Despite his dour expression, those outrageous Swann looks left me tingling. He could easily play a film heartthrob or a brooding Eurasian potentate. No woman would question either choice.

"Ladies," he said. "Your chariot awaits." He helped Anika into the back seat and belted me in beside him. "You behaved yourselves, I hope?"

"We tried, but something happened anyway." I gave him my sunniest smile despite the storm clouds that blew in.

"It wasn't about us, son. Ames Exley started something with Master Moore. Most discourteous." Anika abhorred bad manners almost as much as violence. "They didn't come to blows but nevertheless . . ."

I added my two cents about Justin Ming. "He swears that money came from his patrons, and I believe him."

Deming gave me a measured look. "You do, huh? Maybe Ming-sanity is contagious."

Even Anika raised an eyebrow at that.

"Wait," I said. "You don't understand. His devotion to Avery Moore is fanatical, almost old world. Shaolin City is his life. He'd never jeopardize that."

Deming put the pedal to the metal and sped up Boylston Street. "You realize what that means, don't you? Justin Ming would do anything to save his master. If Phaedra stood in the way—watch out." He swung into the Swanns' circular driveway and stopped. "Anything else, Mom?"

Anika leaned forward and hugged her son. "You two stay close. I don't want Eja having any accidents."

A mile-wide smile split his face. "That's one thing you can count on. I'll put her under house arrest."

Chapter Twenty

DEMING'S CONCEPT of penal servitude was more like paradise. When we returned to my condo, I saw that the love god had paid a surprise visit. The living room was filled with the heavenly scent of my favorite flowers—lilies and orchids—and the Bose spewed soft, sultry jazz. On the inlaid French chest, a Gold Ballotin of Godiva chocolates, food of the gods, beckoned me. A magnum of Veuve Clicquot nestled in the ice bucket next to it.

"Wow! What did I do to earn this?" I could think of a dozen answers, all unlikely.

"You don't have to earn anything. Just be yourself."

My voice quivered. I hate it when it does that. "My feelings for you scare me sometimes. I lose control."

His eyes softened as he stroked my cheek. "How come you never tell me that you love me? Not enough, anyway."

"I do too." My cheeks and every visible part of me flushed. "It's just . . . when I see women like Pam, I feel so inadequate. Like I'm not enough for you. They're so perfect." I took a big gulp of air. "I'm afraid it's a dream. That one day I'll wake up, and it will all slip away."

"Dreams do come true, Eja. I'm not going anywhere. I waited a long time for you." He took my hand and gently kissed each finger. Deming has a romantic side that few would suspect. For years he'd submerged it in a surly shell that raised my hackles and led to pitched battles. I found out much later that he cared for me and always had. That revelation changed my life.

We attended to Cato's needs, although he bristled at the abbreviated length of the walk and the absence of ball throws. After I bribed him with treats, the spaniel settled down, allowing me to focus on showing Deming through word and deed how very much I cared. The rest of the evening was magical, a testament to the strength of our bond. Only one thing marred the experience—the pall cast by the unsolved murder. I tried not to think about it, but Deming, the crackerjack lawyer, knew something was amiss.

"Okay. Out with it. Not thinking of another man, are you?" Deming held me at arm's length, watching me closely.

"No."

He beamed the legal death ray at me. "I'm waiting, Eja. Fess up."

"It's the murder. No one really seems to care, and time is slipping away."

"Why do *you* care so much? I assure you Euphemia Bates is on the case, and nothing gets by that woman. Give it time."

He was right. I couldn't argue with his logic, but something told me the answer was within reach. My reach. Call it ego or a thirst for justice, whatever fits. I owed it to Phaedra and to myself.

"Lieutenant Bates has a big caseload. I can give it my full attention."

Deming brushed his lips over my engagement ring. "You are a writer, not a detective. I need your full attention, missy. Our wedding is five months away, and I already feel neglected."

That inspired me, causing a brilliant idea to bloom in my mind. "You're right. Let's find the answer together. That way you won't have to worry, and I'd have a partner. Plus your mom, of course. She'd never forgive us if we left her out."

Deming pressed his lips into an irresistible semi-pout. "That's not good enough. My client's interests are the only things that concern me. That and your safety."

"Really? If we find Phaedra's partner it would help your client too." I sat down and flipped through the latest edition of *Architectural Digest*. "But that's okay. I respect your decision. Anika and I will handle it alone."

Suddenly Deming took notice. He grabbed a legal pad, jotting down several notations. Then my sizzling sweetie cleared his throat and summarized the case coolly and dispassionately like the brilliant lawyer that he is.

"Listen up, Ms. Kane. Lieutenant Bates said that Phaedra usually worked alone. Safer that way and no need to share the loot. If she changed her pattern, and assuming her partner is someone local, there aren't too many possibilities. My money's on Justin Ming, but I suppose Ames is a viable suspect too."

"You're excluding Horton, I notice. We have to question everything he told us. Who knows if it was true? And what about the women? According to your client, Phaedra never specified whether her partner was male or female. Heather Exley springs to mind."

"Hold on," Deming said. "A woman would have to be mighty

strong to haul those bars."

I leapt to my feet and made a muscle. "Sexist! You should see some of the babes who prowl around Shaolin City. They could take on almost any man. Not someone like you, big fella, but the ordinary garden variety guy."

The more I thought about it, the stronger my suspicions grew. I'd assumed that the catfight between Heather and Phaedra was about Justin Ming. What if it involved something even more precious—gold? Heather mentioned "bullion" as they exchanged blows. Had her partner tried to cheat her out of her share?

Deming cleared his throat. "Earth to Eja. Come in."

"Sorry. I remembered what your mother said. Exleys thrive on money. Maybe Heather decided to stockpile some of her own. Swindling her husband and colluding with his lover would make things extra sweet."

He grinned. "I can see that devious mind of yours will keep me on my toes. Be real. You're giving Heather way too much credit. She's not sharp enough to pull off that kind of scam."

"Okay, Perry Mason, tell me who is." I folded my arms and scowled. Unfortunately, it didn't faze him one bit. Deming laughed in my face instead.

"I don't have the answer. If I did, I'd go straight to Lieutenant Bates. That's her job after all." Deming finally relented and took pity on me. "Here's my suggestion. Let's drop in at the Exley Foundation tomorrow. That's where all this started, and I guarantee that Horton and at least some of the other possibilities will be there. You can nose around as long as I'm there to protect you."

Anika's advice about marital compromise rang in my ears, causing me to stop and push the mute button. Normally I would rail against the idea of protection. Not tonight. I'd asked for a partnership, and he'd agreed. Why quibble?

"Have they left yet?" I asked. "Ames and Portia, I mean?"

He shook his head. "Nope. Frankly, I don't think they will. Just bravado if you ask me. Ames is basically lazy. He has it made there, and he knows it. Portia is your typical accounting drudge—dull and dependable. Not the type to cut and run."

Speaking of accounting drudges made me think of Fleur Pixley. There were one or two questions that vixen could answer for me about the gold scam. With Deming at my side she might just do it.

"How do you feel about having company tomorrow evening?" I

asked. "Just drinks, nothing special."

Deming has a suspicious mind. He crossed his arms in front of him and frowned. "Out with it. Who's the mystery guest?"

"Fleur Pixley. I can't help thinking that we're missing something about this gold scam. She knows all the ins and outs, and with you here, she'll talk."

He wasn't happy, but he agreed with one proviso. "Not here. I'll make an appointment for us to meet in her office. Less complicated that way."

"Good idea," I said. "It's hard to interrogate someone when you're dancing."

He shook his head and moved my way. "You'll pay for that one, smarty-pants. Just wait 'til I get hold of you."

THE NEXT MORNING I decked myself out like a Back Bay matron or a writer's fantasy of one. No one could fault my sober navy suit, high-necked blouse, or sensible pumps. Doing good works made one focus on worthy goals, not appearances. At least that was my theory.

Deming had a much easier task. He wore the impeccable male uniform of corporate America, looking every inch a dreamboat. Foxy men in business attire push every one of my buttons, and Deming Swann in charcoal pinstripes brightened the day like a dose of sunshine.

"You look different," he told me as he straightened my collar. "Very prim and proper, a sort of school marm meets librarian look. The kind I'd love to ravage."

"Down, boy. It takes work to look this plain. Besides, I even wore pantyhose. God, I loathe pantyhose! Some evil misogynist must have invented them."

We could have walked there from my condo, but Swanns never walk when they have other options. Exercise is confined to the dojo, squash court, or polo field, and gratuitous sweat is frowned upon.

The Exley Foundation was located four blocks away on the third floor of a venerable Newbury Street brownstone. Sandwiched between Boylston and Commonwealth Avenue, the structure was so nondescript that I'd passed by many times without giving it a second glance. Only a discreet brass plaque stated the purpose.

As we made our way to the elevator, I admired the dentil molding, high ceilings, and proportions of the house. Once again I was awestruck by the history and timelessness of Boston's Back Bay.

"Do they know we're coming?" I asked. Members of the proletariat fear rudeness. Swanns, on the other hand, assume they will always be welcome.

"Don't worry," Deming said. "Just play it cool and follow my lead. We'll start with Horty and go from there."

He approached the reception desk and flashed the starstruck receptionist a smile. "Mr. Swann and Ms. Kane to see Horton Exley," he said. "We're expected."

The poor flustered creature stabbed several buttons, announced our arrival, and led us through a suite of rooms. Naturally, the palatial corner office belonged to Horton.

We settled into comfortable leather side chairs, refused refreshments, and awaited our host.

"What did you tell him?" I whispered.

Deming crossed his long legs and leaned back. "The truth, of course. What else?"

The man had no concept of stealth or our need to take Horton unaware. "Suppose he's the one?" I said. "You've already tipped him off."

He tapped his foot on the floor and heaved a big sigh. "Horton's no fool, Eja. I told him you've got pull with the cops, and we're trying to help the family. Give me some credit, for crying out loud. I skirted the truth as it was."

Before our tiff escalated, Horton Exley, monarch of all he surveyed, swept through the door and shrugged off his Burberry. I could tell by his expansive smile that Deming had done his job. The scion of the Exley clan seemed delighted to see us.

"Dem, Eja—what a pleasure! Come, come, come. Let's have a chat." He glared at the serf outside his office, who squirmed like a gaffed fish. "No espresso for our guests, Ellen?"

"We're fine," Deming said. "Full up with caffeine."

After a few desultory comments, we got down to business. I harnessed my frustration and let Deming take the lead. He rambled on in lawyerly fashion for a while and finally came to the point.

"We need your help in finding Phaedra's partner. You're the only trustworthy source we have."

I saw an opening and took it. "Her partner had to know the inner workings of your foundation. Chances are he or she killed Phaedra."

Horton's eyes bulged in bullfrog fashion. "How can that be?" he sputtered. "We're all family here."

"Exactly my point." I tried womanly wiles, but considering

Deming's raised brow, I missed the mark. "Phaedra's partner was smart and audacious. Sound like anyone you know?"

"Other than yourself, of course," Deming added smoothly. "We need to anticipate the police on this and avoid unsavory press. Frankly, you're in the best position to help."

Horty furrowed his brow in an earnest attempt to think. "We run a tight ship here. Mostly family with a few employees. You wouldn't believe the waste in some of these organizations. Non-profit doesn't mean profligate!"

"Ames must be a great comfort to you," I said. "Isn't he the chief investment officer? Sounds important."

"Bah!" Horton snorted. "It's just a title. I make the investment decisions around here. You can rely on that."

No wonder Ames was a jerk. His brother's arrogance could drive a saint to the dark side. Fortunately, Deming's profession required him to keep his composure with even the most trying clients. He simply nodded and continued the conversation.

"So, you met Phaedra here—at the Foundation? She was an investment counselor, I believe."

Horty's face lit up. "She was magical—full of enthusiasm and packing some pretty impressive references. I checked, of course." He hesitated. "Or someone did. No matter. I'm a keen judge of character, and that young woman impressed me."

"I presume Phaedra suggested precious metals as an investment?" Deming's question was closer to a statement of fact, and I detected a slight edge in his tone.

"It's not what you think," Horton said. "I brought the subject up myself after watching those television commercials. You know. They're everywhere. Major celebrities endorse buying gold."

My head felt like it was exploding. If not for the tragic consequences, the whole thing would be ludicrous. Horton Exley was a bigger fool than I'd ever imagined.

"Your board of directors agreed?" I asked. "I imagine Portia analyzed everything for you."

"Portia? My dear Eja, I don't need a CPA to vet my decisions. Not when I find a sure thing. Why bother with some tedious proposal process when opportunity strikes?" He gave me the verbal equivalent of a pat on the head. "I judge a person by more than numbers. When I learned Phaedra loved the martial arts, that sealed the deal. Discipline, strength—those are the qualities that count." He nodded at Deming.

"You understand, Dem."

Deming faked a cough to hide his laughter. I'm positive of that.

"Heather trained with her," I said. "Surely you knew that, being a student of Master Moore yourself."

"A happy coincidence," Horton said. "Come to think of it, I first met Phaedra at some Shaolin City event. Chinese New Year, I believe."

Deming shot me an "I told you so" message as Justin Ming's involvement surfaced once more. "You know the players, Horty. Make a guess. Who do you think her partner was? As I recall, you always were pretty shrewd at sizing up such things."

No matter what Deming said, I had to horn in. "Any unexplained money or change in lifestyle? Five million dollars could buy a lot of independence." I thought of Ames' escape plan and poor pitiful Portia, toiling in her cousin's home.

Horton's face resembled an heirloom tomato. "Sorry. I need to speak privately with my attorney. No offense, Eja."

I took the hint and sauntered toward the door. "None taken. Maybe Portia is in her office."

"Yes, yes," Horton said. "You girls have fun."

I kept calm even after seeing the snarky grin on my beloved's face. Surely Horton was too dense to plan and execute this crime. On the other hand, maybe he was just lucky.

THE BELEAGUERED receptionist led me to Portia's office, a lesser space on the other side of the corridor. It was snug—some would say tiny—with none of the benefits of size or location save one: distance from Horton Exley.

Fortune favored me, and Portia was at her desk sorting through paperwork. She answered my knock with a tepid smile and waved me in. To my chagrin, her dun-colored outfit was a virtual twin of the ensemble I had chosen.

"Sorry to disturb you," I said mendaciously. "We were visiting Horton, and I got kicked out. Big male powwow, you know. No girls allowed."

Her reaction was priceless, a faint echo of excluded females through the ages.

"I know all about that," she said. "Horton seldom listens and rarely takes my advice. He's too *manly* to respect me or any other woman."

I smoothed my skirt and sank into one of the tweed chairs. It had seen better days and was missing a few springs. "At least he let you vet Phaedra. That was more than I expected."

Portia did a double take. "Vet her? You're joking? From the moment that tart wiggled her way into this office, Horton was hooked."

"Sorry. I figured that would be your job." I shrugged. "Wonder where she got those glowing references Horton mentioned?"

"Oh, please! You do live a sheltered life." Her face teetered between a smile and a sneer. "Anyone can phony up references, degrees, endorsements. We live in the age of digital magic. Half those things don't hold water if anyone ever checks them. And you'd be surprised at how many supposedly smart people never bother."

Portia was smart—there was no disputing that. How galling to toil under the yoke of the insipid Horton and his sleazy little brother. Maybe the worm had finally turned.

"I'm surprised you're still here," I said.

"Hush!" Her voice turned shrill and panicked. "No one knows about that. It was just talk, nothing real."

"But you said . . ."

"That was Ames spouting off nonsense. Neither one of us is going anywhere, and we both know it." She slumped in her chair. "I'll always be the poor relative living on sufferance. Begging for crumbs from Heather's table."

I lowered my voice to a conspiratorial level and leaned toward her. "Think. Who was Phaedra's partner? When we know that, we'll find the murderer."

A low chuckle issued from her throat. "How ironic."

"Huh?" Not my best response, but I was curious.

"This partner game doesn't quit. That's exactly what Euphemia Bates asked me last night. She's one scary woman, and take it from me, she won't stop until someone's in cuffs."

Chapter Twenty-One

THE POLICE—NAMELY Lieutenant Bates—were way ahead of me. I should have expected it. They are professionals, after all, not midlist mystery writers with a hunch. I slunk out of Portia's office feeling lower than a garden snail at dusk. Some sleuth I was. When Deming finished his conference, he glanced at me and shook his head.

"Why so glum, Sherlock? I thought you got what you wanted."

I tried to be brave and laugh it off, but I couldn't fool Deming. "It's complicated," I said. "I feel like a fool."

He ruffled my hair and helped me to my feet. "Come on. I'll buy you a sumptuous lunch filled with fattening foods. Something chocolate. That should cheer you up. We can discuss ways to eliminate those pesky pantyhose you hate so much." He pushed the elevator button and spoke *sotto voce*. "I've got some interesting news."

I pleaded and begged, but he refused to budge.

"Not a word until we're seated at the table, napkins on our laps and drinks in hand. Come on. If we leave now we can snag a table at Stephanie's." He licked his lips. "Hmm. I can just taste those buttermilk onion rings."

Luck was with us. Deming parked the Panamera on a side street and loped into his favorite lunch spot with time to spare. I wasn't surprised. Swann magic extended to dining as well as other earthly delights.

Despite getting my comeuppance from Euphemia Bates, I was ravenous. Fortunately, Deming claims to like women with a healthy appetite. Encounters with anorexic debutantes had cured him of feeling otherwise.

"Stephanie's is the gold standard for lunch," he said. "Just what the doctor ordered."

He chose Pellegrino and his beloved onion rings as an appetizer. I made the sensible choice despite flirting with several succulent alternatives. The crunchy vegetable salad was actually pretty tasty, and it filled me up. Catch phrases like "healthy and fresh" did nothing to spoil its appeal. Deming opted for the incredibly luscious grilled cheese sandwich, consuming it all without compunction.

"Okay. What did Horty tell you? Unless it's privileged, of course."

He lowered his voice to a near whisper. "Don't worry. He said I could tell you."

"Why all the secrecy then?"

Deming chuckled. "He was embarrassed. You know how Exleys are about scandal."

"Scandal?"

"Heather left him yesterday." Deming kept his face blank, but his eyes glinted with mischief.

"Big deal. We knew that was coming. Divorce is pretty common these days, even in their crowd." I watched him carefully, noting the tapping foot and the biggest tell of all—knuckle cracking. "Okay. What else?"

"She moved in with another man."

I yawned. "B-o-r-i-n-g. Do better, Counselor. Who was this guy, the mayor?"

Deming sipped his Pellegrino. "Nope. Better than that. Heather moved in with Ames Exley."

His comment caught me in mid-crunch, causing a carrot to lodge in my throat. I gulped Pellegrino while Deming prepared to administer the Heimlich maneuver. After the crisis passed, I mopped my streaming eyes and faced him.

"Ames and Heather—no way."

He raised his hand. "On my oath as an officer of the court and your devoted fiancé."

I was befuddled, confused, and just plain perplexed by the turn of events. It took a minute, but my synapses finally started firing again. "Which one was Phaedra's partner? I thought they didn't even like each other. Obviously, I was wrong. Your mom said money motivates the Exleys, and who knows, they might have planned the entire thing together to scam Horty."

"Could be." Deming narrowed his eyes in a determined Judge Dredd scowl. "Heather couldn't do it alone, but Ames has brains to spare and very little conscience. Horton just told us that he met his lady love at a Shaolin City event." He spread his hands. "You do the math."

We temporarily detoured around murder by sampling Stephanie's heavenly chocolate cake. Sharing dessert halves the calories and avoids dieter's remorse. Unless you're Deming Swann, that is. He wolfed down most of it without a scintilla of guilt.

As he scooped up the final crumbs, I made my move. "Now that you've switched suspects, it means you've given up on Justin Ming. I feel vindicated."

"Hold on." He paid the check, added a tip, and helped me up. "I'm still considering the possibilities. Heather reacted emotionally to the news about Phaedra and Ming. She must have. You said yourself that she was obsessed with him. Ames was clearly an afterthought. She may be lovestruck, but money trumps passion every time."

I considered the options as we walked to the car. I hated to admit it, but Deming made sense. Heather was a flighty character prone to dramatic gestures. Ames, on the other hand, had no character at all and five million reasons to throw his lot in with Heather.

"Do you think Mia Bates knows this?" I asked. "She was on the trail of Phaedra's partner only last night."

Deming snapped his fingers. "Good point! I better give Pam a heads-up." He hit redial on his iPhone and spoke urgently to his partner. In short order Pamela Schwartz went into attack mode, ready to unleash her ire on the Boston PD. My money was on Lieutenant Bates.

Our meeting with Fleur Pixley seemed anticlimactic at that point, but Deming insisted on following through. "Got to keep in her good graces," he said. "Horton's not totally out of the woods with the authorities, you know. Fleur could complicate things if she felt slighted."

"You're in kind of a pickle, aren't you?" I asked as we cruised toward Government Center dodging construction crews, pedestrians, and stoned students.

"How so?" His horn blared at an elderly driver who dared to challenge the Porsche.

"You really can't represent Horton *and* his estranged wife, can you? I mean, Heather might try to implicate her husband if things got rough. A murder charge will do that to you."

He pressed his lips together. As he considered the possibilities, I studied him. Deming takes his looks for granted and always has. He found it hard to understand how the rest of the mostly female world reacted to pure male beauty.

"Frankly," he said, "I don't care a fig about Heather. Of course, avoiding a scandal would be in Horton's best interests. The whole Exley clan's actually."

Once again, Deming found a parking spot not far from our destination. His run of luck was beginning to creep me out. Boston was as impossible to navigate as Manhattan, especially when one has a pricey vehicle to risk.

"Better let me take the lead again," Deming said. "Fleur can be prickly."

Something in his voice alerted me that all was not well. "She does know I'll be with you, doesn't she?"

"I'm sure I mentioned it." He lengthened his stride, forcing me to skip after him. "Come on. Don't overreact. Everything will be fine."

"Stop!" Any visit to Fleur had to be closely orchestrated. "Maybe I should catch a cab and go home."

He spun around and pulled me to him. "Be a good sport. I promise you can ask her anything you want."

I mumbled several unkind things, but in the end we came to a rapprochement. Deming would use the soft soap, and I would play clean up.

Fleur's office was typical government issue, one notch up from the police station. We navigated an unending rabbit's warren of orange and brown cubicles before finding the executive suite. Even I had to admit that Fleur's personal space, although Spartan, was impressive. Her private office managed to combine authority with a few feminine touches and some fairly impressive artwork with an Asian theme.

For Deming she was all smiles and girlish glee, but her face hardened the moment she saw me. We sat at her conference table for a few minutes, exchanging pleasantries like the civilized beings that we were.

"Eja, what a pleasant surprise. Dem forgot to mention that you were free. We could have done lunch."

Wormwood and gall, bitch! Deal with it.

"We had other appointments," Deming said. "Thanks for fitting us in. We won't take much of your time."

She glanced at the clock on a side table. "Nonsense. You're always welcome. Both of you. Now how can I help you?"

Deming crossed his long, elegant legs, giving Fleur a full view of what she was missing. "Just a few points on this gold scam. Naturally, our firm has researched my client's situation, but I have several questions."

"Of course. Ask away." Fleur leaned forward, exposing a hint of cleavage.

"How sophisticated would the promoters have to be? Phaedra had a smooth line of patter—she was the bait. Her partner must have been the strategist, and that requires brains." Deming's technique was interesting, cordial but professional.

"Horton thought she was a financial planner, but that's unlikely." I dipped a toe in the conversational pool. "Still, the company she claimed to represent is legitimate. Horton's treasurer told me they researched it. That was the clever part. Sound company, phoney goods."

Fleur's smile was pained. "Didn't he get an independent appraisal of the bullion? That's SOP when a sizable sum is involved."

Deming shook his head. "By the time the bars were delivered, my client was hooked. He did get a certificate of authenticity, though. Ms. Jones insisted on it for his protection."

"Let me guess," Fleur said. "It said the bullion was pure gold."

Deming nodded. "She was quite a cool operator. That certificate looks very impressive. Things fell apart when the foundation's insurer insisted on an appraisal. That uncovered the scam."

Fleur enjoyed the joke. "Bogus, of course. They're so easy to fake. I presume the police are tracing the fake gold bars. Not many places make a quality product like that."

"Yeah. They traced the wire transfer Horton made to a Swiss account. Closed now, of course."

"Nice touch," Fleur said. "Swiss banks inspire confidence. If it had been the Caymans, your client might have smelled a rat."

Deming rose and shook her hand. "Thanks for your time. We'll make sure you get a wedding invitation."

I tried not to smirk, but it wasn't easy. Fleur recovered nicely and faked a smile worthy of Georgetown Law School.

"Make sure I get a synopsis of that scam too. I'll include it in our files as a case study." She shook my hand. "And once again, congratulations to both of you."

"THAT WASN'T SO bad," Deming said after we cleared the building. "Everything went rather well."

"I guess Heather is out of the picture," I said. "No way she fits the role of cunning strategist." That left Ames Exley as the only viable suspect. Even though he made me shudder, I still didn't see him as a villain, let alone a murderer. "Will you notify Lieutenant Bates?"

Deming blanched. "Are you crazy? My first job is to protect my client, not chase criminals. Let Euphemia Bates find her own suspect. That goes for you too, Eja."

I ignored his rant and focused on a larger issue. By the time we reached the Porsche, the answer was clear. We made the assumption that Phaedra's partner and her killer were one and the same. What if it wasn't true?

"Horton or Heather might still be the killer," I said. "We shouldn't presume that the silent partner murdered Phaedra. Plenty of other people had reason."

"Climb in, Sherlock." Deming unlocked the door and tucked me into my seat. "Follow the money. That little maxim never fails. I say that Ames found a way to double his share of the take and eliminate a loose end." He fired up the monster engine and eased into traffic. "Need I remind you that Ames has the skill to administer the *Dim Mak*?"

"You said he's not that good."

Swann confidence surfaced. "Everything's relative, my love. Ames didn't win competitions, but he could still do the deed. Trust me on that."

I scoured my memory banks for something I'd heard recently, a scrap of conversation that bothered me. Unfortunately, my mind was clouded by too many thoughts and not enough rest.

"Wake up, sleepyhead," Deming said. "We're home." He swung into the driveway and left the Porsche splayed across the cobblestones. "I have to go to work, and you need a nap."

"Go on," I said. "I'll be fine. I'm just groggy."

"No, ma'am. I'll escort you to your door and check out the place first. Remember, a murderer is still at large. Ames wasn't at the Foundation today, and neither was Heather."

I protested a bit more even though I was secretly relieved when Deming gave me the all-clear sign. He planted a kiss on my forehead, deftly evaded Cato, and swept out the door with a promise to pick up dinner before he came home.

Chapter Twenty-Two

HOME. THE IDEA of living with Deming day after day felt so comfortable, so right, that it frightened me. I'd once consulted a shrink who told me that my feelings of inadequacy formed a protective barrier against both rejection and happiness. Even though he was the ultimate sleaze, the man made a valid point. I'd vowed to make an attitude adjustment that would widen my world. Thus far I'd only taken baby steps.

I glanced at my watch and lay down for a brief nap. Not too long, just enough to clear the cobwebs from my brain. When the phone rang, I leapt up drowsy and disoriented. Good Lord! It was almost five o'clock! Deming must be calling.

"Eja," a familiar voice asked, "is Deming there? I'm in the lobby with some papers for him from Horton. Typical thing. Big emergency. You understand."

"He's at work, Portia. Come on up and leave them here. We can have a drink."

I gave Jaime the go-ahead, marveling at the success of Deming's carrot and stick approach. The concierge had transformed overnight from lethargic to hyper-vigilant.

My real motive was information gathering, not hospitality. I wanted Portia's reaction to the Heather/Ames alliance as well as the profile of the accomplice that Fleur outlined. Something was missing, and a fresh set of eyes might close the gap.

By the time I bribed Cato with a chicken nugget and hastily untangled my curls, Portia was at the door.

"Welcome," I said, ushering her in. "Don't mind Cato. I'll lock him in the kitchen if he gets too obnoxious."

She lugged a weathered leather briefcase to the dining room table and sighed. "Wow! This thing is heavy. Whatever happened to the paperless office?"

I laughed. "Never going to happen as long as lawyers and lawsuits exist. Come on. Let me get you a drink. Chardonnay, right?"

Portia's shrewd grey eyes looked weary. "I'll take vodka rocks if you have it. This day has been a bear." She placed a thick manila envelope addressed to Deming on the table.

My bartending had improved since hooking up with the Swanns. Nothing fancy. I substituted imagination for skill.

"How about a gimlet? I learned to like them after reading *The Long Goodbye*. If they're good enough for Chandler's ladies, why not us?"

A grin overtook Portia's gloom. "Why not, indeed? Sounds great."

I followed the traditional recipe, mixing Rose's lime juice, a pinch of powdered sugar, and Deming's latest enthusiasm, Reyka small batch vodka, into a shaker.

"Voila! See what you think," I said. "Don't you love cocktail glasses? I'm not keen on the taste, just the look."

"Nice," Portia said. "Just what the doctor ordered." She sipped greedily and sighed. "I guess you heard about Heather and Ames?"

I nodded. "Did it surprise you? You're so observant."

"Hadn't a clue," Portia said. "All Heather blathered about was Justin Ming. She and Ames barely spoke at home."

"Money shouldn't be a problem. Massachusetts divorce laws favor the wife."

Portia rolled her eyes. "Talk about sibling rivalry. I'm sure Ames has feathered his own nest too. He was always a sly one."

"What do you mean?"

"Surely it occurred to you. A five million dollar nest egg would make anyone bold. Horton was so in love, he never even saw it coming. Imagine falling head over heels for someone named Enid."

I felt a jolt in my brain, a reminder of another time she had used that name. "I'm surprised you know her real name. Lieutenant Bates just told us the other day. Quite a step down from Phaedra."

Portia cocked her head to the side. "Why wouldn't I? After all, I did the background check. These days it's almost impossible to hide all your tracks."

"You're right. I must have misunderstood you. I thought you said that Horton wouldn't allow you to check her out." I glanced at the clock, praying that it had stopped. Surely Deming would be home soon to deliver me from Portia's clutches. She was nice enough but tedious in that linear thinking, accountant way.

"Allow?" Portia snorted. "That will be the day! Horton Exley doesn't know half of what goes on there." She drained her glass and stared at the pitcher.

"How about a refill?" I asked. "A few snacks might hit the spot too."

I went to the sideboard, brought over the pitcher, and replenished both of our drinks. Cato remained underfoot, emitting low growls every time Portia moved.

"Time for you to visit the kitchen," I told him. "I'll grab some snacks to hold us until Deming gets back."

Portia's face brightened. "I could use a little something. No time for lunch today."

I forced Cato into the kitchen, found him a bone, and filled a tray with Brie, grapes, and crackers for my guest.

Portia was still planted in the same spot as before, staring moodily at her gimlet.

I cleared the table and placed the platter and serving dishes in front of her. "Here we go. Dig right in."

Portia piled her plate with cheese, but I remained virtuous. Nibbling on grapes would have to suffice if I expected to squeeze into my wedding gown.

"We stopped at the FTC after lunch," I told her. "Let me run a few things past you to see what your take on them is."

"FTC? You certainly have connections." She stopped snacking and gave me the gimlet eye. A nice touch considering our choice of beverage.

I shrugged it off. "Actually, the director there is an old school chum from Brown. She's always been hot for Deming, but I was just along for the ride."

Portia leaned back on the sofa, looking a bit tipsy. "So. What did you learn?"

"I'm convinced that Heather wasn't involved. No way. Everyone says the same thing. Phaedra's partner was intelligent and a master strategist. Now does that sound like Heather Exley to you?"

"Not likely," Portia scoffed, "unless it was a fashion show or some martial arts thing. Heather is crafty in those areas. I have to admit that Ames fits the bill, though. He's smart enough and has a mile-wide grudge against Horton. Cain and Abel, those two."

Something—some inconsistency—was buzzing around my brain, irritating the hell out of me. I sipped my cocktail and nibbled a grape to absorb the liquor. Next time, I'd have to dial down the vodka in my gimlet recipe. Chandler's dames must have been heavy hitters to gulp these babies every night.

"Maybe we're looking at this whole thing the wrong way, Portia. What if Phaedra's partner didn't murder her?"

"Really?" Her reaction stopped just short of a sneer. "What are the odds on that? Follow the money, I say. Everything else pales in comparison. Swiss bank accounts, wire transfers, and phony certificates of authenticity—whew! Why stop at murder after all that?"

I suddenly recalled Anika's words. Exleys are obsessed with money. Always were, always will be. Ames and Horton were Exleys, but so was Portia. I worked hard to control the chill sweeping through me. If I could just bluff, stall her until Deming arrived. He could handle Portia and get Mia Bates involved.

"Does Lieutenant Bates suspect Ames?" I asked. "You must have gotten some sense of it last night."

"Not really. She plays things pretty close to the vest. Focused on the gold scam mostly. I think she suspects Horton, believe it or not. That *Dim Mak* thing ties both my cousins to the murder."

Did Portia know kung fu too? Was I the only person in Boston without fighting skills?

"I'm hopeless at martial arts," I said. "Uncoordinated as hell. Anika is great and Heather too. Phaedra was phenomenal."

Her smile was genuine this time. "You're not alone. I tried one class and made a fool out of myself. It's important to accept your limitations and focus on your strengths. Yours is writing. Mine is making money."

I suddenly realized that my stomach was at war with me. For some reason I felt quite unwell. I gripped the arms of my chair and rose halfway.

"Let's walk Cato before Deming gets here. Frankly, I could use the fresh air. That vodka really hit me hard."

Portia stared at me with glacial calm. "Let's not."

"But Cato . . ."

"Can wait. Unfortunately, you can't."

I tried to move, but my legs wouldn't cooperate. "What have you done?"

"Don't move. It's less painful that way, and we can have our little chat. That's what you wanted, wasn't it?" Her eyes shone with triumph and something else—regret.

"Why?" Every syllable was torture.

"Just so you know," Portia said, "I did not kill her. I've never hurt anyone until tonight. You kept pushing the partner theory until people started believing it. Those dead roses didn't even faze you."

"You?" I gasped.

She preened, showing a new and unpleasant side of her personality. "A nice touch, don't you think? Ames is forever wearing that tatty

Grateful Dead shirt. I knew that sooner or later you'd make the connection. Another nail in his coffin if needed." Portia speared a cheese cube and smacked her lips. "Top flight, by the way. Hits the spot. This is really unfortunate, Eja. I actually like you. You're not one of them. But you're so stubborn. You just wouldn't quit." She shrugged. "What could I do? It's self-defense. Surely you can see that."

The woman was delusional. I wouldn't beg, but perhaps I could reason with her. Get her to call the paramedics.

"I saw through that tart right away," Portia said. "Prancing around the office, calling herself a financial advisor. You were right, of course. I checked out her references and her record. Enid Jones—what a joke."

I croaked out a response. It took effort not to close my eyes and put out the lights. My words were slurred, barely intelligible. "Why not tell Horton?"

"Opportunity, Eja. I sensed my chance to make it big. Phaedra wanted to run at first, but I convinced her to stay the course and share the spoils. With my help, the scam was invincible."

"Huh!" I put a ton of venom in one word.

"That insurance thing was Ames' fault. It almost screwed up everything. So I told her to tell Horton she'd been swindled too. It worked. The dolt actually believed her." Portia checked her watch. "Don't worry, we still have some time. Deming got an emergency call, you see. He thinks that Pamela Schwartz was in an accident. By the time that's sorted out, I'm afraid it will be too late for you."

"W-h-a-t?" My speech was slurred, and I was so weary. If I could hold off, Deming would save me. I knew it.

Portia slipped a pillow under my head and pulled the cashmere throw up to my chin. "There you go, dear. No need to be uncomfortable. Just so you know, I dosed your gimlet with Rohypnol. In small doses it won't kill you. I gave you a whopper, but your luck might hold. Not that you'll remember anything."

Her throaty laughter rang in my ears as I fought to stay conscious. My limbs were powerless, floating in a sea of marshmallow fluff. My last memory was Portia's saucy grin as she unlatched the door.

"Someone did me a favor by eliminating Phaedra. Maybe two's the charm."

I HAD THE WORST headache of my life. Even body parts I'd long forgotten conspired in painful mutiny. Opening my eyes was torture, but

I had to try. In the distance, someone was calling my name.

The voice was familiar. My hand was pressed against a larger one and gently kissed, over and over. Then a woman spoke, urging me to awaken. I knew her too. Slowly, painfully, sensation returned to me and with it a ghost of memory. The scratchy sheets, metal bars, and that light—that blinding light. Definitely not my home. I was in a hospital. The smell of antiseptic gave it away.

Deming's was the first face I saw. His beautiful eyes were misty, the way they looked when CeCe died. But I was alive and planned to stay that way. If nothing else, the excruciating pain proved that.

I blinked not once but twice and cautiously opened my eyes, squinting against the blinding institutional light. Anika and Bolin stood on either side of the bed, their expressions set in neutral. Sprays of orchids, lilies, and baby's breath decorated every vacant space—Deming's handiwork, I presumed.

"Don't try to speak, Eja." Anika leaned forward and felt my forehead. "Just nod if you can."

"I can talk." It was more croak than speech, but to me that meant progress.

Deming squeezed my hand again and grinned. "We'll fill you in on what happened. Conserve your energy. This may be my only chance to ever get the last word in."

"You should have called me, Eja. What else are partners for?" Anika seemed a bit miffed at my facing danger alone. "I could have prevented all this. If Dem hadn't found you when he did . . ."

"Calm down, my love. Let's update Eja." Bolin exchanged tender glances across the sickbed with his wife. "The important thing is that she's just fine or soon will be."

"You're right, darling," Anika said. "Forgive me for being testy. We were so worried about you."

I locked eyes with Deming, wordlessly urging him on as if we were partners in a bizarre game of charades.

"We were lucky," he said, pressing my hand until I squeaked. "When Jaime called me, I knew something was amiss."

"Jaime?"

It takes a lot to fluster a lawyer, but Deming stammered until his cheeks grew crimson.

"Tell her, Dem." Bolin's eyes twinkled. "It saved her life."

"Jaime and I had an arrangement," Deming said. "Just a temporary measure, mind you. He agreed to notify me whenever you had visitors.

A precautionary thing."

"Bribe," I sputtered.

Deming shrugged. "Okay. Whatever. Anyway, when he told me that Portia was there to deliver papers, something didn't sound right. I called Horty, and he didn't know anything about it." A wry smile spread over his face. "Not unusual, I get it, but with all that was happening I got suspicious. This supposed accident of Pam's was just icing on the cake. My dad handled that, and I headed over to your place."

"He got two speeding tickets," Anika said. "Almost ended up in jail until Euphemia intervened."

Deming laughed. "Her name even strikes fear into cops on the beat. Anyway, she met me at your condo. It seems that our favorite police lieutenant was already on Portia's trail."

"Not surprising," Bolin said. "Euphemia is a fine investigator."

When we visited the Foundation, Portia had mentioned a visit from Mia Bates. She'd made it sound as if Horton was the chief suspect, but I now knew differently. Mia was playing games, using a ruse to flush out Portia.

"Please . . . let me finish this saga." Deming was a logical thinker who loved to present things step by step. "We met Portia just as she reached the lobby. I have to admit, she played it cool. Said you were up there taking another nap. Naturally, the lieutenant didn't buy that. She detained her in the lobby while Jaime and I went up to check on you."

His voice cracked as Deming described finding me passed out, unresponsive as the medicos say. He called the paramedics and the Swann family physician Jake Harris. Before long I was logged into Mass General with all manner of tubes and tests invading my body.

"You could have died. Thank God you've never been much of a drinker. Portia gave you a whopping dose of that stuff." He tried to sound casual, but the tender side of the man I love surfaced instead.

Bolin squeezed his son's shoulder and resumed the narrative. "Portia finally confirmed that she'd given you Rohypnol. She claimed that you asked for it so that you could sleep." He shook his head. "An obvious lie. Jake suspected what it was anyway, but it helped to expedite treatment. Don't be surprised if you have some memory loss about that night."

Anika jumped into the conversation. "That's a mercy. Imagine spending an evening in your own home with a murderess."

Something was wrong. I tried to penetrate the brain fog that gripped me, teasing me with forgotten information.

"Horton intends to prosecute her civilly," Deming said. "Family connections be damned. Exleys take money very seriously."

"No," I said. My voice sounded weak, but at least the synapses were firing.

Three pairs of Swann eyes stared at me.

"Portia didn't do it," I sputtered. "Not the murder." My memory was still hazy, but I distinctly recalled sitting across from her, sipping cocktails, and chatting about Phaedra. When I put Cato in the kitchen and got snacks, Portia must have put the drug in my glass. No gratitude for being a good hostess!

"Things look grim for her," Deming said. "Lieutenant Bates is interrogating Portia about Phaedra's murder. Plus, our old buddy Fleur Pixley came through too. Her guys traced that Swiss account right back to Portia."

I did a double take. Weren't numbered accounts in Switzerland sacred? Impenetrable? World secrecy standards had taken a nosedive.

Bolin must have read my mind. "Swiss authorities are much more cooperative now than in the past. Makes stashing untraced money more of a challenge."

"She comes from a good family," Anika said, shaking her head. "Apparently she never forgave them for disowning her. Understandable enough, but murder?"

I shook my head and slowly formed the word. "No."

"Rest, Eja," Anika said. "It will all come back to you."

I gripped Deming's hand with all my strength, remembering Portia's parting shot. I had to make them understand. She bragged that someone had done her a "favor" by disposing of Phaedra. That someone was the killer, and he or she was still at large.

Chapter Twenty-Three

I SPENT ANOTHER restless night at Mass General with Deming by my side. Despite polite suggestions and urgent requests, he refused to leave. The staff finally took pity and brought in a cot for him to sleep on. No doubt the yearly seven-figure donation made by the Swann Foundation influenced that decision.

After a final checkup the next morning, the hospital officially released me to Deming's tender care. Po drove the Bentley to the exit, and with the aid of Anika and Deming I was delivered to the Swann manse for R&R.

I'd opted to return home, but that was immediately vetoed. Deming nearly hyperventilated at the thought of it, and Anika pleaded for me to reconsider.

"You said Portia's not the murderer," he said. "That means someone is out there, and you might be a target. Again."

Recuperating in the lap of luxury was a minor concession. It allowed me plenty of time to hash over theories with Anika, my co-conspirator and eager partner-in-crime. I also received some curious visitors.

Fleur Pixley led the parade armed with flowers, gossip, and faux sympathy.

"I never dreamed you'd be in danger," she said, "but then you always were the impetuous type."

Fleur confirmed that the federal case against Portia was humming along. "She violated at least six federal statutes. Let the local cops nail her for murder. We'll get every penny that she stashed in Switzerland. Count on it." The venom in her eyes was chilling. I'd never realized the depth of her dedication to justice.

That afternoon, we had more callers. Under Po's watchful eyes, Ames and Heather Exley plied me with another Ballotin of Godiva truffles and more expressions of shock.

"Portia never showed an ounce of temper," Ames said. "Who knew she was capable of murder?"

"Sheer jealousy," Heather growled. "Some thanks we get for taking her in. That little thief stole five million dollars from her own family. I hope she gets the death penalty."

"Unlikely in Massachusetts," I said. "Besides, I don't think she killed Phaedra. She had no reason to lie to me about that under the circumstances."

Ames passed the truffles my way. "Here, Eja. Invalids deserve to indulge themselves."

After my dustup with death, I was reluctant to eat anything from an Exley. "I'll save the treats for dinner," I said. "That way the whole family can enjoy them."

He wasn't finished. "You really believe Portia is innocent?"

Anika moved next to me on the couch and playfully wrinkled her nose. "Oh, Ames, I doubt that Portia's ever been innocent. Listen to Eja. She has great instincts about this kind of thing."

"Wasn't she home with you that night?" I asked Ames.

He shrugged. "Couldn't say. I went to Cambridge to meet a friend. Unfortunately, she stood me up."

"I stayed in my room," Heather said. "I suffer dreadfully from migraines."

"My mistake," Anika said. "I thought I saw you at the dojo that night with Horton."

Judging from the look on Heather's face, murder was well within her skill set. "My husband has his own schedule, Mrs. Swann. And so do I."

They left a few minutes later.

THE NEXT MORNING brought an official visit from Euphemia Bates. We assembled in the study, joined by Deming and Bolin, and fortified by cups of espresso. Unlike my other callers, the lieutenant came fully armed with Officer Opie at her side.

"How are you feeling?" Mia asked. She was garbed in charcoal grey with subtle hints of cream at her throat and wrists. Her smooth leather boots were midnight blue.

"I'll survive," I said. Deming sighed at my bravery.

"We need a formal statement," Mia said. "Drop by the station as soon as you can." She handed me a typed list of questions. "Take a look at these and give me your reaction."

I repeated everything I recalled, starting with the conversation at the Exley Foundation and ending with my second vodka gimlet.

"She didn't dose the first drink," I said. "It never left my hand. But she was alone while I went to the kitchen for snacks." Cato sidled up to Mia and gave her his paw. "Funny thing. Cato growled the entire time Portia was there. I should have listened to the little fellow."

"Did she admit killing Phaedra Jones?"

"No. By the way, Portia called her Enid, not Phaedra. Portia was way too sharp not to discover that sham identity because she'd done all the vetting. That's how she got connected with Phaedra in the first place."

Mia nodded to her officer and checked off several items. "You've told people that Portia was not the murderer. Why? She had no problem trying to eliminate you."

"It was an opinion, Lieutenant, not a fact." Deming edged closer to me.

I recalled another scrap of our conversation that evening. "Something else came up. Portia was doing her best to hang everything on Ames, and we both admitted having absolutely no skill at martial arts. It was a throwaway comment, nothing planned, but since Phaedra died from a *Dim Mak*, that made an impression on me."

The look in her eyes told me that Mia was not impressed. No doubt she'd encountered plenty of wily killers during her stint at homicide, and this was nothing new. She rustled papers, preparatory to ending the discussion.

"We also agreed that Heather Exley wasn't intelligent enough to be the silent partner. If you're looking for Portia's weak spot, that's it. She's smart and proud of it."

"Good point, Ms. Kane. If you think of anything else, you can include it in your formal statement."

I saved the best for last. My memory had slowly returned, and one vivid scene haunted my nightmares. "Before she left, Portia tucked me in as if I were sleeping. She gloated and said that someone had done her a favor by eliminating Phaedra." I grabbed Deming's hand. "She had no reason to lie to me at that point. I believed her, Lieutenant."

AS SOON AS MIA left, Deming pounced. "Where did that last comment come from—out of left field? It's the first we've heard of it."

"Calm down, Dem. Eja's memory is gradually coming back." Bolin turned toward me and smiled. "Anything else, Eja? It must have terrified you being so vulnerable."

That memory of Portia was etched in my mind with the worst of my childhood fears. I pride myself on resourcefulness and self-reliance. All my literary heroines are marvels of courage. But fiction and life often diverge. In the end, I'd been a quivering mass of Jello.

I shook my head to avoid speaking. At that point, I was perilously close to tears, reduced to a sniveling stereotype of feminine weakness.

"We'll stop by the police station tomorrow," Deming said. "Don't worry. I'll make all the arrangements."

"Time for me to go home," I said, grinning sheepishly at Anika. "I can't hide out in the lap of luxury forever. Cato's getting spoiled."

That evoked a storm of protest from Anika's distress to Deming's outrage. Bolin remained neutral, but his expression was grave. I knew that flirting with danger brought pain to these three people I held dear. Each incident made them relive, as I did, the loss of their beloved daughter. They couldn't know how fragile my courage was or how tentative my grasp on independence. Deming had once called me brave— foolhardy, actually. He never guessed how wrong that assumption was. I knew if I didn't go back now, I'd never be able to live in my apartment again.

After the storm passed, Deming tried negotiating. "How about this?" he said. "After you submit your statement tomorrow, I'll drive you and Cato home." He held up his hand to forestall his mother's protests. "Don't worry, Mom. I'll stay with her until this murder thing is sorted out. No one has to know that she's there."

Anika beamed her approval. "I'll spend the afternoons with her. We can do all kinds of fun things—shopping, lunch, even our exercise classes." She met Bolin's eye. "Po can go with us. That way Eja won't feel like she's under house arrest."

I'm a firm believer in compromise, and frankly, I was aching to resume my kung fu studies. Deming's proposal seemed like the best of both worlds—freedom tempered with a pinch of caution. I gave them a thumbs up and sealed the deal.

EUPHEMIA BATES WAS gone when we arrived at the station the next morning. I completed my statement under the wary eyes of Officer Kevin Jennings, aka Officer Opie, while Deming hovered protectively. His brusque comments and questions seemed to cow the young officer, who resorted to quoting his boss and blushing furiously.

"When will you formally charge Ms. Amory Shaw?" Deming demanded. His firm no longer represented the felon in question due to conflict of interest.

"The lieutenant met with the DA yesterday evening."

I ignored Deming's instructions and asked Opie a question. As the saying goes, I am not a potted plant. "Any progress on finding the murderer?"

Opie swallowed several times, causing his Adam's apple to bob erratically. "She found the murderer, ma'am. I thought you knew."

"What?" I grasped the corner of the desk to steady myself. "Who is it?"

"They charged Ms. Amory Shaw. That's where the lieutenant is today."

I clutched Deming's arm, squeezing it until he yelped. "Did she confess?" I asked.

Opie blanched, his freckles boldly splayed over pale white skin. "I'm not trying to be rude, but Lieutenant Bates should tell you that."

A broad grin spread across Deming's handsome face. "You see, Eja. No need to worry anymore. I suspected Portia Amory Shaw all along. This concludes the case."

"She didn't do it," I told Opie. "Portia is a dreadful person and fully capable of murder, but she didn't kill Phaedra. She told me so. Plus, how could she have hefted those gold bars without someone's help? Everyone says they weigh a ton."

He exchanged nervous "crazy lady" looks with Deming, beseeching him to deal with me. But my sweetie was far too wily to say anything that might cause a public scene. He preferred to placate me with vague assurances that meant nothing.

"Ask Lieutenant Bates to call me, Officer. She has my number." He helped me with my jacket and herded me toward the nearest elevator post haste.

I loathe pouting, but this occasion definitely called for it. From the elevator to the car, I maintained a stony silence that unnerved Deming. He tucked me into the Porsche and took his sweet time cracking his knuckles and fumbling with his seatbelt.

"I thought you'd be happy, Eja. No more worries, nothing to fear. Case closed."

I tried to analyze the situation calmly and rationally even if it meant that I was wrong about Portia. There were just too many unanswered questions, too many implausible scenarios.

How had a dull, dumpy accountant managed to corner a trained martial artist and administer a deathblow? It made no sense, especially with three black-belted Exleys on the loose. Each of them had the killer instinct and ample motive for eliminating Phaedra. Love and money held pride of place on my murder hit parade, but apparently Euphemia Bates didn't agree.

"Cheer up," Deming said. "Let go of your obsession with this murder. Now we can focus on planning our wedding." He pinched my cheek. "Remember? White dress, big cake, gold rings—the whole she-bang."

"Will you be moving back to your place now?" My voice sounded puny and pathetic. I hated it.

"Not unless you want me to." He leaned over and gently kissed my lips. "Just say the word."

"Don't ever leave," I whispered. "Please. I need you so much."

Actions speak louder than words. I spent the rest of the evening proving just that.

THE NEXT AFTERNOON, Cato, Anika, and I took a long walk on the Common. Spring's beauty was slowly fading into summer, but the fresh, crisp air made even Cato mellow.

"Funny thing," Anika mused. "Phaedra Jones was a serpent in the garden of Exley, luring them to their doom."

"Maybe," I said, "but Horton's marriage was in trouble long before she slithered his way. Remember Justin Ming."

Anika beamed her luminous smile. "Ah, yes. A gorgeous man can do so much damage. I've been lucky with my two. Bolin is the love of my life, and Dem is the finest son a mother could hope for."

Our eyes met in silent tribute to the male Swanns.

"You don't have to babysit me anymore, Anika. I feel guilty. Deming hasn't moved out yet, you know."

She threw Cato a stick and laughed as he tumbled end over end. "If I know Deming, he never will. That boy will be there until you say those vows. He won't take another chance at losing you, Eja. It would destroy him."

"Maybe we can stop by Shaolin City soon," I said. "Strangely enough, I've learned to enjoy all that stretching and sweating. How does tomorrow sound?"

"Perfect. Shall I contact Justin?"

"Nah, I'll give him a call later this afternoon. He left a message on my machine, but I haven't had time to respond."

We parted after Po pronounced my condo safe, and I slipped the bolt in the Medeco lock. I had several hours before Deming came home to finish my outline for *Dojo Death*. At least fiction allowed me to control my characters and determine the plot and the villain. Or did it? I zigged and zagged, unable to point the literary finger at any one person. I vacillated between a Portia clone and a snide playboy ala Ames Exley. As in real life, neither was ideally suited for the role of murderer. Portia was a planner, not a doer; Ames was too arrogant and lazy to make the effort. Even that fabulous married couple Horton and Heather failed the test. He was self-absorbed; she was stupid.

I welcomed the distraction of a phone call, especially when the velvety tones of Justin Ming wafted over the line.

"Ms. Kane, I've been worried about you." The sexy sifu was at it again. Soon even I would believe his patent leather line.

"Sorry I haven't returned your call. Things got a bit hectic around here."

"Heather told me." The man's gift for understatement dazzled.

I took a temporary vow of silence. Men like Justin Ming were accustomed to women babbling nonsensically and drooling over their nicely tailored clothing. Silence upended the balance of power.

"Is it true?" he finally asked. "An accountant murdered Phaedra and tried to murder you as well?"

"So they say."

He sighed. "You don't sound convinced. Why don't we meet somewhere and discuss it?"

Was I dreaming, or did menace lurk at the fringes of his message?

"No need. Mrs. Swann and I will be at the dojo tomorrow for our private lesson. We can sort things out then." I opted for the spunky self-assurance of my literary idol Amelia Peabody. Justin Ming was attuned to every nuance, any hint of weakness. I had to project confidence.

"Of course."

"Will you be teaching us?" I asked. Conversation with Justin Ming required the patience of ten vestal virgins.

"Yes. The master has other commitments."

"Okay then. See you tomorrow."

"Ms. Kane? Please understand that as your sifu, I am responsible for your welfare. I care about you as I do all of my students. Always remember to exercise caution. Phaedra was a skilled fighter, yet even she fell to an attacker."

Justin Ming was up to something. His concern appeared genuine, but his warning chilled my soul.

I waited patiently for him to disengage the receiver and hang up.

It was a long time before I heard that comforting click and the deafening silence that accompanied it.

Chapter Twenty-Four

WHEN DEMING CAME home, we lit a fire and spent a cozy evening listening to music and sipping wine. He did the wine sipping, actually. After the gimlet wars, I confined myself to Pellegrino and let the deep, sexy sounds of Michael McDonald soothe my spirit.

"I played those songs the whole time we were apart," Deming said. "I never thought this kind of happiness would be possible again."

"You're the one who took off for six long months," I said. "Don't blame me."

He ruffled my curls and pulled me close. "Hush, baby," he whispered. "Let's not fight. Focus on our future." He did a quick survey of the living room. "This place has happy memories. Too bad we'll have to sell it."

I pulled away from him. "Sell it? What are you talking about?"

He gave me that measured, prosecutorial look. "It's fine for now, but not when we start raising a family. Kids are noisy, and you have a bunch of old coots for neighbors."

"This place is 4,000 square feet, Deming. That's twice the size of most houses. Besides, my only neighbors on this floor are the Sullivans, and they're hardly ever here."

He pulled me back beside him and rocked me as if I were an infant. "I spoke with a realtor yesterday. It's time to put my place on the market anyway. We can live here for a while and consider our options."

Possessions aren't important. I know that. But my home had been CeCe's, and her spirit still inhabited it. As long as I lived here, she stayed alive too. Metaphysics 101. Anika knew that. Bolin too. Selling would be a sacrilege, an abandonment of my dearest friend.

"Hey," Deming said. "What's this—tears? Don't cry. We'll think of a solution. Promise."

He spent the rest of the evening demonstrating just how imaginative he could be.

THE NEXT MORNING, I was sucked into my own creative vortex. I fired up a continuous stream of Bonnie Raitt ballads and focused on writing. Ironing out plot details in *Dojo Death* and addressing the motives of the principals was therapeutic, far more sensible than revisiting the murder of an unsavory victim who was neither mourned nor loved. I excluded Horton Exley's faux emotion from that statement. When push came to shove, his devotion to reputation and family honor exceeded any temporary allegiance to Phaedra Jones. Besides, the case had already been solved, tied up neatly with a big bow courtesy of Lieutenant Euphemia Bates. I had neither the courage nor expertise to question her judgment. Writers invent crimes—detectives catch criminals. Isn't that the way it goes?

Shortly after noon, Cato forcefully reminded me that he too had needs. We compromised by snacking on chicken fingers and jogging three times around the Common for penance. Despite my recent dedication to martial arts, by the end of our excursion I found myself gasping for breath. I stumbled into the lobby, oblivious to my surroundings until Cato's growls alerted me to trouble. Jaime, paid informer and my erstwhile guardian, was pointing to the seating area and gesticulating wildly.

On cue, Ames Exley folded his newspaper and rose, giving me the snarky smile for which he was famous.

"Eja! So glad I caught up with you." He glared at Jaime. "Your man wouldn't give me any information at all."

I winked at Jaime and turned toward Ames. "Really? I wish I'd known. You could have saved me from an hour of jogging."

"Do you have a minute?" he asked. "I need to discuss some things with you."

His voice was cordial, but something else, an undercurrent of expectation and male privilege, made me bristle. Cato's hackles were already raised at the mere sight of Ames.

"Sorry," I said. "I'm pressed for time. Anika will be here any moment, and I'm not even close to ready."

"You two are certainly joined at the hip," Ames snarled. "Quite the clever one, aren't you, Ms. Kane? That Swann fortune won't get past you."

I controlled my smoldering anger and killed him with kindness instead. "You should join us for dinner sometime. Deming would enjoy your portrayal. Hmm. Greedy gold digger is kind of a new role for me, but what the heck? Oh, and do bring Heather along. Her wit enlivens any conversation."

My sarcasm was wasted on Ames. "Heather," he spat. "That's off. She went running back to big brother the moment he got the five million back. Now I'm odd man out. Horton won't allow me back at the Foundation, let alone his home."

"What a shame," I simpered. "You must miss Portia too. I know you worked closely together. Still, some things worked out for the best. At least one marriage was saved."

Ames clenched his fist and stepped forward. Cato's growls accelerated, growing more urgent by the second. Jaime stood poised by the phone.

Despite the situation, I felt empowered. Ames Exley didn't frighten me. Not in the elegant lobby of my own home with residents going to and fro. I wasn't foolhardy enough to invite him upstairs, but in a public space I felt invincible.

"Next time, Ames, phone first. Better still, wait for Deming. He lives here now, and I know he'd love to see you."

I'd been to the New England Aquarium many times studying the cold dead eyes of sharks. Beneath his civilized veneer, Ames Exley had that same impersonal air of a killer. He shot me a venomous look, pivoted, and stalked out the lobby without saying another word.

Jaime was close to hyperventilating. "I tried, Ms. Kane. Something about that gentleman made me go all cold inside." He rubbed his hands together. "You'll tell Mr. Swann, won't you? I tried to protect you."

I walked over to the concierge and patted his arm. "Between you and Cato, I felt perfectly safe. Mr. Swann will probably want to thank you personally."

Dollar signs replaced the angst in Jaime's eyes. He saw himself as my savior, sure to cash in on Deming's gratitude. He insisted on locking the lobby door while he personally escorted me upstairs.

"If that man tries to get in again, Jaime, call Mr. Swann or his father immediately."

The thought of contacting Bolin Swann was almost a game changer. Jaime gulped but stood his ground. "Okay, Ms. Eja. Don't worry about nothing while I'm here. I'll pass the word to the night man too."

I spent precious minutes doing deep breathing exercises, calming my brain, and lowering my heart rate. A woman's home should be inviolate, not besieged by visitors popping up willy-nilly like toadstools. Maybe a moat would fend off marauders.

My old college chum was toxic, a true biohazard. Both Ames, and Fleur Pixley, for that matter, sowed poison while hiding behind bland countenances and empty smiles.

After a thorough scrubbing in the steam shower, I applied a touch of makeup, tousled my curls, and transformed myself from writing nerd to wushu warrior.

As soon as I stepped outside, I spied Anika, waving from the back seat of the Bentley. A bracing blast of cool air, and a dose bright sunlight immediately lifted my spirits. Let Ames skulk about bemoaning his fate. I was officially out of the detective business. Unless of course he really was the murderer.

I couldn't wait to share my Exley encounter with Anika. She gave the appropriate *ooh*s and *ah*s and added a warning.

"Be careful, Eja. His behavior is peculiar. Very odd. Maybe you should call Lieutenant Bates."

"No way! Deming will deal with him if he gets out of line. Meanwhile, I have a wedding to plan and an exercise program to master."

We bumped fists and chattered about menus for the big occasion. I said the right things, but my heart wasn't in it. The old Eja Kane was tenacious, a soldier in the army of truth. Would Mrs. Kane-Swann become a society cipher absorbed by charity galas, PTAs, and fashion trends? I shuddered as a wave of panic surged my way.

"Are you ill?" Anika asked. "Maybe we should skip our session."

"No. It's nothing that an hour of jabs and kicks won't cure. Hope I haven't forgotten the routines."

As soon as Po rounded the corner on Boylston Street, my anxiety lessened.

Remember Julius Caesar, I lectured myself: "Cowards die many times before their deaths." You are no coward, just a jittery bride-to-be with too much imagination. Deal with it!

Shaolin City was bustling again, a sure sign that the stigma of murder had been erased. Anika told Po to pick us up in ninety minutes and hopped out of the car with the grace and verve of a twenty-something. I checked for traffic and lumbered out behind her.

"Come on, Eja," she urged. "Let's stow our things in our lockers before class."

Ever since we'd found Phaedra Jones, the locker room creeped me out. I couldn't confess that to Anika. Correction—I refused to acknowledge my cowardice. Characters in my novels were fearless, but this was real life. Before Deming had moved in, I slept with a night-light and stashed a hammer under my bed.

The reality of the locker room was less threatening than I had imagined. A row of overhead lights now brightened the space as did the lively banter of several young students. The traces of tragedy had vanished except for those that lingered in my mind. Phaedra Jones was a ghost, abandoned even by her spiritual home. So much for the caring sifu and distraught master.

"Are you okay?" Anika asked. "I think this dustup with Ames traumatized you."

I grinned sheepishly. "Nah. I'm writing a novel about a kung fu murder. *Dojo Death*. Snappy title, isn't it? I sort of got carried away."

Anika rolled her eyes and urged me on. "We'll be late if we don't hurry. Come on."

We scurried down the corridor, reaching our classroom precisely at 3:00 p.m. Justin Ming was there, imperturbable as ever, waiting patiently for us.

Neither time nor grief had withered his dimpled smile and chiseled abs. If anything, the sexy sifu seemed more appealing than ever. Perhaps Phaedra's death had resolved more than a few of Justin Ming's worries and breathed new life into the dojo.

"Ladies," he said with a curt nod, "shall we begin?"

Following an interval of stretching and internal breathing exercises, we plunged into a gut-wrenching series of competency-based tasks. As the star pupil, Anika was permitted to advance from the basic Dragon form to the Snake. She earned Justin Ming's praise by replicating each phase of her training with minimal adjustments. My performance was more nuanced, or in other words, a big mess. The sifu frowned as I fumbled the stances, punches, and kicks that had once come easily. My performance was off the charts. On a ten-point scale it was subterranean.

"Come now, Ms. Kane," he said. "Let me assist you."

For once I had no trouble being humble. "I'm sorry, Sifu. I've lost my focus."

He stepped behind me, bending my arms into the correct posture. "These exercises are designed to build confidence, Eja, not to punish. You are tenacious. Eager to learn. You will not abandon any task you want to master."

He glanced at me, his almond eyes telegraphing a more sinister message. My feelings changed from shame to rage as I watched him. Must every man try to intimidate me today?

Propelled by adrenalin, I completed a perfect set of punches, kicks, and thrusts. When I finished, Anika clapped her hands, and Justin did a double take.

"Excellent, Ms. Kane. I commend you."

I heard more clapping and turned toward the door. Deming stood there garbed in his own wushu outfit with a black belt wound tightly around his trim waist. He nodded to Justin Ming as they locked eyes.

"My pardon, Sifu. I came to escort my mother and fiancée from their lesson."

Anika and I exchanged smiles. The air teemed with testosterone as each man took the other's measure. They were similarly matched— Deming was taller by about two inches, but Justin was more heavily muscled. Both embodied every trait I lusted after in a man.

"You are most welcome, Mr. Swann." Justin gestured toward the practice mats. "You would honor me by sharing a practice session."

FOR ONCE I yearned for my cell phone with its nifty camera. Watching two magnificent creatures in combat was the equivalent of viewing stallions at the starting gate. The very idea was a major turn on.

Alas, it was not to be. Before their match began, another man joined the party. Master Avery Moore glided into the room, beaming his vague, luminous smile.

"Mr. Deming Swann, I believe." He bowed. "A pleasure, sir. You are a practitioner of the Shaolin arts, I understand."

Deming nodded. "I trained with my father, Master."

"Excellent. Bolin Swann has been a most generous supporter of our community." The master gifted Anika and I with a nod. "If you will excuse me, ladies, I need Sifu Ming's assistance." He beckoned to Justin and led him from the room.

"What are you doing here?" I asked Deming. "You've spoiled my surprise."

"Surprise? You've been dragging my mother here for almost a month. It doesn't take a wizard to figure things out."

Anika put her arm around Deming's waist and hugged him. "Now, children, don't quarrel. Eja has been working so hard on this project, Dem. It was her wedding gift to you."

"Really?" His surprise was almost insulting.

"I thought you'd be proud of me. You know, becoming a fitness buff."

His eyes met mine in a look that singed my heart. "I'm always proud of you. You don't have to change anything. Besides, I thought we could walk home together. You too, Mom."

Anika shook her head. "Nope. Po is waiting outside, and Bolin and I have dinner plans." She kissed my cheek and slipped out the door. "I'll get your things for you, Eja. Wait here a minute."

"Hold on," I said. "Don't go alone." I sped down the corridor after her, narrowly averting a collision with Justin Ming.

"We missed our discussion," he said. "Next time, perhaps when Mr. Swann is busy elsewhere."

I paused, just long enough to unsettle Justin Ming. "There's nothing to discuss, Sifu. Phaedra's case is closed. Her murderer has been arrested. The police are satisfied and so am I. Good evening." I faced forward, heading toward the locker room at a leisurely pace. Was the sexy sifu battling Ames for creep of the year, or was something more sinister at play?

The moment I reached the locker room, Anika gave me a quizzical look. "What happened? You're a million miles away."

"Nothing. There must be a full moon tonight or something. Every man I meet is half crazy."

Anika grinned as she handed me my bag. "You underestimate yourself, Eja. Men are drawn to you."

I loved her explanation. Too bad it wasn't true. A different more sinister thought swirled through my brain, making me shudder. Despite evidence to the contrary, Portia Amory Shaw was innocent of murder. She was certainly a criminal, but someone else—someone with a very different motive—had murdered Phaedra. I couldn't prove it, but I knew it was so.

Chapter Twenty-Five

OVER THE NEXT few weeks, life settled back to normal or what passes for it after a murder. Deming and I combined households, Anika assembled our gift registry, and I resumed my schedule on the lecture circuit. Most events were inconsequential—book signings, seminars, and library readings. At first Deming protested, but eventually he agreed that my life was no longer in jeopardy. An audience of bibliophiles was unlikely to harbor an assassin.

One evening after a session at the Boston Public Library, an unlikely duo appeared. Horton and Heather Exley trotted to the front of the line, books in hand, asking for an autograph. He was garbed in Brahmin casual, a combination of cashmere blazer and well-tailored cords. Heather had abandoned her customary black for a stunning red pantsuit that hugged her whippet-thin figure.

"How are you?" I asked, gaining points for originality and sprightly dialogue.

"Nice talk, Eja. Very informative." Horton thrust my first novel at me with a request. "Sign it for Jonathon. My boy likes mysteries."

Heather nodded, adding her own contribution. "My book club meets every month. Maybe you could speak to us."

Book clubs and Heather Exley didn't go together. Still, the quest for customers was unending.

"I guess you heard about Ames," Horton said. "Flew the coop. About time, I say. That boy had to stand on his own someday."

I was flabbergasted. "Where'd he go?"

Heather shrugged. "Somewhere in the West. Hollywood, I think."

Horton curled his lip at the thought of it. "He wrote some kind of screenplay. Said you inspired him, Eja. Calls it *The Family Jewels*. Can you believe it? Kind of a dumb title if you ask me."

No wonder Ames tried to contact me. He wanted my advice, not my life. I recalled the wicked sense of humor he had once displayed. Who knew? The screenplay might be a big success. Certainly the Exley family contained a wealth of material.

"When is your wedding?" Heather asked.

"Soon," I said. "In a few months."

She glanced at Horton, a strange look filled with secret longing. "We're going to Paris next week."

Horton's complexion grew ruddy with either emotion or high blood pressure. "New start. Second honeymoon." He shrugged. "It happens."

I shook his hand. "Congratulations and the best of luck to you both."

They walked away arm in arm, leaving me to think about Phaedra and her tangled legacy. She was now a mound of ashes, while the Exley dynasty motored on. Portia hadn't confessed to anything, but despite some craters in the evidence, the Suffolk County District Attorney had charged her with first-degree murder. Both he and Euphemia Bates were convinced of Portia's guilt. Why wasn't I satisfied?

When I left the library, there was Deming sitting on the library steps waiting. As usual, he was hunched over his iPad, glued to the latest fiscal news from Wall Street doomsayers.

"Wow! What a pleasant surprise!" I bent down and kissed his cheek. "How do I rate a personal escort?"

He leapt to his feet with a panther's grace. "Get used to it, toots. As Mrs. Deming Swann you're entitled to that and much more."

My reaction was mixed. The feminist part of me bristled, but the romantic side of me melted like triple cream Brie. True, I was and always would be Eja Kane, married or not. My guilty secret was the pleasure I felt in hearing my name linked with his. Mrs. Deming Swann. It sounded heavenly.

"Come along now," he said. "Even famous authors need their rest." He took my hand and scrambled down the steps, his toned glutes inspiring lustful thoughts in any sentient female.

We wandered through Copley Square, turned on Dartmouth, and made our way to Newbury Street, reveling in the starry sky and cool, fresh air.

My scoop about the Exleys rated a big yawn from Deming.

"Old news," he said. "I meant to tell you. They're back together now, bound by hoary tradition." He waved his hand dismissively. "It will never be a love match, but as Horty's lawyer, I'm relieved. Divorces are messy affairs, especially when a family fortune is involved."

Messy affairs. Exleys knew all about that. I wondered if Heather had quenched her wanderlust, or if Horton would find a new "soul mate." Maybe Ames was the smartest of the bunch after all. He was well equipped to deal with Hollywood soul-suckers, no matter what nonsense they threw at him.

"A dollar for your thoughts," Deming said. "Inflation, you know."

I shook my head. "Nothing special. It seems like Phaedra Jones got the worst of the deal while everyone else made out just fine."

"Portia's not so happy," he snorted. "They may not nail her on murder, but that gold scam is a lock. She had the audacity to ask Pam to represent her. Impossible, of course."

Ethical claims aside, I knew that Pamela Schwartz refused any client without a hefty bank account. Portia Amory Shaw was virtually indigent.

"Your esteemed sifu didn't fare too well either," Deming sneered, "although I'm sure some empty-headed heiress will come through." He tightened his grip on my hand until I yelped.

"You really don't like him, do you?"

Deming peered into the window of Loro Piana, fixated on the incomparable cashmere. "What do you think of that jacket? Maybe I'll stop by there tomorrow after work."

"Answer the question, Counselor." I folded my arms and risked a mini-frown.

"Ming doesn't interest me at all," Deming said, "but he doesn't fool me either. That guy is a charlatan, and he's way too interested in you for my taste."

"Pooh! Would you really have fought him that night?" I had to admit that the thought was thrilling.

"Sparring, Eja, not fighting. And to answer your question, yes, absolutely. I would have won too. If you and my mother insist on learning kung fu, go someplace else."

"What about Master Moore?" I asked. "Is he a charlatan too?"

Deming's jaw tightened. "According to my dad, Avery Moore is the real deal. Old school. Big on honor and tradition. Lives for that whole Shaolin Law stuff." He nudged me toward the sidewalk. "Come on. We'd better hurry. Your dog is waiting, and we both know what that means."

We walked the final block in silence, each of us bound by our separate thoughts.

THE FOLLOWING MONTH, murder charges against Portia Shaw were dismissed. Lack of evidence was the official reason, although the

DA dropped dark hints about eventually reinstating them. Both state and federal authorities charged ahead with the gold scam cases, or as the *Boston Herald* famously dubbed them, the "Gilt Trip." Portia's claims of innocence were largely ignored by the popular press, particularly after news of her Swiss account was leaked on Twitter. While Horton and Heather honeymooned in France, Deming handled the many requests for interviews and insights into the Exley family, refusing all of them with a firm, "No comment." The Internet was awash with stern images of his handsome face as he deflected inquiries with a luscious frown.

Then came the news that a novel, a tell-all roman à clef by a family member, had been auctioned to a major publisher and optioned for a movie. *Family Jewels* by Ames Exley became a literary sensation well in advance of its publication date. The author embarked on a media blitz-krieg, granting interviews to all the major outlets. I watched him smooze with Ellen, charm the ladies of *The View*, and ingratiate himself with nationwide audiences. Brown University had taught him something, but a lifetime with the Exleys had taught him more. He was sensational.

Anika and I lost our fervor for the martial arts, substituting the ri-gors of wedding planning for physical conditioning. I occasionally practiced the kicks, thrusts, and squats at home, but my heart just wasn't in it.

Two months before the wedding, I received a call from Justin Ming. "I bring sad news, Ms. Kane. Master Moore is no longer with us."

"You mean . . . he died?" I was stunned into silence.

"His passing was peaceful and without pain," Justin said. "But he entrusted me with something for you. Will you join me for tea so that we may discuss it?"

I spoke without thinking. "I'm so sorry, Justin. I know the master was very dear to you. Of course we can meet. How about this afternoon at the Courtyard Restaurant in the Boston Public Library?"

"Very well. Please bring Mrs. Swann with you also. That will please your fiancé I know."

"Two o'clock, okay?"

"I will be there, Ms. Kane. Thank you."

It took several spates of yogic breathing before I assimilated the news. Avery Moore seemed immortal, a creature immune to human frailty. How had he died, and why had he left a message for me, a virtual stranger? I hardly knew him, yet oddly enough his absence created a spiritual void in me.

Anika was shocked by the news but eager to join the action. She immediately rearranged her schedule in order to accompany me.

"Count me in," she said, "but maybe you should check with Dem first. Or I can call Bolin."

"They're both in Manhattan for the day," I reminded her. "It would only worry them. Besides, what can happen in broad daylight?"

I found Cato's leash and spent an hour power walking around the Common, trying to anticipate the day to come. Perhaps the master left words of wisdom, rules for a happy marriage. Surely Shaolin kung fu had something to cover every type of union.

As usual, choosing an appropriate wardrobe posed a challenge for me. Black seemed pretentious, but bright colors suggested disrespect. I made the safe choice, opting for a sober charcoal-grey sweater dress with black buttons and a high neck. An engagement ring and watch were my only jewelry.

It pained me to take a taxi, but nerves made it a necessity. Plus, it would earn points with Deming and showcase the newly cautious Eja Kane, wife-in-training. Not surprisingly, I arrived far too early for our appointment. Call it the residue of parental strictures on promptness or a sign of social anxiety. Either way, the habit was deeply ingrained in my character and no surprise to anyone who knew me.

I checked my watch and realized it was early enough for a visit to the mystery section. Seeing my works on those revered shelves was unreal, a dream come true. I caressed the spines of the books like a lover and smiled with secret satisfaction.

"I thought I might find you here, Ms. Kane."

Justin Ming loomed over me looking larger and more muscular than ever. Despite the hour, this section of the library was deserted. I moved back, bracing myself again the shelves for confidence. Early birds get worms, not praise. Why hadn't I remembered that?

"You followed me up here, Sifu." I said. "Tea doesn't start for an hour."

His smile highlighted a striking set of dimples. "I also arrived early. When I saw you, I decided to surprise you. Besides, our business doesn't require tea, Eja. Come. Sit down with me." He pointed to a couch hidden away from the main thoroughfare.

"Mrs. Swann will be looking for me. She'll be worried." I took a deep breath, trying to forestall a tide of panic.

Justin stared at me, more predator than sexy sifu. "Don't fear me. We have time enough to do what must be done."

I reached into my purse, cursing the tiny clutch I'd exchanged for my shoulder bag. A lipstick wouldn't deter Justin Ming, but my pen might help. How ironic if I were saved by a writer's tool. May the pen be mightier than the sword just this once.

"Don't be silly, Justin. Shaolin Laws prohibit violence toward women." I gulped, remembering the injuries that Phaedra had suffered. An army might not stop him if he chose to hurt me.

He nodded and took another step toward me. "Sometimes even a righteous man can err. My master knew that."

Should I scream? Would my vocal chords function? No one could hear me if I did, and that might anger him even more.

His bright eyes mesmerized me. I was the hapless victim, the tethered goat awaiting sacrifice.

"Whatever Phaedra was guilty of, she didn't deserve to be murdered. Your whole belief system teaches that." I squared my shoulders and swallowed my fears. Control over women or the illusion of it fueled his every move. I refused to gratify that need.

"Time is running out, Ms. Kane. Follow me, please."

Justin reached for my arm and pulled me toward him. He was strong, but I had the element of surprise on my side. If only I could remember some of those self-defense forms that Anika had demonstrated. The Snake might work if only I were able. My legs were leaden, and the hand that clutched the pen felt stiff. I uncapped it and pointed the nib toward his extremities. Even a sifu would feel pain when stabbed in his tender parts. Justin Ming would learn that lesson if he came any closer.

Before I acted, I heard an angel's voice.

"There you are, Eja. I thought I'd find you here." Anika, a blinding vision in white, stepped toward us. "Sifu Ming! I'm so sorry about the master." She gestured toward the restaurant. "Shall we discuss things over tea?"

AFTERNOON TEA IS a highly civilized ritual that infuses calm and good behavior into those who partake. Suddenly, the idea of murder in a historic public library seemed like an absurd reaction to my own imagination and Justin's sudden presence. Anika's arrival had saved me from making a fool of myself.

Logic alone failed to satisfy my rubbery legs and rapid heartbeat. I leaned against Anika for support as I took my seat.

"Yum," Anika said. "Look at the menu. So many choices."

To my surprise, I was hungry. Famished. I helped myself to cucumber with herb cheese and smoked salmon canapés, determined to nibble, not gobble, the tasty treats. It felt unseemly to gorge oneself when discussing death.

Justin pointed to the menu. "Look, they have wedding tea. It is a very special blend, Ms. Kane, a favorite of brides throughout China. White tea, pink rosebuds, and lemon."

"Perfect!" Anika clapped her hands. "It's so delicious. They served that on the day I married Bolin." She chose Dragon Pearl Jasmine tea; Justin ordered Earl Grey.

With the preliminaries over, it was time for the sifu to take the stage. Justin reached into his jacket and produced a thick vellum envelope that was addressed to me. The calligraphy was beautiful, the product of an ancient art and a skilled hand.

"It's lovely," I said. "Did Master Moore write this?"

Ming nodded. "His skin was brown, but his heart was all Chinese. My master was the most honorable soul I have ever known."

I was unsure of how to proceed—open the letter now or wait for privacy.

"He asked me to tell you first," Justin said, "because you were a truth seeker. He knew you would do the right thing."

That was a grave responsibility, depending upon what the note contained. I nodded in silent assent to the proposal.

Justin closed his eyes for a moment as if he were meditating. He placed his hands on the table, fingers touching, and began to speak. His voice was hoarse, barely audible in a room full of chattering people. "Master Moore saved me more than once," he said. "He gave me a home and something to believe in—Shaolin Law, the creed by which he lived."

"He was proud of you," Anika said. "That was obvious to everyone. He thought of you as a son."

Justin uttered a harsh sound that was more like a sob. "I betrayed him."

"How?" I dreaded hearing the answer, but I had to know. "Did you murder Phaedra?"

That ended his fugue state in a hurry. "Me? Of course not. Why would I do that? My crime was far worse." He raised his head, gazing at us with misery-filled eyes.

The tension at our table was palpable. Anika reached for my hand and squeezed it.

"What then?" she asked. "Surely Master Moore forgave you."

For a moment I feared that Justin Ming might weep.

"He had a generous heart filled with compassion. Even when he learned of my sins, the master embraced me."

I said nothing, even though my mind teemed with all manner of thoughts. Our conversation was attracting the attention of those around us. Several women at the surrounding tables were revving up the lust factor, boldly eyeing Justin Ming. I had no desire to cause a scene or participate in one, but Anika seemed perfectly at ease.

"According to the Bard," she said, "mercy shows a true nobility of mind. I think that describes Master Moore perfectly. He had a special presence, an aura, if you will, that comforted people." She leaned forward and patted Justin's hand. "Tell me, Sifu, how did he pass? We had no inkling that he was ill."

Justin closed his eyes once more and shuddered. "He did not suffer. Only those he loved were left in pain."

The use of bromides and vague phrases breached my tolerance threshold. Either Justin was incapable of a direct answer, or he was still hiding something. Even a death certificate would be helpful at this point. Anika's use of tact and diplomacy had failed. Time for a frontal assault.

"Bottom line, Sifu, how did Master Moore die?" I channeled Euphemia Bates, hoping for a firm, authoritative tone.

A curious transformation had taken place. Justin Ming was diminished, no longer the sexy stud that thrilled sentient females. He raised his head and stared at me.

"I'm responsible for his death," he sighed. "I killed my master."

Chapter Twenty-Six

I GULPED AN ENTIRE cup of wedding tea before speaking. "You *murdered* Avery Moore? You're confessing?"

Anika clutched my arm and leaned toward him. "Explain yourself, Justin."

"My actions dishonored the dojo and my master. I brought shame to Shaolin City. He tried to protect me, but it was too late. Too late." Then Sifu Ming, that monument to male pulchritude, pushed back his chair and fled the room.

I took my time, studying the beautifully lettered writing and the red wax sealing the envelope. Master Moore had entrusted me with his written words, and I would honor his wishes. Besides, at that point my curiosity was almost crippling.

"Maybe you should wait for Dem," Anika said. "There might be legal issues."

I shook my head. "No. I'll read this no matter what the repercussions. Let's take it back to my place where we can have some privacy."

After paying our bill we stepped out into brilliant sunshine where the Bentley, accompanied by the ever-faithful Po, was parked at the curb.

Anika rattled off instructions in Mandarin and cushioned herself in the glove-soft leather seat. "I don't know, Eja. This could be very tricky."

"Probably. But knowing Master Moore, I feel rather honored that he chose me."

She gave me a hug. "Integrity and courage. That's what Avery saw in you. It's one of the many things I've always loved about you."

We said very little on the ride back to Beacon Street. Even Jaime's effusive greetings and Cato's sharply worded protests failed to rouse us. We were focused on only one thing, and until that duty was discharged, nothing else mattered.

To my surprise, we found Deming sprawled on the library sofa, snoring lustily. When Anika roused him, he bounded to his feet, grumbling like a wounded bear.

"Our client signed the settlement," he growled. "An early day, for a change."

I outlined our meeting with Justin Ming and dangled the master's letter before Deming's eyes. Immediately he morphed from sleepy son to quizzical lawyer.

"I wish you hadn't accepted that, Eja. You might have put yourself in legal jeopardy."

"So be it. Aren't you the least bit curious about this? Anika and I certainly are."

"Let's call my dad first. He might as well be in on this thing too."

I chafed at the delay, but Anika nodded and dialed Bolin's private number.

"He'll be right over," she said. "Meanwhile, I could use some cognac."

Deming played bartender, filling four snifters with Courvoisier. By the time Bolin arrived I was more ready for a nap than a final scene.

Bolin Swann was coolness personified as he smiled my way and stepped up to kiss Anika. "This is your show, Eja. Why don't you read Avery Moore's message and decide what you should share with us. It's up to you."

Even before opening the letter, I'd made that decision. "You are the people I love and trust most in the world. I'll read his letter out loud."

We know each other only slightly Ms. Kane, yet I trust you to read these words and do the honorable thing. Unlike so many of us, you observe the precepts of Shaolin Law as they were intended. I have tried to live my life by the Moral Way and to inspire others to do so. Unfortunately, as in so many things, I have failed.

I knew Justin's weakness. We all have them, but his was based on kindness not malice. He traded pleasure for the funds of frivolous women who wanted more. He did so to sustain me and the dojo. It violated Shaolin Law, yet I could not condemn him.

Phaedra Jones was a predator, a temptress who found moral soft spots and burrowed in. She abused her fellow beings and entangled men in evil.

I too fell victim to her charms. For the first time ever, I was captive to the flesh, willing to sacrifice everything I believed in for her favors. I gladly gave my money and my heart and helped her with her schemes. She discarded me when I no longer served her and turned to Justin. She vowed to trap him, implicate him in scandal if he refused her advances.

That was why I killed her.

I feel no guilt, though you may judge me harshly. Either way, I am at peace.

Please share this with the authorities and anyone else you so choose.

Grand Master Avery Moore.

Tears streamed down my cheeks, and Anika dabbed her eyes with a tissue. She buried her head on Bolin's shoulder and sobbed.

"We should have known," Deming said. "It was the logical solution. The killer was conversant with the dojo, skilled in martial arts, and probably one of Phaedra's victims. It makes sense."

Bolin showed no emotion save for the tenderness toward his wife. "Avery Moore was an honorable man. He made a choice and took responsibility for it. I respect that."

"Dad!" Deming said. "That's why we have a legal system. Avery Moore should have exposed her and made Phaedra pay for her crimes."

In the silence that followed, Bolin answered his son. "That's exactly what happened. Phaedra chose that path and paid with her life. Avery did too. A different kind of justice but a satisfying end."

I couldn't help but wonder if justice or another master had been served.

WHEN WE MET with Euphemia Bates that next morning, I was dry-eyed and calm, aided by a soothing night in Deming's arms. Mia listened without comment to my narrative and scrutinized Avery Moore's dying declaration.

"We'll verify the handwriting, of course," she said, "but this puts paid to the murder of Phaedra Jones." An impish grin transformed her face. "Men! I thought a spiritual being like Avery Moore was wiser than that. Just goes to show you."

Deming folded his arms across his chest. "What about the autopsy results? Any news?"

"According to the medical examiner, our master died of natural causes. No obvious signs of trauma." Mia's eyes were depthless pools, impenetrable to outsiders. "Toxicology results are still pending."

"You're not satisfied, are you?" I didn't expect an answer.

"I'm a cop, Eja, trained to be suspicious. Justin was a son to Master Moore, and most parents would shield their child at all costs."

"It makes sense though," I said. "Phaedra broke just about every Shaolin Law there is. At least this explains how she transported those gold bars."

"I wonder . . . but I suspect we'll never know for sure." Mia stood and shook Deming's hand. To my surprise, she bent down and kissed my cheek. "Best wishes on your marriage. I hope you'll both be very happy."

AS OUR WEDDING grew near, Deming tackled the issue we had both avoided. We were comfortably settled in the home that I loved, CeCe's home, now ours. Even Cato had opted for a temporary truce with Deming and his shins. His bachelor pad sold quickly to a childless power couple that reveled in urban life. That left only one issue unresolved.

"We need to talk about something," Deming said. "I know it's on your mind."

"Really? Is mind reading part of your repertoire now?"

He lobbed a pillow at me and stood hands on hips. "This is serious. Stop fooling around."

I gave a mock salute and faced him. "Yes sir, Counselor. Take your best shot."

Deming patted the sofa cushion. "Come on, baby. Sit next to me. Please."

My heartbeat quickened as I stepped his way. I loathed cowardice, especially when I was the coward in question. Better to confront the issue head-on.

"We discussed what to do about this place. Once we start a family, that is." He raked his hand through that lush Swann hair. A sure sign of nerves.

"As I recall, we were miles apart. Discussion implies give and take."

He gave me that blank, lawyerly look. "Let me finish, Eja. Anyway, I mentioned it to my dad, just kicking around ideas, nothing sneaky. He suggested something I think you'll like. Naturally, he ran things by my mom too."

A shiver quite unrelated to the outside temperature ran down my spine. Was this a Swann conspiracy? Was I the last one to know about issues affecting my life?

"Go on," I said. "This sounds interesting."

He pulled me close and kissed my hand. "Just listen for a change. Dad saw old Mr. Sullivan at some charity lunch, and they got talking."

"Fergus Sullivan, my neighbor?"

"Yeah. Anyway, it seems that Mrs. S wants to split their time between Paris and Palm Beach. Better weather or something like that."

"Okay." I refused to make things easy for Deming. Let him suffer.

He swallowed hard and continued. "Bottom line, Dad made him an offer for his place—cash of course—and Sullivan accepted."

Here's where my brain fog started. Would Bolin and Anika be my new neighbors? I was dumbfounded, and for once, I had nothing to say.

"Don't you get it? My parents are giving the place to us as our wedding present. Subject to your approval, naturally. There'll be some renovations, probably a whole bunch of them. The Sullivans lived in that place for forty years, and you know how old people are. But that way we'll have the entire floor to ourselves. Plenty of room and privacy for whatever comes our way."

Eight thousand square feet was a hell of a lot of house, kids or no kids. It meant preserving CeCe's space and adding a bunch more that was exclusively ours. Despite the inevitable construction and confusion, I liked the idea.

"There's more," Deming said. "Just one proviso. If we ever feel for whatever reason that we need a house, Mom and Dad will swap the one they live in for this one. That way, it will never leave the family." He shrugged. "You know how they are about anything to do with Cecilia."

I try to avoid sloppy sentimentality, but all rules have their limits. At that moment I felt CeCe's presence more than ever. She was somewhere close, clapping vigorously and cheering us on.

Deming cracked his knuckles until I grabbed his hand.

"It's not a good idea, it's inspired! I love it Deming, and I love you. Thank you. There's no better present I could ask for."

We sat in front of the fireplace, toasting that bargain and our future life. One chapter had concluded, but the best remained unwritten.

THE END

About the Author

Arlene Kay spent twenty years as a Senior Executive with the Federal Government where she was known as a most unconventional public servant. Experience in offices around the nation allowed her to observe both human and corporate foibles and rejoice in unintentional humor.

Those locations and the characters she encountered are celebrated in a series of mysteries including *Intrusion* (2011) and *Die Laughing* (2012) both from Mainly Murder Press; *The Abacus Prize* (available now on Amazon); and the Boston Uncommons Mystery Series (*Swann Dive*; *Mantrap*; and *Gilt Trip*); now available from Bell Bridge Books. She is currently writing the fourth installment of the Boston Uncommons Series—*Lookback*.

Ms. Kay holds graduate degrees in Political Science and Constitutional Law.

CPSIA information can be obtained
at www.ICGtesting.com
Printed in the USA
LVOW08s1814150317
527323LV00004B/973/P